The

Doctor's Daughter

BOOKS BY SHARI J. RYAN

The Bookseller of Dachau

LAST WORDS

The Girl with the Diary

The Prison Child

The Soldier's Letters

SHARI J. RYAN

The

Doctor's Daughter

bookouture

Published by Bookouture in 2022

An imprint of Storyfire Ltd.
Carmelite House
50 Victoria Embankment
London EC4Y 0DZ

www.bookouture.com

ISBN: 978-1-80314-373-6
eBook ISBN: 978-1-80314-372-9

To my grandma—
I can feel it.

PROLOGUE

MAY 1945

With one last step up to ground level, a wave of emotions ripple through me as I silently recite the words spoken through the dusty speakers of the radio: "The war in Europe is over! The Nazis surrender unconditionally." I reach for the door and my hands feel detached from my body as my fingers tremble against the cold rusty latch. The war has been ongoing for more than a third of my life, and I can't remember being free. I can't recall if I was old enough to understand the perception of peace before it went away.

The wooden door creaks open like the first morning yawn after a long night. Daylight spills in around me and I can hardly see anything.

When hours of darkness are what we've known for so long, the sun feels so extravagant and eternal. At twenty years old, I believe I'm seeing the world as it should be seen for the very first time.

The colors surrounding me are alive and brilliant; dense patches of leaves dangle from tree branches, lush sprouts of grass are rooting from newly thawed soil, and the cloudless sky —it comprises colors from a peacock's feathers, all the variants bleeding into one divine hue of blue that could never be replicated in a photograph or a painting. There is beauty all around us, and upon the first breath of clean air, a new story awaits.

Some might see this moment as an opening to Heaven's gates while others could argue we are stepping away from the depths of Hell. I'm not sure if we lost track of the minutes, hours, weeks, months, years, or if time simply stopped moving forward while we were held captive in the dark.

I was once told that I didn't belong in a world intended for a certain type of people—a type defined by what only one set of eyes could see.

Perhaps I was blind before, but now my view is untarnished. This is my world, and only I will determine what's to come.

Because I am the creator of my own destiny.

CHAPTER 1

MAY 1941

SOFIA

The first morning of a new month feels as if it deserves recognition; it's a new start we're fortunate enough to experience twelve times a year. Yet, no one ever says much about it because life revolves like a wheel—spinning until it hits a hill or loses momentum.

My eyes tire as I stare at a calendar, one I've carefully drawn up on a piece of typewriting paper by tracing lines along the edge of my schoolbook. My teacher taught us about the importance of tracking dates—she says it helps us keep our minds moving in a productive direction. This will be the third month I've attempted to do this, but the last two months only show red x's through each day's box. I would prefer to be busy. Without any plans in the foreseeable future, I'm not sure I see the point of keeping track. I can't even count down the days until the war ends.

Still, the empty squares encourage me to add an event or something special I shouldn't forget. Tomorrow is Friday, and Shabbat, or it should be for us. We don't speak much about the holiday in our house, never mind celebrating as we had for as long as I can remember, but it belongs on the calendar.

My hand is unsteady as I write each letter across tomorrow's box. The curves and lines of my handwriting have ridged edges, proving the everlasting nerves I endure. Shabbat deserves to be noted. Maybe if my parents were to write it down, they too would reconsider how we tend to our practices.

I pull open the drawer of my rickety writing desk and drop my pencil on top of the others, but I can't hear the rattling clunk above the loud chatter growing downstairs from what sounds like several men. I wasn't aware we were expecting company, especially this early in the day.

Papa's voice isn't the loudest, not like it normally is. He would argue that it's not that he has a more powerful volume than anyone else, it's that he has a uniquely baritone sound, like rumbles of thunder.

I take my robe from the edge of my hand-carved four-poster bed and pull the warm material over my shoulders. With a slight twist of the doorknob, I tug the door open just enough to fit through, then follow the muddy-brown floor panels from my bedroom that flow into the hallway, which lead to an oak stairwell. The railing, though clean, always feels sticky from whatever varnish was used during the latest round of minor renovations to our eighteenth-century farmhouse. Although the last updates were completed well before I was born, this house has been passed down from generation to generation on my mother's side of the family—originally built by my great-great-grandfather.

The first flight of stairs complains with creaking groans that could give away my footsteps, but rusty-red tiles cover the second stairwell. I could run up and down those steps all day and no one would hear a peep. In fact, there have been many times where I've been able to hide behind the curve of the white-stucco wall and listen to conversations carrying on in the

foyer, perhaps ones I shouldn't always be priv·
rather know than be left in the dark.

I'm still in my lime-green evening pajamas an
unruly auburn hair is in knots, but I must know more abou
what's happening just a few steps away.

"You must understand, I can't abandon my patients per
your say-so, gentlemen." There is a change in my father's
voice. It may be because he's speaking in German rather than
Polish, but we are all quite fluent, or so we've become over
the last couple of years since Germany took over our country.
We still speak Polish among ourselves and the other locals in
town. I don't see why we should change the way we talk
because the Germans don't feel the need to speak our
language. "As the primary physician here in Oświęcim, I have
a commitment to the folks in this town. They depend on
me."

The pause in discussion feels minutes long even though
only a few seconds pass before one of the other men responds.

"Herr Amsler, certainly, you must know we will make it
worth your trouble. You are, indeed, the best physician around,
and we need a man with your skills. You would be doing your
family and country a great service, as well."

Our country—a confusing term since the Germans have
overruled Poland and taken it as their own. Papa is not in the
Polish Army, and definitely not a part of the German Army.
Therefore, I'm not sure what more he could do to help Poland
than being of aid to the residents here.

"I understand quite well, but I insist you allow me time to
speak to my wife before offering you an answer."

Papa would never consider leaving—or worse, closing his
practice—the one I planned to join after nursing school—for
whatever these men are offering him. I'm sure he's saying what
he must to make them leave.

"Of course, Herr Amsler. We will return tomorrow

morning for your answer. Please tell your wife and daughter we send our best. Take care. Have yourself a pleasant day."

Foolish men. It's quite clear there isn't such a thing as a "pleasant day" in Nazi-occupied Poland.

"Will do, gentlemen," Papa replies. "Allow me to get the door for you."

The front door closes with a deafening thud, cueing me to continue down the steps, where I find Papa gripping the doorknob and staring at the door as if he could see through the thick wood.

"Papa, is everything all right?" I ask, keeping my voice low so I don't startle him.

His shoulders slouch forward before he turns to face me. He's already dressed for work in his tweed brown dress pants, white button-down shirt, and favorite maroon tie with small white polka-dots. But there is sadness in his eyes and a crease between his eyebrows—not the way he typically appears before leaving in the mornings.

"How much did you overhear, Sofia?"

"Enough to make me wonder why there were men in our house so early in the morning, especially men who were asking you to give up your practice for 'our' country."

"It's complicated, *mały myszka*," he says, placing his hand down on my shoulder. He hasn't called me "little mouse" in years. I'm sixteen now, nearly a grown woman.

"Who were they?" I press.

"No one I want you to be concerned with, but I must go talk with your *matka*. Go on and get yourself ready for school so you aren't late." Whatever he must talk to Mama about, it will not be a pleasant conversation.

My stomach churns with apprehension. Papa hardly ever shows his nerves, never through his expression, which declares a state of fear now. He will likely take the conversation into their bedroom, where he knows I can't overhear them. Their large closet sits between my bedroom and theirs, blocking out all sound.

He's already halfway up the first stairwell when I make my way to the front door, wondering if the men are still outside. The narrow glass window alongside the door is foggy, so I rub my elbow in a small circle, spotting two men in gray uniforms, complete with knee-high shined black boots and tilted head-caps. They aren't just men from one of the Armed Forces; I can see they are of a higher importance, especially by the looks of the Mercedes they are stepping into. We avoid men in uniform at all costs around here. It's something we've done since they moved into our country over a year and a half ago.

The car loops around and kicks up dirt upon leaving our property. I didn't realize how long I have been staring out the window at the men, but sometimes I feel like it's the only way I can catch a glimpse of the truths these walls protect me from.

The conversation between my parents must not be going well as I hear their door open and close with force.

"Sofia, where are you?" my mother calls out.

I head up the steps, being quick about it as it sounds like Mama might be in my bedroom waiting for me. My heart pounds as I mount the top step, facing my room.

"I'm here," I say, finding her hovering over my desk and scrutinizing my calendar.

"What is this?" She points down to the one box I wrote in.

"Shabbat—it's tomorrow night and I thought—"

Mama lifts the piece of paper from my desk as if she's holding a document that could dictate our fate. Her eyes widen and her bottom lip falls ajar. "No, no, no." She tears the paper into pieces, over and over until the scraps float to the floor, creating a mountain of snow. Mama sweeps her short auburn hair behind her ears, showcasing the pink tinge of her cheeks. "There is no more Shabbat. We've been over this." She says so with her teeth gritted.

"I don't understand why it matters what we do in our house?" I question her.

Mama's sharply shaped brows knit together, and her head falls to a slight angle. She's looking at me like I'm guilty of a sin. "You know why it matters. Your father is not Jewish like we are, and it's not right that we force him to celebrate a holiday of our faith."

Someone might as well sock me in the stomach because I feel winded, and all I can do is stare down at the pieces of shredded paper between us. "We've lost all of our rights. I must have forgotten," I say, folding my arms over my chest as if she deserves my aggravation. She doesn't.

"You did not forget," Mama snaps. She takes my hand between hers and squeezes tightly. "You are angry, Sofia, and rightfully so, but for now, we must forget who we are and stand behind your father. Believe me when I tell you, we have not lost all of our rights, and we should be grateful."

When I look up at Mama's face in search of empathy, I notice tears forming at the corners of her red-stained eyes and she lifts my fist to her lips, giving me a kiss. "Why are you angry with him then?" I ask.

She shakes her head and releases a lungful of air. "Your father is not who I'm angry with. I, too, resent the world we are living in, and there is nothing I can do except comply for our safety."

Denial is like a glass wall, easy to see beyond, but impossible to walk through. If I give into the fear, it will consume me. Therefore, I must continue to focus on the present.

Because we are safe. For now.

CHAPTER 2
MAY 1941

ISAAC

When I open my eyes each morning, I search for the silver alarm clock I used to keep on my nightstand. It looked like one half of a tin can, with a yellow-tinted dial encircled with Roman numerals.

For years, the repetitious ticking would keep me up at night. My heart would race, and I would hold my pillow over my head until the sound was silent, and I could finally fall asleep. It wouldn't be until morning that I would hear the tick, tick, tick, just before the hollow bell pierced through my head. I would slap my hand over it, usually knocking it onto its side. Mama and Papa both had early work duties and I was responsible for making sure my little sister, Olivia, and I made it to the schoolyard on time.

The responsibility at a young age wore on me, or at least I thought it had worn me down, but I didn't know better then.

Now, I must rely on my internal clock to wake up each morning. I would give up my last few belongings just to hear the ticking of that old timepiece again. No one warned me there would eventually be a last tick.

We've been living in the ghetto of Warsaw for just over a year since we were forced to leave our home in Krakow. We were told Jewish people were being relocated to a community specifically for our kind. When Germany invaded our country, we had no say over what we were entitled to after Mama and Papa had devoted their existence to giving Olivia and me a life many would do anything to have. Neither status nor stream of income makes a difference to the Germans. A Jew is a Jew, and nothing can change that. Their promises of safety and shelter were lies. We live like sewer rats, hoping the food we procure keeps us alive—praying Papa can continue to supply extras for us with his diminishing connections on the outside of the walls. The sewers have become our only means of passing items from one side of the city to the other, and the Germans are now aware of our activity. We aren't allowed out of the ghetto—the space enclosed by a wall, one twice the height of any person, and topped with barbed wire, closed off to a city square made up of a dozen blocks in each direction. Our habitat is the definition of a prison. We are Germany's prisoners.

Mama is already awake, crouching over Olivia, who is still sound asleep among the warmth of the clothing-filled pillow-cases we use as mattresses. When she was a little girl, she would wake up if one of us blinked too loudly, but these days, she can sleep through a shrilling air-raid siren. I'm sometimes envious of this twelve-year-old girl.

"Lu-lu, it's time to get up, darling," Mama whispers in Olivia's ear while brushing away the sweat-ridden curls draped over her forehead. It hasn't been warm down here in longer than I can remember, but the air is stale and thick, and it seems to settle between the four brick walls we occupy.

Olivia rolls onto her back and blinks to see through the

darkness. "Where is Papa?" she asks as she does every morning, hoping for a different answer than the one Mama replies with.

"He got an early start. There was a meeting of some sort." There's always a meeting, but he's secretive about them.

"A meeting for what?" I question, rolling up the flattened pillowcases I slept on.

Mama glances over her shoulder toward me. I can only see the glisten within her eyes. "A meeting," she repeats. I wonder if she knows who he meets with or if she's wondering like we are. I'm not sure she'd say either way.

Papa refuses to give up or accept being trapped between the stone walls that imprison us within the beautiful city we had always loved. Warsaw is no longer a community filled with cheerful residents; it's a holding cell for Jewish people. Whoever he meets with must feel the same, but I'm not sure what can be done about our situation: we're too few against the German forces.

I don't blame Papa—in fact, I wish I could go with him. Mama needs me more, though. Therefore, I don't fuss over what I do throughout the day.

While I pull up my pair of slacks and button my shirt, Mama helps Olivia with her dress—one she used to love, but now despises because the colors are no longer bright, and the hem has begun to fray.

"Papa was able to obtain enough eggs and potatoes yesterday to feed a good amount of people today, but we have a lot of work to do," Mama says, running her fingers across the sides of her hair that she has pinned up. "Isaac, I need you to peel the potatoes, and, Olivia, I'll need you to help me keep the fire burning."

Though we have next to nothing, we have more than many others do and, for that reason, we help whoever we can with what Papa is able to exchange in the underground market.

I pull the loose bricks out from the accessible hole in the

wall, one by one, until there are eight full-size bricks stacked on the dirt-covered ground. Olivia squirms through the wall first, then Mama. I hand her the bricks, one at a time, and wriggle through into the short corridor that leads to an above-ground exit. It only takes me a couple of minutes to replace the bricks before we're scaling up a sewer line ladder that will bring us to the storage space of an old ice-cream shop.

I'm first up the metal rungs so I can move the grate above our heads. I pull Olivia up and place her down on her feet, and help Mama up, then replace the sewer plate.

"The potatoes are up in the back-left ceiling panel," she tells me. We have a distinct ceiling panel for each variety of food we manage to bring in, and then there is a large metal can hidden in the corner behind the old broken freezer. Mama uses it to keep foods as cool as possible before cooking them.

Olivia makes her way to the storefront windows to peek outside. I sometimes wonder if she's hoping to find a different scene. At twelve, I suppose she's still full of hope—another reason to be envious of her.

"It's raining, but there's a line of people outside," she reports.

A line of people once meant men and women standing shoulder to shoulder or front to back in orderly fashion. It has a different meaning now. The hungry Jewish people outside don't have the energy to stand for long, and they often huddle together against a wall for comfort while they wait for a scrap of food. There was no way to know who would be in the lower class or higher class of a ghetto, but some had everything taken away from them, and others found means of holding onto the little they had left. No matter what anyone has or doesn't have here, everyone is hungry, cold, filthy, and miserable. Some are just more so than others.

The three of us move as quickly as we can to prepare the extra rations. By seven each morning, we open the front door just enough to allow in a slight breeze along with the first few people waiting for mercy.

It's been about seven months since the stone walls went up, and in that time, people have lost everything, including most of their body weight. Some aren't fortunate enough to have shelter and sleep on the sidewalks. Roads are filled with ravenous bodies morphing into skeletal figures. The small bit of extras we distribute still aren't enough to keep people alive.

Two women and a young boy standing before us are holding onto each other for support. Their eyes are bulging from the lack of fat in their flesh, and their cheeks are sunken, drawing a precise line around their jawbones. The boy must be around Olivia's age, and it takes everything I have not to scoop him up and offer him some of the life I somehow still seem to have inside of me. We are all suffering, but the children—they don't understand. They shouldn't be able to comprehend the true meaning of hatred at such a young age, but within these walls, there are orphans who not only lost their parents, but watched them starve to death as they fed every morsel of food to their little mouths.

There's no end in sight, just dilapidated bodies waiting for their last breath, the scents of body odor and rotting flesh, and the sounds of cries that carry on from dusk to dawn. I suppose starvation might be a better solution than fighting for survival. It seems clear, the Germans don't intend to let us out of here alive.

For the next couple of hours, fellow Jewish men, women, and children continue to trickle into the muggy shop until there is no food left to serve. The worst part of every day is when we must turn away those who had been waiting with hope that there's something left.

When I see their pleading eyes and their empty faces, my heart feels like a lead boulder bearing heavily on my ribcage. It's hard to push through the weakness to clean up just so we can make it look like we were never here. These moments steal my desire to push forward, and it seems when I'm at my lowest, something surges in me to take on this battle.

Then I hear it, a scream—not one from bodily pain, but from a shattered soul. I can't stop myself from moving toward the cries, wondering if I can help whoever it is. With a few steps out on the street, I watch as a man falls to his knees in grief before a woman I assume to be his wife. Her frail hands shake as she covers her open mouth. "My baby," she cries. "Why?" The woman's knees give out and she falls to the ground too. The couple fall into each other, crying so hard, the veins pulsate across their foreheads.

All I can do is stare and assume their child died from starvation, sickness, or was shot while trying to find food in the underground tunnels like many children are sent to do.

When I come to my senses and realize I'm gawking with no right to witness their intimate pain, I turn back, catching a glimpse at the watchmaker shop toward the end of the block. The sign dangles by one hinge instead of two, highlighting the varying degrees of damage throughout this city. With a quick look, the image of a timepiece on the waving banner looks real, but the minute and hour hands never move. It's the worst kind of reminder that my life may stand forever still.

CHAPTER 3

MAY 1941

SOFIA

The kitchen doesn't hold the same scents as it once did. Fresh bread, pastries, and dumplings would make the entire house smell like a bakery. Mama used to cook and bake all day because it brings her so much happiness, but with the ration cuts, it's difficult to make the same recipes we used to. I smell the floral aroma from yesterday's tea mixed with a hint of cabbage from last night's soup.

"Could you check to see how much flour is left?" Mama asks, pulling other baking supplies out from the cabinets above her head.

I take the yellow canister out from beneath the windowsill and drag it across the kitchen counter to pry open the top. I can feel by the weight that we don't have much left. "There isn't enough to make the babka, we need more." I would do just about anything for a taste of that sweet cake Mama makes so well.

"Yes, well, we'll make sponge cake instead," Mama says, taking the canister from between my hands to reseal the lid. She isn't usually this impatient with me or angered so easily, but I can't blame her.

"When can we buy more?" We've never had money troubles, but there is a shortage of all common food items, and there's no end in sight.

Mama places the palms of her hands on the sides of her face and bows her head. After a sigh of frustration, she replies, "Sofia, we need to have a talk."

Something catches in my throat and it's hard to swallow while conjuring whatever she is about to say—whatever it is they have obviously been hiding from me. She and Papa haven't been speaking to each other a lot over the last couple of weeks. Everything seems to be a secret lately. "What about?"

A clatter from upstairs draws my attention toward the foyer just outside the kitchen. Papa should already be at work since I slept in later this morning than I normally do. School isn't in session today due to some maintenance issues.

"Who's upstairs? Did you hear that?" I ask.

"It's your papa. That's what I need to talk to you about." Mama walks over to the small table on the opposite side of the kitchen and pulls out two of the four chairs. "Sit down for a moment." My mother rarely makes a big deal over a conversation, which means whatever this is about must be as serious as I've been fearing.

"What is it?" I ask, my throat sounding rusty. I take the seat and pull myself in closer to the old worn table we use for all casual meals.

Mama follows and eases down beside me, then rests her hands gently on top of the burgundy linen placemat. Rather than look at her face, waiting for her to speak, I only manage to focus on the twisted fraying tassels that border the seam of the placemat.

"I'll get right to the point since there's no need to drag this out any longer. I'm sorry to have to tell you this, but your papa is leaving his practice. He's going to be working elsewhere. The money will be better and there are other benefits to the new position too." Mama's words sound snipped and shorter than necessary, although I understand perfectly well what she said.

I'm still digesting the information, longing to comb my fingers through the placemat's tassels. They all need to be straightened out so each string can lay flat.

I recall the impromptu meeting Papa had with those men. "Elsewhere? Where will he be working? Papa has been working there my entire life, since he moved here from Germany before you two met, right?"

Mama rests her chin on her balled-up fists. "The Waffen-SS —they need a good physician training their incoming doctors. Your papa's name came highly recommended to them, and the offer isn't something he can afford to turn down. He's closing the doors for now, and when time allows, he will reopen the practice, I'm sure."

How can I comprehend something as ridiculous as Papa accepting an offer to work with the evil people who are trying to rid Europe of all the Jews? He would never do such a thing. She must be mistaken. "I don't understand," I mumble. The more I try to understand the meaning of Papa doing such an unthinkable job, the blurrier the tassels on the placemat become.

Mama inhales sharply through her nose and points her chin toward the ceiling. She's trying to be brave—I can tell that much. "You see, if he is to help the SS, we have a better chance of remaining safe, you and I. This would be on top of me having a 'Privileged Marriage' since your father isn't Jewish."

I can't fathom who came up with these rules, but they were all made unjustly.

While resting my hands on my lap beneath the table, I clench my fists and bite my tongue. We've spoken about the development of new laws arising more often than anyone can predict. There's no saying if or when there might come a time when we are no longer protected by a "Privileged Marriage." Because of this, Papa has begged Mama to consider moving out of Poland to go somewhere safer, but she can't fathom the thought of leaving generations of her family's farm behind. It's the reason Papa wanted to plant his roots here with a medical practice. Future generations of our family will always have a place in this town. But things have changed. Nothing is what it was, and this town is no longer a part of who we are.

"Mama," I say, "we both know we shouldn't be here in Poland. We should have left when we had the chance. We can't act as if we are always going to be exempt from Hitler's power. We are safe for now, but what if those rules change too?"

The same frown lines along her cheeks deepen each time I mention leaving Poland, but she won't accept the thought of running in fear.

Mama stands from her chair, the wooden legs scraping jaggedly across the tiles. "We have no choice in the matter, Sofia."

"Is that what you truly believe?" I question, trying to remain calm, though the panic I'm feeling is much louder than my words.

Mama rests her hands on the back of the wooden chair, then leans in as if cowering in pain. "You already know the answer to this question. Please don't make this harder than it already is. Please."

Papa's footsteps echo between the stairwell as he descends the last couple of steps into the foyer. "Lena, Sofia, I'm heading to the city now. I don't expect to be back until suppertime."

"The city?" I ask, standing from my seat to face him. "What city? I want to join you. There's no school today."

"No," Mama snaps. "You are staying here."

"Lena, it's fine if she wants to come along for the ride. I just need to pick up some paperwork from an office clerk. It's the driving distance that will take most of the time today."

The look on Papa's face is different somehow. Maybe it's that I see him in a different light, knowing what he has agreed to. Even still, there's an unnatural arch to his brows, and his mouth is parted as if he has more to say but won't dare.

"I'm heading to Warsaw. You're welcome to join me," he says, taking heavy steps across the kitchen.

Papa reaches into a cabinet above the counter and retrieves a glass. Mama and I both watch him as he fills it with water from the tap, then guzzles every drop down just as fast. He's stalling until he doesn't have to fill the dense air that's seemingly suffocating each one of us.

Mama closes her eyes—perhaps so she doesn't have to face him and the decisions he's made. I understand why she doesn't want me to go with him, but the time in the car will allow me to ask the questions I need answers to. He can't avoid me if we're cooped up together for hours.

"I'll be fine," I assure Mama, placing my hand on top of hers and squeezing gently. "I would like to join you, Papa. Maybe we can find some flour along the way too since we've almost run out. Mama can't even make babka for us."

"Yes, I'll see what we can do about finding flour. That's fine." He looks as preoccupied as he sounds. Normally, he'd respond to a statement like that by reminding us we must make do with what we have.

"You are dancing with the devil, Friedrich. You know this," Mama sneers.

Papa clears his throat and drops his gaze to the tiled floor. "Yes, well, there isn't much to hide—this has been made clear to me. Sofia's coming and that's that. I'll be leaving in a few minutes. We need to get on the road as soon as possible," he says, rinsing his glass under the running faucet. "Go on and get ready."

"Friedrich," Mama scolds him as I walk out of the kitchen.

I race upstairs to my bedroom and change into a daytime dress, one comfortable enough to sit in for a while.

The arguments between Mama and Papa are becoming louder and more emphatic. I can hear them through most of the walls in the house now, but I can't seem to make out their particular words. I can only tell that Mama doesn't agree with Papa's decision. Nor do I, but I need to know more. I must know more about what he hopes will be the result from this unthinkable job.

I'm ready to go within a few short minutes and trot back down the steps into more uncomfortable silence. Mama is leaning against the arched opening of the kitchen, staring through the glass of our grandfather clock across the way. Papa is straightening his tie in front of the mirror just a few steps away from where Mama is lost in her daze. They have always had a strong marriage, loving, and full of understanding, but the war has changed everything for so many. I didn't think it would have this kind of effect on my parents' marriage too: we all need each other right now, and that should be the only thing that matters.

I step in front of Mama and place my hands on her shoulders, giving her a kiss on the cheek. "Don't worry. I'll be safe, and back soon."

"I love you, darling," she croaks without blinking a single eyelash. "Sofia, wait. I have some finger sandwiches you can take with you for the ride." She disappears into the kitchen and returns within a few breaths, holding a paper-wrapped bundle.

I take the sandwiches from Mama's grip and give her another kiss on the cheek before turning to leave her alone with her thoughts for the day. "Love you, Mama."

CHAPTER 4

MAY 1941

ISAAC

When the morning rush for scraps of food is past us, we're left with the rest of the day to absorb the world around us—every sight, smell, and sound. It's hard to ignore the truth when we are living in a narrow, never-ending tunnel.

Papa has offered to help clean up the streets today, something many of the able-bodied men do in their free waking moments.

"Mama, if you are settled, I'm going to find Papa to see where I can lend a hand."

I'm not sure what the look in Mama's eyes means these days. If I had to assume, hopelessness, fear, regret, and misery, but she would never admit to any of those feelings out loud, not when she's telling us to keep our chins up.

"You don't have to do that, darling, I'm sure they have enough hands today."

I clear my throat and duck my head, knowing what she's saying isn't true.

"I want to go too," Olivia says. "I'm strong and capable. I can help just as much as Isaac."

"Absolutely not. You aren't going anywhere. Neither of you are," Mama says, looking up at me from where she is sitting on the edge of the curb. She flattens her hand over her eyes to block out the sun.

"Lu-lu, stay with Mama and keep her company. She needs help sewing up some holes in our clothes."

Olivia's shoulders fall as if someone stole her energy. "What fun is it to sew up old rags? I should be playing with colorful fabrics that shimmer and shine beneath the sun, not dirt-stained cotton."

Olivia has always loved dresses and fancy clothes. Before we were forced out of education, she was known to wear dresses far too formal for a school setting. Her teachers would sometimes approach Mama with complaints that Olivia's clothing choices were a bit of a distraction. Mama would respond with something along the lines of: "Olivia is a girl who knows what she likes." She didn't want to discourage her from having a "wonderfully unique sense of style." This was only until the school decided to require uniforms. Mama didn't always see eye to eye with Olivia on her outfit choices, but she felt strongly that she had a right to wear what made her happy. That, and there were far worse things to argue over in life.

Olivia's favorite clothes were left behind when we were told we could only bring the necessities here to the ghetto.

"No one said it was going to be fun, but I could use your help," Mama says.

Olivia twists around to face me again and tilts her head to the side, narrowing her eyes. Her left braid swings into her cheek and she swats it away. "Just because I'm a girl doesn't mean I can't help you with strong-person stuff."

She thinks the definition of cleaning is using a broom or a

mop. That isn't the case here. "I never said you aren't strong enough," I correct her.

She folds her arms over her chest and purses her lips. I know this is hard on her, in more ways than it probably is for me. At least I had somewhat of a normal youth. Hers is being completely stolen. If we ever find our way out of here in one piece, God only knows how old she'll be and how much she will have missed.

I lean forward to whisper in her ear, but she tries to step away. Nothing I say will make a difference. Once she has made her mind up, that's that. I have hope that will be a helpful trait for her someday. I take her by the elbow and stop her from backing away any further. She's so tiny for twelve years old, it would be easy to knock her off her feet if I'm not gentle enough.

"I need you to stay and help Mama because something doesn't seem right with her today. Papa has been exhausted from cleaning so much and it will be considerate of both of us to each help one of them out today. I'm positive Mama would prefer your company over mine. We both know this."

"You're her favorite," she bemoans.

I flick one of her braids. "I can't argue with you on that, but this will be the best plan for now."

Olivia rolls her eyes at me, something she's become very good at doing over the last few months. "Fine. When will you be back?"

"When the work is done," I answer.

"If I find out you're playing with a deck of cards somewhere in between these buildings, I'm going to haunt you in your sleep tonight."

"Fair enough," I say, patting the top of her head. "I'll be back soon, Mama. Lu-lu is staying with you, but Papa needs help. I need to go."

Mama bobs her head, an automatic response when she doesn't have the energy to argue.

I leave her with a kiss on the cheek before heading down the crowded streets. With as many people as there are in the roads and on the sidewalks, the conversations should be much louder and echoing between the rows of buildings, but the chatter seems to become quieter each day. People stare at one another without purpose. I don't think anyone wonders much about the person beside them—what they're thinking or how they're feeling. It can't be much different from what we feel.

I hear the wagon before I see it. The wooden wheels are clumsy while carrying a lot of weight across uneven stone. The sight of a motionless body draped over the curb tells me that Papa hasn't made it down to this area yet. My chest aches knowing I will likely spot a dozen more bodies scattered in no particular place, but everywhere at the same time. Each day, there are so many bodies to clear off the street. They're bodies—humans—people just like me, and they're dead—left for the crows and rats that have a better life on these streets than we do. We're not even allowed to fight for the chance of survival. If our bodies can sustain the torment, we live. Yet, those who keep us confined to this ghetto can't be bothered to clean up. We must take care of our own before, during, and after life—not only for their sake, but for the health of everyone else too. We're running out of places to pile up the bodies, but we continue with the effort because it's what we hope someone would do for us.

Mama doesn't know Papa has been carting away bodies, nor does she know I'm helping him. She would be furious that I've been seeing these inhumane sights.

Papa says that if we are able-bodied and capable, we should do what others here can't. We're fortunate enough to have age on our side and the bit of extra food we manage to get our hands on.

Once the men start taking the wagons with piles of skeletal figures away, I begin scooping up the nearest bodies to haul over to the others. The strength of the stench doesn't falter or weaken. It's the strongest reminder of what we're facing. The thought of what a dead body smelled like never crossed my mind until a couple of years ago. Now, I'm afraid I'll never smell anything else again.

The flies are relentless, swirling around us and taunting us like the Nazis do. If it isn't enough to carry human remains around on our shoulders, needing a free hand to swat away the bugs adds insult to injury.

I don't wish to see this truth—this nightmare every day—but who am I to have the luxury of hiding within the walls of an old ice-cream shop all day? No one wants to be cleaning up this mess. We just do as we do because it seems like the only option. Nothing will save us and there isn't anything that can bring these poor people back to life. Cleaning up their reminder is the humane thing to do and it's more humane than those outside of these walls act. If I die with respect, it will be more than they can say.

"Isaac," Papa shouts through a tired groan. "You've come to help your old man. What a mensch you are, my boy." As he approaches me, he's cowering forward, placing one hand on his back and the other on his thigh. Papa has had a bad back since he was young. He was injured from falling off a horse when he was my age, but the long-lasting damage failed to present itself until after I was born. He refuses to speak a word of it now. I'm not sure if it's for the sake of pride, or for the purpose of forgetting the pleasant memories of riding a horse through a field. He never let his injury get in the way of what he loved, not until all our rights were robbed from us. "Is everything fine with your mother and sister?"

"Yes, but I assumed you needed help, especially after the number of bodies we found yesterday."

Papa shakes his head and releases a heavy lungful. "It's bad, son. Real bad, and I'm afraid it's only going to get worse. There's nothing left of these poor people. They're all skin and bones." He speaks of what I've seen for myself, what we've all had to witness. It's hard to look at any corner of a street block without spotting another lifeless body. "That alley—we haven't gone down there yet today," he says, pointing off to the left.

As I follow his finger along the damp cobblestones, I notice smog rising from the sewers just as a light breeze stirs up the mild warmth from the sun with the dank air. A bitter stench floats around me, hinting at how many decomposing bodies might be concealed in the shadows down there. I can't understand why so many of them seem to be in one place at the same time, but I wonder if their final thought is that they don't want to be alone when they take their last breath.

Once the bodies are piled up as high as we can stack them within the wagons, we push forward to the current disposal location.

People no longer look over in the direction of the wagons. No one is curious about the loud racket. It isn't a scene that needs to be witnessed when we can feel it down to the very core of our souls. We all have a last day and not a clue as to when, but the hope we once had has slowly disappeared into a faraway distance. Our eyes won't allow us to see that far ahead, all we have to hold onto is a desire to live for just one more day. It's enough for now, enough to carry us through to nightfall again.

CHAPTER 5
MAY 1941

SOFIA

Papa hasn't said a word since we left town, and I've been staring out the car window for miles. Maybe he knows I'm already aware of the truth behind his actions.

"How far are we going to drive before you ask me how my studies are, or how the new lambs in the barn are getting along?"

We have been sitting here as if we are strangers. I've had to sit on my hands to stop them from fidgeting. There's so much I want to ask him, but I don't know where to start.

"I apologize, my darling. I didn't realize you were waiting for me to talk. Usually, you'd be content carrying on chatting with a wall if given the option," he says with a snicker. I know he means to be humorous, but there aren't many people left in Poland who find much to laugh about these days.

"Why did you do this, Papa? I feel ashamed for asking, but I think I deserve to know."

My father shifts around in his seat as if he's just noticed he hasn't moved a hair in the last few hours. He must be stiff, gripping the steering wheel so tightly. I notice how white his knuckles are. "I assumed you figured it all out on your own. There isn't much that goes unnoticed by you."

"I listen to the radio daily. I'm well informed of what's happening all around us, and I know I'm in a peculiar situation, being the daughter of a Protestant man and a Jewish woman. However, it doesn't seem as though there are intelligent reasons for the decisions that have been made against other Jewish people, so I can't help but wonder what part of our situation is keeping me safe."

Papa hasn't blinked since I began to explain. I'm not sure he's even focused on the winding road in front of us. I dig my fingernails into the upholstery, waiting for him to realize he's veered off too far to the right and is hitting the pebbles on the side of the road. The uneven terrain startles him into straightening out the wheel to redirect the car.

Maybe he'd rather avoid an answer, but I can't just stare at the side of his face, waiting until his lips move to try to form a word. With frustration running through me, I swivel in my seat to stare out the window once again. The green pastures in this area are endless. We could have been driving for just a few minutes or hours and I wouldn't know the difference if I didn't keep checking my watch.

Papa releases a heavy sigh. "I'm not Jewish. That's the only reason you are safe. It's a horrible truth. The last thing I want to do is cause you unnecessary fear. As your father, it's my job to keep you safe, Sofia, and that's what I've been doing since the day you were born, and something I intend to do until the day I die."

"Or, when *I* die," I reply, interrupting.

He shakes his head and takes in a deep breath. "This is exactly why I didn't want to discuss the topic with you. It will only scare you. Let me protect you. All you have to do is trust me. It shouldn't be that much to ask of you."

I turn my head to look at him again. "This isn't about my

trust for you. I'm more curious about how you expect me to be so naive. You've stopped asking about my studies because you don't think I'll ever become a nurse, never mind a doctor like you. Am I right? Jewish people are losing value and credibility every day this war continues. That's what my future looks like now."

Papa inhales sharply and squeezes the steering wheel tighter. "That's not what I think. I know you will achieve all your lifelong goals in due time. I have faith you won't give up until you are exactly where you want to be. Though, right now, you are only sixteen, and I want you to live without so much worry about the world around you. Adulthood is just around the corner, but I don't want to rush your youth away."

"It's easier to dream of a future when we are not in a war," I argue.

"In any case, my hope is that by helping these men, I will be giving them one less reason to consider us a problematic family, being of mixed-religions."

"You're practically holding your Jewish wife and daughter as bait in front of them? How do you figure this is going to help?"

"You sound just like your *matka*. You must have more trust in me than you do. My only plan is to keep us safe and alive, Sofia."

The next hour—the final hour of our drive—is as quiet as the first two. I'm no longer fighting for information. I understand enough and it's painful to even attempt to comprehend.

The city of Warsaw looks different from what I remember when we came years ago to visit Mama's extended family— more links to our so-called unfortunate circumstance. Papa has very few roots left to his family since they are either still in Germany or have emigrated to America within the last decade.

He would have liked to go to America too, but Mama can't leave the legacy of our family farm behind. I see both of their sides very clearly, and while I think we would be safer elsewhere, I can appreciate the heartache of abandoning a part of what made us who we are, and only for the reason of hatred. I know we all want to be stronger, but it seems impossible.

"I don't recall there being a wall in the middle of the city like this. Do you?" I ask, finding block after block of stones stacked higher than any wall I've ever seen.

Papa clears his throat and shifts around his seat again. "Uh —I believe the wall is fairly new, as of the last couple of years."

"Why would they do this to such a beautiful city?"

I should have expected he wouldn't answer.

We pass a broken piece in the wall, an opening the size of a large gourd. There's a line of cars in front of us, slowing down to allow pedestrians to cross the road, giving me just enough time to catch a glimpse of what exists on the other side. There are children looking out of the hole, an arm reaching for something or someone, and for a split second, it looks as if we are on the daylight side and they are on the nighttime side. It's dark and the buildings are corroding, but why are people in there when there is a perfectly good part of the city here?

"Sofia, keep your eyes on the road ahead of us," Papa says.

The sound of a hollow slap, following a striking ping from what sounds like a gunshot shocks me into straightening my posture and facing forward. "What was that?"

"We're in a city. There's a lot going on around here," Papa says, talking quickly as he squeezes in between the curb and the car in front of us to turn down the next street.

As we round the corner, I look over my shoulder, back toward the direction where the sound came from, but all I see is a group of Nazis marching alongside the wall, blocking the view.

"When we go into this building, I need you to keep silent

and speak only if someone asks you basic questions. Do you understand?"

"Or what? Will they shoot me too?" I utter from the shock rippling through my nerves.

Papa pulls into a spot to park and pounds his fists against the steering wheel. His jaw tenses and his nostrils flare. "Obviously, this was a bad idea. Stay in the car. I will only be in there for a few minutes."

"They are trapping Jewish people on the other side of that wall, aren't they? That's the ghetto I heard about. It was in Warsaw, I remember now."

Papa presses his fist against his mouth and closes his eyes. "I will keep you safe and alive. Stop fighting against me, Sofia. It won't help." He huffs and peers over at me as a look of realization pulls his shoulders down. "For God's sake—I don't even know what I'm saying anymore. You obviously shouldn't be in this car out here alone. You're coming in with me—just keep quiet."

"I'm a Jewish girl. They might mind me being in their building," I say.

"Sofia, if a man has nothing to hide, they are less likely to go looking. It's better off this way."

I scoot across the front seat and slide out the door. I feel sick, wondering what life must be like on the other side—just a block from here.

The air doesn't smell clean like it does at home. There's a sour scent floating through the air along the tail end of each breeze. The odor makes my throat tighten.

The building we enter feels larger inside than it looked from the outside. The click and clack from my heels echo between the walls and I find myself studying every inch of the grand entryway as if I were no larger than a mouse walking through the Amazon. Tall plants in oversized vases line the walls, and the chandelier in the center of the ceiling seems overwhelming for a business setting, but it creates an atmosphere of elegance and luxury.

We're escorted into the elevator and taken to a high-level floor, just one down from the top. Another grand entryway welcomes us off the elevator. SS officers are in clusters, scattered around taking part in various discussions outside of meeting rooms and offices. No one seems to notice us at first, giving me an extra moment to look around. My gaze is drawn to the floor-to-ceiling arched window, inviting in an abundance of sunlight. It's just across the way and I make my way over to see the view from up here.

"Sofia," Papa scolds in a whisper.

"I'm just looking out the window," I reply, mouthing my words to keep quiet.

Upon settling my gaze on the wide view, a chill climbs up my spine. Remorse—it's all I feel now. I could have gone on living in ignorance, but now I know the answer to all the questions that have been running through my innocent mind. The windows on this floor overlook the wall in the middle of the city... almost too perfectly. People are lined up against buildings, sitting, curled onto their sides, or hunched over. The sight of children selling goods like beggars, while others hold each other, limping down curbs where they are forced to step over another person's ragged limb reveals how much these poor people are suffering. It's as if they're trapped in a container without holes for air, and it's only a matter of time before they all waste away. The officers can watch what is happening on the dark side of the wall. I can't understand why anyone would want to bear witness to so much desolation, but the people working in this building—they are the creators of the scene outside. It must be like watching a play in a theater for them. The brutality of the life they are inflicting on Jewish people continues spinning on an endless reel, all for their viewing pleasure.

I glance over my shoulder in search of Papa, wondering if he was aware of what I would see. In either case, he must notice a change in my disposition. I feel like the blood has drained from my face. I'm sure I look pale as a trail of sweat wraps around the curves of my neck like a form of strangulation. There is no irony of looking at what my life is intended to be, nor the fact that I'm being spared by hiding behind Papa's last name. I shouldn't be in this building, I should be behind that wall.

CHAPTER 6

OCTOBER 1941

ISAAC

Every single day feels like ten, but without a future to look forward to. It seems inconceivably obvious what lies ahead—with bodies failing, the healthy waning as starvation and disease take over—it's all there is in front of us. Death and morbidity, sickness, and the end of someone else's beginning.

Even when a person is sent to prison, they are sentenced with a duration of time. I can't understand what an entire religious group has done to deserve less than what a criminal receives.

The moment I feel the cold, wet air hit my face each morning, I wonder what new enemy we will be forced to face. The people in the buildings surrounding this cage must watch us like rats in a maze, placing bets on who's next to die, and who might outlive us all. It's hard not to assume there is a person standing at a tall window, holding a cigarette between his lips and a cup of tea in his hand, telling the person beside him to watch what happens next. It's all a plan. They have us right where they want us and watching us is their favorite form of entertainment—the SS officers, all of them acting all high and mighty in their freshly pressed uniforms with their chins angled toward the sky.

They don't care what we think of them, but if one should know, we think they are the most disgraceful, unintelligent creatures who have ever roamed the face of this earth, and forever, they will be known for the torture they have delivered to so many innocent men, women, and children. Jealous cowards, that's what they are.

It's been a week since Papa was able to retrieve extra supplements from the personal connections he has outside these walls.

"There's still nothing," I tell the line made up of ragged people, all leaning their weight against the edifice of the building.

The familiar face of an elderly woman peeks out from the queue. If she wasn't dressed the way she is, she could easily be confused for a child from behind. She's barely the average height of a young teenager, yet she is likely one of the oldest on the block here in the ghetto. She must also be the strongest person here, surviving this long without age on her side. She's here every morning in the mix of people hoping that we have extra food to spare. The others look distraught to hear my news, but the woman steps out of line and ambles toward me with her broken cane. Everyone is so quiet this morning I can hear each thump of the hollow stick grinding against the rubble between stones. She has her charcoal gray scarf wrapped around her head, tied in a knot beneath her chin. The fabric casts a shadow over her eyes, but I can see that the definition of her chin and jaw has become very prominent over the last several weeks. Her dress, the one she's always worn, is hanging like drapes from her shoulders.

"Isaac," she wheezes. Mrs. Ackerman gently swings her cane beneath her arm, freeing her hands. She reaches out for my hand that isn't holding the door to the ice-cream shop open.

"Yes, madam, how are you getting along today?" I ask her.

"Isaac, my boy," she says again, squeezing my hand between her warm, spindle-like fingers. "How is your mama feeling today? Is she any better?"

My gaze drops to our clasped hands. "Not well," I reply. "I will make sure to tell her you asked about her."

"Does she have a fever?" Mrs. Ackerman continues.

"I believe so. She's very warm to the touch, but shivering at the same time. The cough has progressed too. I'm just glad she has a dark space to rest her eyes. It's the only time I've been grateful for the lack of light."

"The headaches are quite bad, I remember well."

Mrs. Ackerman was ill with typhus just a couple of months ago. We've all said if that virus didn't take her down, nothing here will. If only I could put a bet on that statement.

My family and I thought the worst was behind us—the most severe impact of the bacterial spread has been coming to an end but isn't completely gone yet. As careful as we tried to be in a helpless situation, we managed to make it nearly nine months without one of us becoming sick, but a few days ago, Mama became unsteady while sweeping the curb. Thankfully, Olivia and I were outside, sweeping as well, and caught her before she went down. I knew right away. Olivia didn't want to believe it could be typhus, not after as far as we'd come, keeping the disease out of our small space. But there's no denying the symptoms, and there's no use in wondering what the outcome will be: all we can do is pray.

"Do you need wet compresses?" Mrs. Ackerman asks. The

scarf on her head billows upward, riding along with the breeze bouncing between the walls of this alley. The fabric folds back over her head, exposing her sad light gray eyes, baggy skin sagging beneath each set of lower lashes. She may not be as old as we assume, but we've all aged a great deal from living in these conditions.

"I've been tearing an old sheet and keeping them damp," I tell her.

"I have something that can help with the rash," she says. "I don't have much, but I have some baking soda we can mix with a little water. It will give her some relief."

I haven't been one to accept items from others, not when we all have so little, but if it's going to give Mama comfort, I must accept the offer. "I would be ever so grateful, Mrs. Ackerman. Thank you. Thank you very much."

"You're a kind boy, Isaac—a very kind boy." She clasps her fingertips around my chin and gives me a little pinch. "I'll be back in a moment with the baking soda."

Mrs. Ackerman limps off down the curb. Even the weakest still have strength to help others. It speaks volumes for each one of us holding onto what we have left here.

Everyone else who was in line has now dispersed, leaving me alone, half inside the ice-cream shop and half outside.

Mama doesn't want Papa, Olivia, or I to be near her, but I refuse to let her suffer alone. We are taking turns watching over her, covering our mouth and nose with a small piece of fabric to protect ourselves. We won't do each other any good if any of the rest of us become sick too.

It takes me a few minutes to make my way through the sewer line that brings me to the false bricks used as our door-way. I can hear Mama coughing from behind the wall. She needs medicine, and there's nothing for her—there's nothing for anyone.

Olivia is sitting by Mama's head with a nearly dry compress that I left her with. She's holding a cloth over her mouth and nose and rubbing at Mama's cheeks.

"When did Papa leave?" I ask her.

"He only left just a few minutes ago. He said he wanted to wait until you returned, but he was worried about the time." Olivia continues to move her hand in machine-like circular motions. "I think it's because he's planning to travel down the other sewer line—" Olivia's statement ends abruptly, as she seemingly needs to take a deep breath to continue, "the bad one."

I do my best to control my expression, so I don't scare her, but from what I've heard, that underground pathway is lined with traps and *Wachmänner* guards hiding in the shadows of every nook and cranny. It sounds as if that route has the same chances of survival as typhus. Though I couldn't ask him not to do everything possible to help Mama right now, my worst fear is walking away from this place without either of them.

"Papa will be okay, he knows what he's doing. Hopefully he can find something that will help Mama," I force myself to say.

"She's going to die, isn't she?" Olivia mouths in a breath of whisper. She asks the question as if she's casually wondering when Mama might be going to the market next.

I wish Mama would speak up in response, but the fact that she is silent scares me. "How long has she been asleep?" I ask, ignoring Olivia's previous question. "Did she wake up at all when I was gone?"

"No, she hasn't moved at all," Olivia replies, turning back to focus on holding the crumpled cloth against Mama's cheek.

I squat on the other side of my sister and place my hand on the curve of Mama's neck. It looks like an endearing gesture, but I'm actually checking for a pulse. She's pale and I can't tell if her chest is moving or if I'm imagining the slightest movement.

"Are you going to answer me?" Olivia says.

"We just have to help her fight this off. She's stronger than the two of us combined, right?"

Olivia doesn't answer, nor do I expect her to. There aren't many ways to see a brighter point of view while being held captive within this never-ending darkness.

CHAPTER 7

MAY 1942 – SEVEN MONTHS LATER

ISAAC

Whispers in the dark were something of a nightmare years ago. Today, it's the only form of communication we have inside these walls. It's likely the middle of the night, not a typical time to be overhearing a conversation, but sleep seems harder and harder to find lately too. I spend more time staring up at the dark concrete ceiling than I do resting.

"But where have you been all day?" Mama asks Papa. "It must be two in the morning."

"We came across some information today," Papa says.

We, as in the Jewish partisan. He has made it clear that we aren't going down without a fight, but I don't know how he plans to defend us against an entire country full of hatred.

"Ludwig," Mama shouts in a whisper. "What on earth are you talking about?"

There's a long pause, giving me a minute to wonder what could have kept him out so late.

"The Germans—they are going to start deporting us from

Warsaw," he says, his whisper ending with a sigh of apprehension.

"Where to?" Mama asks.

"Perhaps somewhere else like where we are, maybe worse."

Worse. Even after all I have seen over the last few years, I'm not sure how I could comprehend something worse than the state in which we are living. No one speaks about the purpose driving the Germans to treat us like an infestation, but it's easy to silently assume.

"When will this start? How much time do we have?"

"It's hard to say, my love. It could be weeks—possibly a month or two. We shouldn't assume the worst, but we should prepare for whatever may come. There was a lot of talk about forced labor, and not just for the men. We need to prepare the children for whatever may lie ahead."

I consider speaking up, telling Papa I'm awake and listening. He should know I have been watching him very closely to follow in his footsteps.

He was an accountant before the war. A talent for seeing numbers in ways others don't is what carried him to his success. We lived a good life, never needing much. Having food on the table was never a concern. Friends would always join us for tea in the afternoons. Whoever was over, they brought their children, and Olivia and I always had other kids to play with. We would sing, dance, smile, and laugh—moments I took for granted, never assuming they could be stolen from us.

At some point between those days and today, I was forced to become a man at sixteen. Papa knows I'm capable of labor. I've proven myself time and time again, but Olivia, she knows how to serve food with a ladle, and I'm not sure that's enough for what Papa is talking about.

"How much more can we endure?" Mama asks. "As if typhus killing off over twenty-thousand people wasn't enough. They won't stop until they take our blood."

"Hush, darling," Papa says, trying to soothe her with a calm tone. "Let's be thankful you survived. We thought we were going to lose you, but a miracle carried you through, and for that, we must believe God is watching over us, and keeping us alive for a reason."

I know what Mama is likely thinking. Why would God choose to keep us alive over the others? What are we offering the world more than them? It isn't a choice on who lives or dies, it's a test of strength and endurance. It's a race to a finish line where a cliff over a bottomless pit awaits. Some may say those who have already died are the lucky ones. We're still fighting to stay alive, only to end up in the same place at the end.

"What will we do with Lu-lu?" Mama asks. "She knows nothing more than serving a bowl of food." Olivia was just ten when we arrived here. She went from playing imaginary tea parties to living in a hole where we consider stale bread a luxury.

"She must learn everything we can teach her, from sewing to first-aid and using tools she's capable of maneuvering."

Mama sniffles during a moment of silence. "This isn't fair of them. We had everything we could have wanted and more. You worked so hard to give us a wonderful life, and now—we're here. I don't feel right about remembering my carefree days as a young girl, knowing Lu-lu will never be able to experience the same. Her childhood has already been robbed."

I know with Mama's final words, there is nothing left to say. Papa can't make the truth better or deny a word of what she said. All he can do is hold her and let her feel the same pain we all feel.

A couple of hours of sleep found me, in the quiet following Mama and Papa's conversation, but with the shuffle of my father moving around the small space between the lumps of bedding, I know it's morning.

"I'll be ready in a moment, Papa," I mutter as I pull myself upright. Lately, he hasn't been asking me to join him as much. I assume this is due to the scene outside becoming worse each day, but I feel it's my responsibility to do my part. Plus, it's only a matter of time before the *Wachmänner* find me. I'm too old to be sitting at home with Mama. The other boys my age have either been sent to a labor camp or one of the manufacturing facilities for textiles or carpentry. I've been fortunate they haven't come for me with an assigned job yet.

Papa takes a moment to respond, and I know it's because he'd rather me stay here than endure the burden of life outside, but I can't let him do what he's doing alone. "Okay, then. Thank you, son."

The rustling of fabric stirs a couple of steps away. A quiet groan rumbles in Olivia's throat before she asks her usual question of, "What about me?" Her words are raspy from the dry air we inhale all night.

There's a pause before a response since we didn't realize Olivia was awake just yet. "Oh, Lu-lu, Mama needs your help today," Papa says.

"Why do you say this every day when we don't have extra food to hand out? All we do is sweep the curb or look for raggedy pieces of fabric on the streets. I want to help, I want to do more."

She doesn't know what she's asking. I know she is aware of the deceased bodies on every street corner, but I'm not sure she knows what happens to them or where they are going—where Papa and the others cart them away to. She might already have an idea, but just as Mama feels guilty for Olivia's childhood being torn away, I feel the same about the extra four years of youth I was given.

"I'm going to teach you something very important today, Lu-lu," Mama says, kneeling by her head.

"What's that?" she asks. An inflection of interest highlights her question.

"You're going to perfect your sewing skills. You already know more than the basics, and you could become quite proficient with a needle and thread just like you've wanted."

"I wanted to sew beautiful clothes, not scraps of dirty rags," she scoffs.

"We all have to start somewhere, sweetheart. Someday, you will be able to make all those beautiful dresses you used to admire so much. Won't that be wonderful?"

I can't see Olivia's expression with Mama in front of her, but I assume she's not buying into our mother's talk about the future. Instinctually, none of us can think that far ahead—not with the truth surrounding us like slowly closing walls lined with daggers.

"Do we even have a needle and thread?" Olivia asks.

"Ah, I almost forgot," Papa says, scooping his hand into his pocket. "I came across a sewing needle yesterday."

"We can take the thread from some of the fabric we've picked up along the streets," Mama adds.

"I can hardly see more than shadows in this space. How will I thread a needle?" Olivia asks.

"Don't worry about that now. Let your papa and brother go, and then we'll find a quiet place with more light."

The only source of light we have down here, between the basement and the main sewer line, is from the crack in the corner of the ceiling joint. There's a small window vent in the storage space on the floor above us. It's enough to allow us to see shadows and some details, but never much more during the day. We have candles for emergencies, but we try to avoid using them whenever possible. The longer we stay out of sight from the parading Nazis, the safer we'll be.

I pull on my pants over the thin layer of shorts I wear to bed and button my shirt while slipping my feet into the worn boots that are far too tight.

Mama's hand touches my back as I lower my pant leg over the first boot. "Be careful, dear, please," she says, placing a kiss on my cheek.

"I'm always careful," I remind her.

I fix my other pant leg and lean down to ruffle Olivia's hair. "Once you learn to sew, you can make me new clothes. If that doesn't lift your spirits, I'm not sure what will," I say to her.

"Make you clothes?" Olivia questions. "Maybe after Old-Bear has a new coat."

When we were told we could only bring the necessities and our valuables, Olivia took her favorite stuffed bear that Bubbie made for her before she passed away. She believes our grand-mother's soul lives within the stuffing of the bear and keeps us all safe.

"Fair enough," I say. "Old-Bear is in need of a new coat, I suppose."

Olivia squeezes the stuffed toy under her arm and scrunches her nose. At thirteen, I might tease her about the love she has for an inanimate object, but we all need to find comfort where we can. I wish I had something warm and full of memo-ries to squeeze at night too.

Once Papa and I leave Mama and Olivia behind, I confess to being awake last night when they were talking. "How accu-rate do you think the information is?" I ask.

"Quite accurate," he replies. "However, like I always say, we must focus on today and not worry about tomorrow just yet. I need your strength more than ever now, son."

"I understand." I know not to ask more questions, including the source of his information. If one wrong word is spoken out loud near the wrong set of ears, it could end badly. We can't afford to take any chances, so I trust what Papa says is for our protection. "Will we stay together if and when the worst is to happen?"

Papa looks at me as we step out onto the street. As usual, the whites of his eyes are lined with red webs of veins, encircling the amber hues that could once convince anyone of anything. "Yes, of course, son."

It's at this moment I come to terms with the fact that he can no longer convince me of the truths he wants to believe.

CHAPTER 8

JULY 1942

SOFIA

The house is never quiet anymore. We always have guests—
each one in uniform with a red band emblazoned with a white
swastika around their arm.

Shortly after Papa accepted the position to train doctors of
the SS, he was informed that Mama and I are to wear *Jude*
patches when in public or in the presence of any Germans.
Papa didn't elaborate on the conversation he'd endured to
receive this information, but it was shortly after our visit to the
building in Warsaw. We are still considered to be "privileged"
but not as "privileged" as we would be if I wasn't being raised
Jewish. I wanted to ask Papa if they made up a new rule right
then and there because the details of a "Privileged Marriage"
had not been broken down so clearly for us before. Now, Mama
and I are branded in our own home, as if we are nothing but
house pets each time a man in uniform pays a visit.

Often, I stand outside whichever room they are in and stare
at the men, each relaxed in a chair with a leg folded over the
other, a cigar pinched between their fingers, and laughter

bouncing between the walls. Papa smiles and nods at what is intended to be humorous chatter, but when he spots me, the blood drains from his cheeks. He is aware of the thoughts brewing in my head. The voice inside of me would like to step up to any one of the officers. "Why don't you do to me what you've done to the others?" I would say with an arched brow.

In truth, I fear each of them, and for that, I know I have lost my greatest personal attribute: bravery.

"More cognac?" Papa asks.

Yes, let's offer them more of our finest liquor in hopes they will leave here as smitten as they arrived. I hate to believe that Papa is creating an ally with the devils. It appears he enjoys some of his time with these men, and for that reason I have nothing to say to him. We haven't spoken in nearly two months. It was a slow decline at first after we visited Warsaw, but since then, with each guest that has seen the inside of these walls, I desire less and less to converse with my father, the man I silently call a traitor. We would have been better off fleeing the country than standing by while he keeps the evil healthy. It isn't a secret as to how many Jewish lives were stolen by typhus just a few months ago, but Papa oversaw the health crisis by assisting the SS doctors who were not properly trained to treat their comrades who were falling victim to the pandemic. I can only imagine what was happening within those walls of Warsaw, or any other walls imprisoning my kind across Europe.

Mama serves a meal to these men, as per Papa's orders—promising that by her doing so, we will remain safe, even with a star sewn to the black sweaters we wear over our dresses.

When our gazes meet, the pain deepens in my chest, as I'm sure it does for her as well. After she places a new platter of meats and cheeses on the linen-covered table, she mutters, "Why don't you go on upstairs, Sofia?" before continuing into the kitchen.

"It's Shabbat, in case you have forgotten," I whisper as she walks away.

Mama spins around on her heels, her eyes wide, her brows high, and her mouth slightly parted with a look of horror.

"Sofia," she scolds.

I drop my gaze to the ground and make my way toward the stairwell. When I close my bedroom door, the feeling of freedom embraces me. The walls don't have eyes or ears, and no one can stop me from what I am thinking or believing—not here.

The sun is melting against the horizon outside my window. The sky is lit up like an oil painting, with splotches of red-wine, fresh orange peels, and a hint of ripe plum.

It's about the right time.

I open the drawer to my writing desk and slip my hand-drawn calendar out for the month of July. With my red pencil, I write the word "Shabbat" in today's square.

I place the calendar face-down in my drawer and kneel in front of my bed, pulling out the sterling silver tray I had set up this morning. It's an old rusty tray, a family heirloom we have been forced to try to forget about. Along with it, there are two matching candlestick holders I polished this morning. I place a white candle in each and light a match to give life to the fresh wicks.

Mama is the person who should light the candles and recite the prayer, but it's up to me to continue the tradition if she is to fear what we believe.

I place my hands over my eyes, wishing the act was in fact closing on the truths I'd like to leave behind. Mama always said: "We cover our eyes so that when we uncover them and see the new light, we have reached our much-earned day of rest."

We no longer rest, not any day of the week, but I can't give up on hope because it's all I have left now.

With a mutter of my breath, I recite the prayer that used to feel like a blanket of warmth on a cold night—something to welcome after a long week.

> "Blessed are you, Adonai our God,
> Sovereign of all, who hallows us with
> mitzvot, commanding us to kindle the
> light of Shabbat."

I lift my hands away from my eyes, staring directly into the flickering lights. "Shabbat Shalom," I whisper to myself.

My grandfather left me his family's Shabbat wine cup before he passed away several years ago. I should be grateful he isn't here to see what this world has become. I've kept the beautiful gold patterned cup safely wrapped in cloth in my bureau to use with a family of my own someday, and since I can't ask Mama for the cup we would normally use, it seems appropriate to use Grandfather's. I uncork the small crystal glass I siphoned some wine into a few weeks ago and drop a splash in the bottom of the cup. I kneel onto my folded legs and take in a deep breath while lifting the cup. "We praise You, Eternal God, Sovereign of the Universe, who creates the fruit of—"

My door swings open, the gust of air stealing the candle's flames. The startling commotion makes me spill the wine on my lap and my heart pounds against my chest like a mallet against a gong.

"Dear God, what are you doing?" Mama mutters harshly under her breath, closing the door behind her and twisting the key in the lock.

"What am I doing?" I ask. "Is this sight no longer familiar to you? Does this cup bring you no reminders?" It's her father's. How can she act as if this wasn't a part of our life—as if it wasn't her entire life before these last few years?

"How long have you been doing this?" she asks.

"This?"

Mama closes her eyes and kneels next to me. A sigh spills from her lips. "Sofia, this isn't the life I want. You must know this."

"It's just one we're supposed to accept, but I can't. I refuse to give up who I am," I say.

"Those men downstairs—if they knew—"

"They don't."

Mama folds me into her arms and places her cool hand on the side of my face. "I'm not sure what else we can do."

"We should continue to believe what we always have. There is no other choice for me, Mama. If we give up who we are, we are allowing them to have their way."

"We live in the shadow of their footsteps. They have already gotten their way," she argues.

I understand, but I refuse to speak those kinds of words out loud.

"Do you have a loaf of Challah hiding under your bed too?" she asks, curling her lip into a small smile.

"I didn't think there would be someone to break bread with, so no."

Mama's body shivers and she squeezes me a bit harder. "Next Friday night we will have a proper Shabbat dinner, even if it has to be up here in your bedroom."

Her words bring a smile to my face, something I thought I was incapable of after what we've been bearing witness to. "How much longer will this go on?"

Mama takes my hand in hers, forcing me to twist my body toward her so I can look into her eyes as she answers my question. "Things are not going to get better anytime soon. They are becoming worse by the day. I know you have a hard time thinking so, and it feels wrong to say this with fairness to any other Jewish family, but we should consider ourselves lucky for the moment. Your papa, he isn't the person you believe him to be. He's doing what he must to protect us."

I close my eyelids, unable to look at Mama when I say what I feel. "He's playing the part a little too well. He's made a believer out of me as well as all those officers. He's a doctor—a man of medicine, a healer, someone I've wanted to become, and now a Polish traitor."

CHAPTER 9
JULY 1942

ISAAC

We are no longer able to help each other here. We can't afford to participate in trades on the streets anymore because there's hardly anything left to trade. We are all just another person waiting, hunched over from never-ending stomach pains while we clutch a ceramic bowl between our boney fingers as we stand in a long queue outside of the public kitchen in our quarter of town. When there are so many people that we wrap around the corner of the small brick building, the wait often feels like an eternity. The chatter is minimal, and the steps forward can be measured by grains of dirt until we reach the narrow set of wooden doors leading into a barren, musky room with another long line of famished people. Once we make our way up to the front, the women with ladles and deep metal basins serve us the broth we've been patiently awaiting. Without a moment to pause, we shuffle back out of the building to make space for others. At last, we can slug our soup on the curb like the vagabonds we have become.

Papa has told us to hold onto faith because there is a future, one we are unaware of—the possibility of finding freedom once again. He's the man I have looked up to for as long as I've been alive, but I worry something in him has snapped. I'm not sure he's able to think clearly anymore.

"Each day, we are closer than the one before, son," he says.

"Yes, Papa," I respond, "I know."

"There's a world out there waiting for us," he says.

I refuse to open my mind to the hope he speaks about. He has had faith in the Jewish partisan since the beginning of their conjuring, but only he knows what their plans consist of. I want to have faith, but too many have already lost the battle. However, I can't steal Papa's outlook, so I agree for his sake.

"Of course," I reply.

"What does that poster say? It's new, isn't it?" Olivia asks, pointing toward the end of the block.

"It must be an announcement from the *Judenrat*," Papa says. "The local council probably has to inform us of more laws imposed by the Third Reich. What other announcements do we see here?"

I hadn't noticed the poster, but with the few changes that occur around here, I can say for certain, it's new. "Stay here with Mama and Papa. I'll go look."

Before stepping out of line, I turn to face my parents, wondering if they even heard Olivia speak. As usual, Mama's eyes are half-lidded. It's hard to tell if she can see straight in front of her anymore. The fight she had brewing inside of her seemed to burn out during the time she was suffering with typhus. She recovered but never returned to the woman she was prior to falling ill.

Papa is nervous, or so he constantly appears. His eyes dart around as if there is action occurring in every direction, within each building overlooking our town, and every sewer hole below street level.

I move down the street quickly to take a quick peek at the poster, where others are now gathering to do the same.

There's a lot to take in all at once, so I scan each line to grasp the important facts listed beneath the bold letters spelling out "NOTICE."

By the time I reach the bottom part of the poster where it lists out punishments, my stomach is churning into tight knots.

I feel the need to hold my breath as I run back to Mama, Papa, and Olivia. They have an eager look in their eyes, wondering why it seems like I just saw something more terrifying than anything I've seen over the last few years.

"What is it?" Papa asks.

Mama places her hands on Olivia's shoulders and stares at me, forcing her eyes to open wider than usual.

"As of today, the Germans have the authority to relocate any Jewish person who lives here in Warsaw. There were some exceptions, but I'm afraid we don't fall under any of them." The hair on the back of my neck rises just as my pulse echoes between my ears.

Papa's nose flares. "If we choose not to go—" he begins.

"Any person who attempts to bypass the resettlement will be shot," I say, lifting my chin to only speak to Papa, rather than allowing Olivia to hear me.

"Where are they taking us?" Mama asks.

"I'm not sure. The poster said we are allowed to take up to fifteen kilograms of luggage, but anything more than that will be confiscated."

"We'll be taken to our—" Papa swallows the last word he was about to speak and closes his eyes. "I know what they are doing with the Jewish people they are relocating. Unless we are of value to them, we are not worthy of being on the same soil as them."

"We are worthy," Olivia argues against what I hope she doesn't understand. "I can sew now. Mama said I'm the best sewer she's ever met, and Isaac, he's strong and can do any of the work you can do, Papa. Mama can cook and sew and fix things too. We should be worthy—we are."

Mama squeezes her hands around Olivia's shoulders and kisses the top of her head. "You're right, we are worthy." She turns to Papa. "They can't take us all at once."

"They won't take us," Papa says, pressing his shoulders back with a force of confidence I don't think we should have.

The line in front of us has bled out, people disappearing back into whatever hole or crevice they came from.

We don't have much more to give or fight with. We're all bones with loose skin, walking around as if life will suddenly take a turn for the better. The Nazis likely thought we wouldn't last as long as we have, and they're plotting their next move.

As we stand in the line that has stopped moving forward despite all the people who have left, a sound in the distance grows. It's hard to decipher at first, but as seconds pass, there is no question that we are listening to screams, cries, and the hollow thud of air replacing a bullet in a pistol's barrel. There's no saying what direction the alarming sounds are coming from, but they are here somewhere within this confinement.

"We must get back inside," Papa says. "You must. I have to go find out what's happening."

"Papa, I told you what they're doing. What more do you need to know? Now is not the time for us to split up. Please, stay with us," I beg.

"Son, I need to do what will ultimately keep us safe. Take your mother and sister inside, seal the bricks, and pad the walls with whatever you can find."

I'm staring at my father, desperate for him to change his mind. We don't know where he goes to meet with the others who are invested in fighting this battle, but I fear the worst will happen.

"You need to trust me," he says.

The man I've known, I would trust with every fiber of my being. The man standing before me at this moment, I'm not sure he should trust himself. None of us are in our right mind.

Staring at him does nothing. He doesn't budge or falter and I know for every minute longer I keep Mama and Olivia outside here in the open, the more danger I'm putting them in.

"I wish you wouldn't do this," I tell him. "Some things aren't worth the fight when minutes are all we have to cling to."

"I understand your disapproval. Please, do as I ask. Once I know more, I will return. Take care of them, Isaac. I need you to do this now."

I take Olivia's hand and place my other hand on Mama's shoulder. Her chin is quivering, but she won't turn her head to look up at Papa. She has shown so little emotion lately, I wasn't sure what she was feeling anymore, but I see the pain in her eyes—the struggle she is enduring.

Papa takes her by the arm and kisses her cheek. "Everything will be fine, darling. Go on."

Mama presses her fingers to her lips and glances up at him for a brief second. "Please come back," she says, lunging forward to wrap her arms around his neck. "Please." Her whisper trails off, like a haunting moan from the wind.

Papa gives Olivia a kiss on the head and squeezes the back of her neck. "My princess."

My sister moves forward while trying to look over her shoulder, watching Papa walk away as we leave in the opposite direction. I hate wondering what she fears the most, what she knows too much of, and what I can't protect her from, but she always seems to take everything in her stride as if she somehow knows life will pan out in the end. If it's true and she can see past this, I am envious. I hope it's all she will see as we move forward toward whatever darkness lies ahead.

SOFIA

Tonight is the first time Papa has been home in time for supper in weeks. The tension at the table is palpable. Mama's fists are clenched, resting on her placemat.

Aside from staring at her wedding band that has been twisted around her finger, hiding the diamond, I've kept my sights on the pieces of onion floating around my soup.

"Why is everyone so quiet tonight?" Papa asks.

I'm positive he doesn't see tonight as any different from the other nights we've spent together.

"What would you like us to say, Friedrich? Should I ask you how your day at work was?"

I don't need to lift my head to imagine the look swimming through Mama's eyes.

"For God's sake," Papa snaps. "If I thought supper would be this cold, I would have stayed late again today."

"What has happened to you?" Mama mutters. Her voice is weak, but I know she is trying to remain as strong as possible. "Do you think we are ignorant to what is happening just down the street from us? Do you honestly think we don't know what those monsters are doing to the Jewish people? We are frightened beyond belief. Do you understand?"

Mama and I try to avoid conversation about what's happening in our town, but it's hard to block the thoughts out of our nightmares. I'd rather sacrifice my safety than know other Jewish people are being tortured because of the hand Papa is playing in this game with the Nazis. There's no reason to keep these officers healthy. Perhaps if they all fell ill and died, it would be one less person to torture the innocent. He must be able to see this.

"How many times do I have to remind you why I do what I do, Lena?" Papa drops his spoon into his soup, causing a splatter of broth to hit the white tablecloth. "You didn't want to leave Oświęcim," he says to Mama. "Do you recall that conversation, or do you only see this situation from one angle?"

"I can't desert my family's farm, but I didn't think you would turn on your family and essentially become a hero to the Nazis. Never in my wildest dreams could I have predicted this would be the punishment for keeping our home safe."

"There is a death camp three miles down the road," Papa grunts. "You left me no choice when the opportunity came up."

"Friedrich!" Mama scolds Papa for using the words "death camp." The two of them have tried to be quiet about the truth of what exists just a short distance away. But with as much as Papa hears while spending days among the SS, he comes home nearly foaming at the mouth, needing to tell Mama of all the horrific happenings. Even if I hadn't overheard my parents talking, there was a prominent change in the air last spring. A strong, sickly-sweet odor funneled into a cloud that would float over our house multiple times a day. Papa told Mama they had to burn the bodies of the deceased because they were running out of space to bury the bones.

It's hard to know how many new people arrive at Auschwitz

each day, but there isn't a question of how many must be dying with the constant streams of ash-filled smoke. Often, there is a thin residue of dust on our windows, and though I try to look through the hazy view, it's not something I can see past.

At night, I used to open my windows to listen to the crickets in the field. They would soothe me to sleep. The last time I opened my window, I could hear faint cries and screams floating along the passing breeze. If I didn't know what was happening so close by, I would think they were ghosts singing in the night. I suppose the sounds could be both.

"This is my fault?" Mama questions. "I should have figured this to be the case since Sofia and I are Jewish. Every horrible uprising in Europe is because there are Jewish people walking this planet, right?"

Papa runs his fingers through his chestnut brown, perfectly combed hair. "You know that is not how I see any of this. Why would you say such a thing?"

This argument has no solution. No one started it, and no one will end it. We can fight over the matter, but in the end, none of us have control over the outcome. There is no guarantee that the law excusing "Privileged Marriages" from losing all of our basic human rights will remain intact. It seems like a temporary loophole. Spouses of non-Jewish faith have still been advised to leave the Jewish members of their families behind. Some already have. Papa has heard the stories of sudden divorces and new marriages to interfaith partners. The Third Reich doesn't have consideration for other lives, and they wouldn't think twice about killing the man in charge of training their doctors. In truth, no one in this country or this continent is safe.

The silence returns and, within minutes, the sound of spoons clattering against our bowls and slurps of broth hitting our teeth is all there is to listen to.

Mama dabs a linen napkin to her lips, then places it down before collecting the empty bowls.

"I'll help," I offer.

I begin to clean the soup bowls in the sink while Mama scoops servings of shepherd's pie onto three plates. We're fortunate to have the selection of foods we do. It's an advantage Papa earns from working with the officers. We could be starving like the other Jewish people. Papa said we would have far less food had he not taken the job, and that other families of mixed marriages are being forced to adhere to strict rationing allowances.

We should be starving. We are no different from the others.

Once we're all reseated at the table, Papa takes a few mouthfuls before placing his fork down on his plate.

"I'm sure this conversation will go just as the last one, but I've been asked if we can prepare the farm to grow more crops in the spring. The shortage of food will begin affecting more—"

"More of those who have been eating feasts three times a day?" Mama asks.

"Affecting everyone," he replies. "We have the largest farmland in the town and can help."

"What more can these ingrates ask of you, really? Haven't you offered enough at this point?"

"If I say no, they will want to know what the reason is, and we don't have a reason if they are willing to supply the materials we need."

"Who will manage the extra farming labor? Is this where Sofia and I become slaves of our home?"

She's right to ask. I was thinking the same way, but Mama has never been one to sit back and bite her tongue, and I wouldn't expect that to change in a time like this.

"They will supply the workers," Papa replies, dropping his gaze to the hole he has made in the center of his mashed potato.

"They will supply the Jews, you mean?"

"Why are we having this discussion if there is no say in the matter?" I add.

My question ends the conversation as quickly as it began. I can't sit here with the two of them any longer. Our family is broken and I can't see how to fix the damage.

No one is right. Everyone is wrong.

We're all puppets, moving along with each pull of a string.

I clean my dish and fork, towel-dry them and put them away.

"Goodnight," I offer, before retreating upstairs.

They mirror a mumbling reply. Each night after dinner, my legs feel heavier, as if I'm lifting them up each step rather than them carrying me. The weight on my shoulders never ceases and I'm not sure I will ever feel free of this guilt, not for as long as I live.

I have peered out the window each night over the last year. It's hard to guess how long Auschwitz has been in development, but it became public knowledge to the locals last year when all residents of the Brzezinka village were expelled from their homes, forced to give the Germans more land to build upon. We are fortunate enough to live outside of this zone.

What's been worse than knowing is seeing... Throughout the process of the Germans acquiring that land, we witnessed prisoners being led to town to work on the construction site. It's hard knowing there are only a couple of acres of trees and the narrow Soła river that separates our land from the atrocities. My eyes play tricks on me, and it seems like the trees stare back at me. All the pairs of eyes belong to people who are imprisoned behind a barbed-wire fence, and they are asking why I am in the comfort of my home when they are waiting for their nightmares to grow worse.

If there is anything I could do to help the prisoners of

Auschwitz, I would give up all my "unlawful" rights in the blink of an eye.

There must be something more I can do to help. I can't continue to stare out at the trees masking the truth that lies directly ahead.

CHAPTER 11

JANUARY 1943

ISAAC

It isn't a matter of if, just when.

I knew there would come a morning when I would wake up differently than I had become used to, or there would be a night I never fell asleep.

"Isaac," Papa whispers my name, snagging my attention, while Mama continues her nightly sewing lesson with Olivia. This has become our routine, I suppose. I help where needed during the day, Olivia shadows Mama, and Papa leaves at night and doesn't return until the early mornings in time for an hour or two of rest before we start the same day over again. He pulls me into the farthest corner of our living quarters, behind a makeshift mattress. "I have to leave."

"You do every night," I remind him.

"No, it's different this time." The sound of Papa ruffling his hand through his pants pocket makes me wonder what he's doing, but it isn't much more than a few seconds before I hear a match scraping against a metal zipper. He lights a tapered candle and holds it between us. "In the morning I'm going along with the others in the partisan. We plan to take action before the next round of deportations. We're out of time, and it's now or never."

"Action? What do you mean?" My voice carries and Papa cups his hand around my mouth and his eyes bulge.

"I need you to be the man of the family right now, take care of your mother and sister. Isaac, you know I can't lay down in the middle of that God-awful road without trying to do everything I can to shield your lives."

"Papa, there are too many of them. It's a death trap. You have to understand," I plead through ragged breaths.

"There are enough of us to show we aren't as weak as they perceive us to be. If we don't show them our strength, what will all this have been for?"

Papa isn't in his right mind. We are outnumbered, malnourished, weak, and without powers to fight. We are mice standing in the shadows of lions, trying to roar through insignificant squeaks. They'll laugh before they retaliate.

"I wish you wouldn't," I say.

"I must," he replies without hesitation. "If there is any chance, no matter how slight, I need to be a part of the revolt. I need you to have faith in your old man, son."

It isn't a matter of faith. I want him to understand.

"What will you tell Mama and Lu-lu?"

"That I'm keeping us safe for another day. That is what I'm doing."

I drop my head, hoping to think of something I can say to stop him. We have a place to hide. For now, we are lucky. We shouldn't tempt our chances, not yet.

Papa grabs the back of my head and kisses my forehead, then pulls me in and wraps his arm around me tightly. "You are every bit the man I prayed you'd become. I know you will keep your mama and sister safe. I love you very much, son. Never, never forget."

I have the urge to be a child and fall to the ground in a fit of tears, wave my arms around and scream for a different answer. But all I can do is stare Papa in the eyes and pray to wake up from this ongoing terror.

"I love you too, and I'm proud to be the person you have taught me to be," I tell him.

"Isaac, your mother and Olivia will think I'm going off to the same place I go every night. There's no sense in worrying them." The heaviness of his words falls against my hollow stomach. "Get some rest, my boy, and tomorrow, stay in this room. Do not leave, no matter what. Do you understand?"

How could I understand?

"Yes, sir," I murmur.

The flickering light between us disappears before I see it floating across the room toward Mama and Olivia. "Here's a little light for you tonight, to spare your poor fingertips for the needlepoint, my sweet girl."

"Oh, thank you, Papa," Olivia says with a sigh of relief. "How wonderful."

"Must you go again tonight?" Mama asks.

"Darling, I'm all right. It's for our safety."

I don't know if Mama believes what he tells her.

They say their goodbyes, as they do each night at this hour, and I count the sound of bricks as they scrape against their opening, one by one, and then again as they are replaced upon his departure.

It appears the Nazis are making their way from street block to street block, taking wagons of Jewish people at a time, taking them somewhere we have only heard rumors about, rumors I hope are exaggerations.

They have been taking people for months, and each day we awaken with a new breath is another day of starving and fighting to survive. For all we know, it may be better than what comes next.

. . .

It feels like only minutes have passed when all the bricks around us vibrate with the sound of falling wooden toy blocks.

"Isaac," Mama calls out.

I roll off the bedding and crawl across the room to her and Olivia. "I'm here," I say.

"What was that?"

"I'm not sure."

A succession of muffled pops filter through the bricks in the wall. "Are those guns?" Mama asks.

"It sounds that way."

"Your papa should be home by now," she continues, her hands covering mine, trembling as her breaths quicken. "What's happening?"

"I don't know." I'm lying. I think I know what's going on outside.

The sounds of shouts and boots hitting the pavement with force shuffle by in groups. The train tracks where they round up transports are just a few blocks north from here.

"We need to find your father," Mama says, standing up quickly.

"No, Mama. We can't leave, not now."

"He could be out there, Isaac. What if he's hurt? What if—"

"Papa knows how to take care of himself, and we have to have trust in that," I tell her, trying to be as quiet as possible for Olivia's sake. I'm not sure if she's still asleep or silently listening to Mama panic.

"Do you know where he goes at night?" she asks.

"No, but he's safe. I'm sure of it." It's another lie.

"They're attacking the *Wachmänner!*" People are shouting from within the building, but from where we wouldn't know since the sewer pipes carry so much sound in every direction.

"Who is attacking the *Wachmänner*?" Mama whispers. She asks like I can see through the ceiling and walls.

I shrug. There is no one else to fight for us here—none other than the prisoners of Warsaw who are strong enough to fight the German soldiers.

"Your papa—this is what he's doing?" she growls with anger.

"Mama—"

"He is. I know he is. This is where he has gone every night, to encourage the others to fight back in a war we cannot win. Why, why would he do this?"

From the corner of my eye, I notice Olivia stirring as she struggles to open her tired eyes.

"He's doing what he thinks is right," I reply. I don't have another answer. I was asking Papa the same questions.

"We can run! We can be free!" Another voice echoes through the pipes. "Now is our chance. We must go!"

Mama has a wild look in her eyes. "We have to go, Isaac. Lu-lu, come on, sweetheart. Get up."

"Mama, no. We must stay here where it's safe," Olivia says, pulling Old-Bear up against her chest.

"No. No. We can run. If this was his plan, we must take the opportunity."

"He wouldn't want us to leave," I argue, grabbing her by the arm to stop her frenzy of pacing.

"How do you know?"

"He said so last night—he said to stay here, no matter what."

Mama's eyes bulge as if her fingertip has made contact with an electrical current. She places her hands on her cheeks and her chests heaves as if she's been starved of air.

"Will this be our only chance?" Olivia asks. "We won't be the only ones still in this building after this is over, right?" I was hoping Olivia would continue to side with me, but it's understandable why she is questioning all of this.

"We're leaving, Isaac," says Mama. 'I'm your mother, and

you are my child, and so is Olivia, and you will listen to me."
She sounds unsure, and terrified. To go against Papa's wishes
doesn't feel right, but to miss an opportunity to escape seems
worse.

"What if we end up leaving Papa behind?" I question.

"Papa won't find us?" Olivia asks.

"Your papa will always find us. He wants us to be safe, and
we are doing what we can to remain that way."

Before I can argue any further, Mama is pulling the bricks
out of the wall, exposing our hiding place, giving into the echoes
in the pipes with hope their words are true. But what if it's a
trap for retaliation for whatever Papa and the others have tried
to accomplish?

"Olivia, grab Old-Bear and your belongings—put them in
the suitcase. Isaac, please do the same as your sister. There's no
time to sit here and think any longer."

"What if there are *Wachmänner* waiting outside of the
building?" I ask.

"What if there's not?" Mama replies.

CHAPTER 12
JANUARY 1943

ISAAC

To know that a split-second decision could impact the rest of our lives is the most frightening thought I've ever had. Before we were sent to live here in Warsaw, we were told to think long and hard before doing something that may get ourselves hurt. Long and hard, that's what it takes to make a decent decision. Yet, our lives are hanging in the balance, and there's no time to think.

But Mama isn't listening to a word I'm saying. She has her mind set on taking this chance.

It's now or never, I tell myself.

"Lu-lu," I say, pulling her up the ladder through the sewer line that leads to the ice-cream shop's bathroom. "Don't let go of my hand, no matter what you do, okay?"

My sister is pale. There's no doubt in my mind she's terrified, squeezing Old-Bear as if she were still a little girl with bouncing pigtails. She hasn't grown much in the time we've been here. Thanks to the lack of food, she is frail and weightless, but her freckles are the same, darker than her golden-hazelnut eyes but lighter than her lashes. She still looks up at me as if I'm a hero.

Mama is the last to make her way up. The panic is still written in her eyes and sweat covers her forehead like an oil slick. "Let's go, let's go," she hurries us as I replace the sewer cover into its correct spot.

She's behind us, with a hand on each of our shoulders, digging her nails into our skin.

I have our one suitcase in my left hand, and Olivia's hand in my right.

The moment we step out onto the street, there is commotion coming from every direction. It's hard to know which way to avoid.

"Umschlagplatz," Mama says. "Where they round up the daily deportations—it's the only way out."

It's not entirely true, but most people who try to escape through the sewer lines that lead to the German side of Warsaw are shot, just like those who try to climb over the wall.

We walk North, toward Umschlagplatz, where the volume of shouts and screams grows louder. People are rushing toward the street as if there are only seconds left to survive what's catching up to us.

"Whatever you do, don't look behind you, just keep moving forward," I whisper in Olivia's ear.

The three street blocks lined with worn and eroding buildings feel endless, but there are thousands of people running and scampering in different directions, creating chaos. Sounds from explosive blasts, screams of terror, and groans of destruction—air escaping bodies that fall heavily to the ground or against a wall, and momentary sighs of relief from both the prisoners of this ghetto and German soldiers, surround us. Fights are breaking out everywhere, but it's a battle between strength against weakness, and weapons against whatever materials the resisting group of Jewish people were able to scrap together.

I want to think we, as a united front, have a chance to make a mark against the soldiers, but from where I stand, I see a lot of blood and more Jewish people falling than German. While some prisoners and soldiers are engaged in nothing more than fist-fighting, others are making a run for the opening between the barricades, where the daily transports have been departing. The exit appears free of *Wachmänner* for the moment. *That's where we need to be.*

Olivia stops running the moment she notices what's happening in front of us and pinches Old-Bear beneath her arm. "It's too late," she says.

"It's not. Follow me," Mama mutters, running ahead to lead the way.

As the crowd grows bigger with each step we take, the three of us slow our pace.

My gaze darts around, trying to spot Papa among the hordes of people. It would be impossible to find him now, but I can't help but look.

"Over here," Mama says, pulling me by my coat. Others are funneling down a narrow street, and we can only hope it's because they found a way through the battling crowd.

Shots are fired. German profanities are echoing between the buildings above our head, and men, women, and children are screaming for their lives.

It isn't long before we come to the dark reality that this street doesn't have a clear exit either. Some seem to be slipping through the cracks, but the Germans have already moved in to block off this path. They're forcing those who just ran down the street to push back, shooting several along the way.

Without much thought, I yank Mama back and pull Olivia into my side, spotting a sewer hole without a cover.

"Drop your bags, now. Leave them. Just leave them," I shout, breathlessly. We won't make it out of here alive by pushing forward with all our belongings.

They listen and drop their bags, but I feel Mama's resistance, pulling against me. She doesn't want to leave Papa. I understand, but we're all going to be caught if she doesn't follow me. I wish we would have stayed put.

I spot a metal rail just inside the hole and grab a hold of it to lower myself in enough to pull Olivia and Mama down too.

"We'll end up trapped here," Mama cries out. "No, no, we can't—"

Olivia is already beside me on the ladder when I reach up for Mama's arm, pulling her to follow.

"Mama, we're going to get shot up there. Please. Don't fight this. We won't win. Come down here."

I know she can see what might look like freedom ahead, but there is no way to be free now.

"There's still a chance we can make it through," Mama says, tugging my arm.

"No, there isn't," I argue. "Dammit. Listen to me, will you? You're going to get shot. You must believe me, Mama. Please."

My gritting teeth and grunting words seem to have no effect on her. I know I'm stronger than she is, and I can easily pull her down here, but I don't want to lose my grip on the rung we're standing on, and I don't want her to fall into the darkness below us either.

The seconds of our heaving breaths feel like much longer, but we do not have time on our side. The gunshots are too close by. Each pull of a trigger causes the metal to clink in the tube surrounding us. It's mind-numbing.

Mama must see my decision is best as she places the sole of her worn boot just beside my hand.

"Come on, I don't think it's too far down," I tell her.

"*Halt genau dort,* street-rat!" A whistle screams in the distance, or maybe it's the sound of multiple whistles.

It's too late.

Mama's whimpering, "Go, go now. Take your sister and go, Isaac. Now. They're here. The Nazis—they see me. Please, go."

She releases a cry and I grab the back of her coat, trying to pull against her grip on the concrete. With a forceful tug on her jacket, the fabric is unexpectedly torn from my fingers. Mama's feet swing against the top of my head as she is pulled out from the hole by Nazis whose obscenities are so loud and voracious that I can't make out what they're saying.

Everything inside me wants to scream, follow her, get her back, but it would be a sacrifice for Olivia's life, and mine. My instinctual reaction is to capture my sister's attention before she yells out for Mama, but instead I release my hands from the ladder, holding Olivia as tightly as I can to protect her from the fall we're going to endure. But I know it's the only way to disappear from the daylight shining down the sewer hole. It's the only way to protect the two of us—the only members of our family left.

The sewer cover drops heavily over the hole just as we fall into the inky ice-cold water.

"Mama, Mama, Mama," Olivia cries between her chattering teeth. "We have to go save her."

I place my hand over her mouth, trying to hush her.

"We can't," I tell her. "Papa will find her. If he's out there fighting, he will find her and protect her. They didn't shoot her. We would have heard a gunshot." The truth is, I don't know if we would have heard a gunshot, I doubt Papa is still battling, and I'm nearly positive we will never see either of them again.

"I'm so—so—scared," she trembles as I pull her up to her feet.

"I know. I know. We need to move. We have to get as far away from these bordering streets as possible."

I have no clue what direction we're facing or where these sewer tunnels might lead. All we can do is walk into the darkness and feel along the walls for metal rungs.

"When will I wake up?" Olivia asks.

My heart is pounding with grief, and pain. I want to collapse and give up, but I must save her. No matter what happens, she's all that matters right now. She deserves a life— more years of freedom like I had. I don't know if I can keep her safe, us safe, but if it means staying down here until we're at the brink of hypothermia then that's what we'll do. I pray Mama and Papa find their way back to our hiding spot in the wall. It's all we can hope for.

"I want to go home," Olivia cries.

I don't know if she means the hole in the wall, or the beautiful cottage we used to live in on the outskirts of this city. Perhaps, both. Either would be better than where we are now.

"I'll get us out of here," I say. "Just don't let go of my hand. If you have my hand, we are safe, okay?" I shouldn't be saying something as ignorant as that, but I need her to stay calm. "We need to walk as far as we can to ensure we've gotten away from the fighting up there."

With each step we take, the foul odor of rotting sludge grows thicker, filling my lungs, forcing me to taste the putrid air.

"I can't, Isaac," she says while coughing so hard she gags.

"We haven't got a choice," I argue. Her body is shaking so hard, probably from a combination of the cold water around our feet and the fear tearing her to shreds inside. "Hop on my back so you can give your feet a rest." I hardly have the strength to keep myself upright, but the tunnel wall is offering me the little support I need to keep going.

"Are we going to die down here?" Olivia asks, looping her arms around my neck, with Old-Bear hanging from her clenched fist. After a moment, she rests the side of her face on the back of my head.

"No, but you need to keep your voice down."

It's like a maze of mirrors, but ones that don't offer any sort of reflection. I can only see as far as the cement entrapping us, but even that might be a figment of my imagination. There isn't a speck of light or any sign of a way out of here.

CHAPTER 13
MARCH 1943

SOFIA

I wouldn't have thought living in this house could be as uncomfortable as it has become.

Papa doesn't come inside the house when he finishes working. He goes directly through the barnyard doors, and we don't see him again until either late at night when he's pulling a blanket over himself in the sitting room, or in the morning just before he leaves for work again.

He has a gaslight lantern burning in the barn and I can't help but wonder what he's occupying himself with for so many hours every evening. It's cold, and the darkness of winter continues to loom with its heavy clouds.

Mama refuses to speak to him. The anger she feels is justified. My resentment toward him feels unfixable. Words can't undo what he's done, and actions can't be forgotten. Part of me wonders if he flees to the barn each night with shame, unable to look at us. The other part of me wonders if he can't stand the thought of looking at two Jews living with him.

The longer I stare at the barn from my window, the more

curious I become, especially tonight as I see dirt spraying out the barn doors. The flickering glow from the lantern makes the dirt look like shimmering speckles of sand.

Mama and I have done all we can do to prepare the ice-cold land for more seedlings that we should be able to plant toward the end of April if the weather cooperates. Papa has brought in a dozen more chickens, goats, and cows, all of which we feed and clean up during the day. There's nothing more he could be doing at night.

Maybe it's my imagination playing tricks on me, but I hear a sound that resembles a growl. The wooden planks of the barn shudder and the doors shake. I stare for another minute longer, wondering what could have caused that much of a disturbance. The following silence makes my stomach pinch. I can't just go to bed, not knowing if everything is all right.

The drapes fall from my clenching fists, and I spin around in search of where I tossed my robe this morning. In the mess of blankets bunched up toward the foot of my bed, I spot a hint of the sky-blue fabric. I slip the robe over my shoulders and tie it in place with a loose knot.

With another glance out the window, everything appears still. Even the flicker of the gas lamp is steady, uninterrupted by the passing shadows.

I tiptoe down the stairs to avoid waking or worrying Mama. She wouldn't want me to go outside at this time of night, especially in search of Papa. Thankfully, my boots and coat are by the front door so I'm able to slip out without making a sound.

My feet crunch on the frozen grass and, as always, I feel like I'm on display in front of the trees that see everything. The light from the gas lamp isn't visible from where I'm standing, and I can't help but worry about what I'll see when I step inside the barn. I pull open the door, listening to the latches whine and squeal.

I spot the gas lamp resting on a bale of hay with nothing out of the ordinary to see in the glowing light. The barn is always clean and tidy. The bales of hay are lined and stacked against the worn wooden walls, tools are organized by size and type, either hanging from a hook or nail, and each shelf Papa has built has a unique purpose. The only thing about the barn I dislike is the smell of musty mildew that becomes overwhelmingly strong in the winter months. At this point of the year, it will get worse before it gets better.

"Papa?" I call out. My voice wavers from a combination of the cold and the nerves running through my body. "Are you in here?"

There's nowhere else he could be.

I take the lamp and walk further into the barn. A high-pitched clatter startles me into tripping. I catch myself on another bale of hay, saving the lamp from crashing too hard to the ground.

Once I right myself, I turn in a circle, but nothing is moving, not even a hanging tool beneath the dust-covered window.

The sound of a sneeze makes me feel like I've lost my mind, so I climb up the ladder to the loft, where we store extra-large tools we don't use in the winter months. My arms and legs shake as I reach the top rung, but aside from a pile of metal, there's nothing up here.

A heavy muted thud causes a storm of dirt to cloud beneath the ladder. I climb back down as quickly and carefully as I can, but the sight of a moving shadow beneath the loft is enough to disturb me. I fall from the ladder, but I'm caught just before landing on the cold dirt. I clench my eyes, terrified to face the truth of what's happening.

"What in God's name are you doing out here at this time of night?"

My eyes flash open, grateful to find Papa placing me down on my unsteady feet. He keeps his hand beneath my arm for support but stares at me with an angry look matching my own.

"I heard a noise and I got worried," I say.

"You heard a noise? From your bedroom?"

"Yes, it sounded like a growl, and I saw the lamp on. I came to make sure you're okay, but you weren't in here when I walked in."

"I'm surprised you cared enough to check on me," he mutters, releasing his grip.

Any response from me will result in another argument, but I want to know what I heard and where he was for that matter.

"Where were you just now?"

"Outside, making a new workbench. I caught my thumb beneath the hammer, which must have been the sound you heard."

I struggle to believe him, mostly because the line across his forehead seems to deepen. I'm sure there's a new workbench out there, but I doubt that's what he's been working on every night for weeks.

"I saw an explosion of dirt too," I say.

"I must have dropped something."

"Papa, you're not telling me the truth—something we always promised to do. It's hard to fall asleep at night wondering what else you might be hiding from me these days."

"Sofia, I'm not hiding anything from you. You have no reason to say such a thing."

"I know when you aren't being truthful, but I won't try to drag anything else out of you. I wanted to be like you—more than anything else in the world. I wanted a life where I helped others because I've always looked up to you, knowing how many people you have cared for over the years. But now, I'm not sure I feel like that anymore. Maybe I don't want to be just like you, after all."

I know my words must feel like daggers, but I can only speak the truth of what I'm feeling inside.

Papa's gaze falls and he squeezes his hand around his pulsating temples.

"Don't talk that way, please. That hurts me deep inside. Please understand that I can't tell you everything just because you want to know things a girl your age has no place knowing."

"I'm going to be eighteen soon. Age has nothing to do with the secrets you keep."

Years ago, I might have gotten answers out of him if I stared into his eyes long enough, but his soul seems to have been stolen and I don't think any amount of staring will help.

"Goodnight, Papa," I say, lowering my head before walking past him.

"My *mały myszka*," he says, giving me an ounce of hope he might let me in.

I glance over my shoulder, finding him still avoiding eye contact.

"I love you."

Those words hurt—words I would never expect to cause pain. Before the war, no one could have convinced me a person could speak those words in vain.

Rather than say something I might regret, I'll let him assume that somewhere deep inside of me, I still love him. After all, I came outside to see if he was okay. If I hadn't, I might have spared myself more heartache tonight.

When I close the front door, my heart catches in my throat at the sight of Mama hugging herself beneath the hanging chandelier in the entryway.

"What were you doing out there?"

"I heard a strange sound," I explain. "I was just checking—"

"You shouldn't be out there at night."

"Neither should he," I argue.

"Well," Mama sighs, "your father must sow the seeds for his future. It's a choice he is making, not one we are."

I nod my head with disappointment, silently agreeing with her. "I know. I'm off to bed, Mama. I love you."

"I love you, sweetheart."

I'm not sure how many more nights I can lie in bed, trying to fall asleep while wondering when and how our lives will change. Will Papa give up on us and turn us in? Will he reap the benefits of feeding the Germans with more slave laborers? Are we even worth the risk? He's slowly changing into someone neither of us know and I'm not sure how much skin one person can shed before they are completely unrecognizable.

CHAPTER 14
MARCH 1943

ISAAC

Almost two months have passed since the initial attack from the Jewish resistance against the Germans, and I can't understand how Olivia and I are still alive, living in the conditions we are in. We have remained underground in the sewer system, in a dark corner with a few others—a man and his wife, and a second man who was separated from his family. We haven't seen the sun or sky since Mama was torn from my arms. All we have is the glow from a nearby sewer grate, which allows in just enough light to keep us from walking into one another. Our corner is at a higher pitch than some of the other tunnels, and it remains fairly dry, unless it's a rainy day and we aren't able to start a proper fire. Those are the days we don't eat—days like today.

Josep, the man who was separated from his family, has been able to start small fires with pieces of flint. Lujan, the other gentleman, and I spend most of the daytime hours searching for mice and rats, but there is little meat to go around so we are doing what we must to survive.

Dosia, Lujan's wife, has taken a liking to Olivia and occupies her with riddles and stories, but Olivia doesn't speak much. She's heartbroken, and there's nothing I can do to repair her pain. Just after we made our way down here and met these folks, she spent days refusing to eat the charred meat off a rat, but, like us all, our hunger forces us to put the thought of what we are ingesting to the back of our minds.

At night, we poke our heads out of the sewer grate to see what's happening on street level. It almost seems as if no one is left up there, but in the daytime, we hear the boots marching back and forth. There isn't a doubt in anyone's mind that the eyes of SS guards are set on every corner of every block, waiting and watching for any new signs of resistance.

With a dismal day like today, there is no use in looking for rodents as the rain has been relentless since the break of dawn yesterday. The days we don't eat, we typically sit in one position for hours on end, staring at the dark wall across from us. Josep had other plans this morning though. He went to look for others to see if there was any information he could obtain.

The crunch of wet rubble beneath footsteps could mean a lone person has stumbled upon our spot, or Josep is returning. If it were the Nazis hunting us down, there would be several pairs of pounding feet, flashlights, and shouting. There's nowhere for us to run. Sneaking up on us is pointless.

"*Hallo*," Josep greets us, the sound in his voice is forlorn.

"What is it?" Dosia questions. "Did you find anything?"

"Did you find my mama or papa?" Olivia asks, squeezing Old-Bear under her chin. Her voice merely escapes in a whisper. She knows these three don't have a clue what Mama or Papa look like.

"No, sweet girl, I'm afraid not," Josep replies, sitting down on the other side of Olivia. "I found this, though."

"What is it?" she asks, a flicker of curiosity emphasizing her question.

"Open your hand," he says. I can't see more than a few

inches in front of me, but I can make out a shadow of Olivia staring down at her open hand.

"What is it?" she asks again.

"It's hope, sweet girl. It's all I want you to have. Can you hold onto it for me?"

"Hope?" Olivia questions. "I love hope. After we're free from this war, I will now have extra hope to fill my life with beautiful dresses, teacups, and jewelry," she says with a wishful sigh.

"It's all yours. I hope it lasts a lifetime," Josep tells her.

While Olivia is tentatively distracted, staring into her empty hands that are filled with Josep's invisible gift of "hope," Josep turns his head toward the rest of us, muttering what we're all desperate to hear. "There's word that there are more attacks on the horizon. Our options aren't good, and it might be wise to turn ourselves in now rather than wait."

Day after day, I wonder which poison is worse: staying here or finding out what comes next.

"If we turn ourselves in, won't the Germans think we took part in the attack? We've been hiding out all this time. We don't appear to be innocent," Dosia says.

"We will look far more guilty if a larger revolt begins before we make our way out of here," Josep argues.

"Darling, I agree with Josep. If there is a chance that there are more imminent battles, we won't be safe down here either. The punishment will be worse," Lujan says to Dosia.

"What are you saying?" I ask. "We climb out of the hole after all this time and walk out with our hands up in the air?"

"If we try to run—they will—"

"Correct," Dosia interrupts her husband's statement, clearly trying to shield Olivia from the horrors of the truth. We all wish to be blind to this reality, but it's too late for that.

"What was the purpose of staying down here for so long?" Olivia asks.

There is no real answer to her question. What we didn't know couldn't hurt us, so we hid from what's happening up there. If we know of something coming, and avoid the truth, we won't be helping ourselves in the end.

"We can only take each day as it comes," Dosia tells her.

"In the morning, we should make our way up," Josep states.

"I agree," Lujan says.

"Me as well," Dosia follows.

"We must do the same," I say, speaking in Olivia's direction.

She doesn't respond, but I understand. She doesn't have faith in anyone or anything, and no one can blame her.

Olivia sleeps with her head in my lap and my arm wrapped around her for the slightest bit of warmth I can offer. I never thought I would miss my clothing-stuffed pillowcases from the hole we were living in, but I do, and I miss Mama and Papa dearly. There's a hole where my heart should be and I'm not sure I will ever recover from this, even if we were to find a miracle of an escape.

My nerves were not as fraught last night when discussing the plan of turning ourselves in so that the Nazis might have mercy on us, but now that I've had a night to think over every possibility and the ones I can't imagine, I'm terrified.

It's clear that we all feel the same as we rise to our feet this morning, stretching our arms over our shoulders, then wiping away the grease from our eyelids. We've been covered in filth for so long, the only thing we try to avoid is our eyes burning from whatever may seep into them.

Josep leads the way toward the grated metal cover. There are metal rungs in the cement wall to make it easy for us to climb out.

It takes both Josep and Lujan to break the rusty seal from the metal and move it off to the side. I have Olivia's hand locked tightly within mine, staring up at the light as if it were a torch rather than daylight. Everything looks like an oil slick above ground, and I don't know if it's my eyes playing tricks on me, or the air hitting the ground above us.

One by one, we make our way onto the street. Olivia's fingernails pierce my palm, silently screaming out her fears. We walk like demon ghouls trudging through a cemetery, limping, weak, and covered from head to toe in black grease.

The air smells sweet in comparison to what we've been forced to breathe for the last couple of months. It feels like a refreshing mist, though dry. The sunlight is piercing against my eyes.

"Halt!"

I didn't think we'd get as far as ten steps before an armed soldier, clad in a gray-green coat, matching slacks, and shined black boots, would spot us.

He shouts over his shoulder, likely calling for backup. Though I'm not sure why anyone would look at the five of us and think they can't trip us all with one swift kick.

"Put your arms up above your heads," Josep mumbles.

We do as he says.

I wonder how many others are hiding, how many are left. I'm not sure we'll ever find out.

We hide Olivia behind our backs as we take slow steps forward, giving up our every right; whatever that may be.

"I found Jew attackers," the Nazi shouts again. I'm not surprised they would assume we were part of the revolt rather than innocent bystanders. I knew we would be safer in the sewers, but it isn't a permanent solution, and there's no saying when or if we would ever be free of danger up on the streets.

Several other Nazis round the corner, marching toward us as if we're about to put up a fight. Not one of us looks as if we are trying to attack.

"I have information that you may find helpful," Josep says while squeezing his eyes shut.

My pulse throbs in my temples as I try to steady my expression. This wasn't part of the plan. He's going to get us all shot.

"The others with me have no idea what I know, but I ask that you have mercy on them in exchange for my knowledge."

The Nazis speak over him as if he's not talking. I'm not sure what they heard or didn't hear. A few of them laugh as if Josep said something humorous.

"*Dreckige Ratten*," one of them hisses, calling us filthy rats. "What could you possibly know? You're just a bunch of sewer rats."

Josep straightens his shoulders, standing a bit taller. "It seems that the Jewish people of Poland might become the least of your worries soon, and this rumor I've overheard has made me fear the foreseeable battles that are likely to ensue on these streets. We don't know what will happen if we stay here, so I've decided to turn in myself and my friends."

One of the Nazis presses two fingers to his lips and releases a piercing hoot down the street. He waves someone or something forward. A wagon half filled with other prisoners pulls around the corner. It's seconds before we are all shoved toward the flat opening in the back—all of us but Josep. He is being pulled by the arm toward the door of a nearby building, and I fear what he has sacrificed for us. I may never have the chance to thank him for possibly saving us over himself.

I lift Olivia in first, never releasing her hand from mine, and pull myself up behind her.

The others in the wagon look as if they were hiding in the sewers too. Maybe they heard news of what's to come too.

"Where are they taking us?" Olivia whispers, tugging my hand.

"I don't know," I reply softly.

"Pawiak," one of the Nazis shouts, slapping his hand against the wooden part of the wagon.

"That's the prison, where bad people go, isn't it?" Olivia asks, fear lacing her voice as she tightens her arms around Old-Bear.

"Shh," Dosia hushes her from behind us. "We haven't done anything wrong."

Except for being born as Jewish people.

In the wagon, no one lifts their gaze. Everyone is fearing the worst, as we should.

CHAPTER 15

MARCH 1943

ISAAC

Like livestock, we're shuttled from the wagon to the back of
what looks like a prison. The ride seemed to be around half an
hour long and felt as if we were moving in slow circles. A stone-
covered courtyard in front of a wide block-like building is
sprawled out before us. In the center of the courtyard, there's a
line we have been directed to join. At the front of the queue is a
Nazi soldier, questioning those ahead of us. Beyond, I spot a set
of railroad tracks through the slats of an iron gate.

"Keep your responses short and be honest if you don't
understand what they're asking. Also, keep Old-Bear tucked
into your coat. I don't want you to lose him," I utter to Olivia.
It's all we've managed to hold onto since we were forced to drop
our luggage when we were trying to escape with Mama.

"I'll never let him out of my sight," Olivia says. "He's all I
have left besides you."

We were separated from Dosia and Lujan when we were
pulled from the wagon. They may be in the line somewhere
behind us, but we were told to face forward.

"Where will we go next?" Olivia asks beneath her breath.

I swallow hard, wishing the tightness in my throat would release for just a moment. "I'm not sure." There's no saying whether the sewer will be better or worse than what happens after answering these questions.

I wish I could hear what the Nazi soldiers are asking the others, but there's so much noise, it's hard to focus on one conversation.

What seems like an hour passes before I step up to the officer waiting to speak to me. His cap is lowered just enough that I can't see through the dark shadow over his eyes. His hands are clasped behind his back, and his jaw is square and tight. There's no discernible expression to read, no weakness to spot, no remorse to sense. He's just another heartless monster.

"What street were you assigned during your time in Warsaw?"

When we first arrived in the Jewish quarter, we were assigned to an apartment, but it wasn't long before we were sharing with so many others that it became uninhabitable. Papa said if we didn't find another place to claim as our own, we could end up on the street. About a year into our new life, he found the space underground, beneath the old ice-cream shop. We had to keep quiet as to our whereabouts or others would want to do the same and we'd lose our space underground eventually too.

"Karmelicka Street," I answer.

The officer leaves a long pause to follow my answer. "Where were you when you were directed to leave for the transfer station?" The calmness in his voice should alleviate a bit of fear, but I don't think calmness or quietness means anything better than volume.

"After the attack in January, I took my little sister to hide, to keep us safe. We were separated from our parents at that time. I wasn't sure what to do." I hate having to sound ignorant, but playing this role is important.

"Your sister?" the officer questions.

I twist my head over my shoulder, glancing back at her in the line, awaiting her turn next. "Yes, *herr*. That's my sister."

"Your parents' names?" he continues.

For a million reasons, my heart begins to race faster than it already is, and I can feel my pulse through every inch of my body. If Papa was caught, his name will likely be on record. We are associated with him regardless of what we did or didn't do.

"Ludwig and Ania Cohen," I answer.

The officer rambles something off in German. He spoke so quickly, I couldn't make out what he was saying, but another soldier joins him, standing to his side with a clipboard. Mama and Papa's names are repeated through their silent conversation. The second officer searches through the papers on his clipboard. I'm not sure what he's looking for, but I assume it's their names.

The men give each other a look, one that evidently supplies orders to the other. The second officer whistles and points to Olivia, shouting at her to come forward.

"*Auf get es*," he snaps at us both to follow.

After the initial round of questioning, we were sent to a new line against the stone wall of a nearby building. We were told to wait, but we don't know what we were waiting for—what comes next. Each prisoner, refugee, nomad, whatever it is we are now, stands raggedly in a state of exhaustion.

No one moves about much when steam from a train pipes over the horizon to the left of where we're standing. The ground beneath our feet vibrates, and the low rumble of metal against metal grows by the second. The screeching halt of the train burns my ears as a blur of red cattle cars fly before us until the engines halt.

"Where are we going?" Olivia whispers.

It's the fourth time she's asked me in the last hour, and I don't know any more now than I did hours ago. I shake my head and close my eyes, wishing she would stop questioning what they obviously don't want us to know.

Within minutes, we're being shoved into a line, boarding one of the dark cattle cars. By the time we make it inside, there's hardly any space to move. There's still a line of at least two dozen more behind us, all of whom they plan to squeeze into this car that can't possibly hold any more people.

Olivia is groaning, but has her head buried in my side and hands squeezing mine. "It's hard to breathe," she says.

They haven't even closed the door yet. There are no windows—just cracked openings between the boards of wood that make up the car. There's a rotten odor of cattle, but the scent will soon be covered with the filth dripping from everyone's bodies.

"Where are they taking us?" a woman's voice echoes just as the door slides closed.

"Who knows," another person answers. "Most likely to a farm, seeing as we're no better than the animals they pack into these crates."

With the cracks between the wall panels allowing in a bit of light as the sun sets, I can make out the whites of Olivia's eyes as she stares up at me in fear.

The light disappears completely within the first hour of our travels. My legs are worn and tired from standing.

"I'm tired," Olivia says.

"I am too, but we can't sleep now."

My only assumption is that they are taking us to a camp of some sort. It was said that's where the Nazis were deporting the other Jewish people from Warsaw. I want to assume it's where they will force us to do strenuous labor, but that might be wishful thinking.

"I don't know how much longer this ride will be, but I need you to listen to me carefully," I tell Olivia. "Whatever they tell you to do, don't argue. If there's a way to prove a skill you have, prove it wisely without overstepping any bounds. Don't speak out of turn. Clear your face of all emotion and stare straight ahead, no matter what is happening. The less eye contact, the better."

"Are they going to take me away from you?" she asks, knowing I don't have the answer. She'd be happy if I lied and made promises to her, but it's not something I can do right now. Olivia seems so much younger than she is. These years have made me feel older, but I fear she is clinging to the last memories of a normal childhood she had.

"Listen to me. You are fourteen now. You're old enough to take care of yourself if need be. You are capable of more than you give yourself credit for, and you must remember this. We have to fight to protect ourselves, but to fight this kind of battle, we need to use our minds the best we can."

I can only hear Olivia sniffle softly. "But I've only been fourteen for a month. Please don't leave me, I'm so scared."

All I can do is close my eyes and pray no one tries to take her away from me, but I know better. I know the chances of us receiving little of anything we hope for.

I wrap my arm around her and pull her in. "Mama and Papa would be so proud of you right now. You know this, right?"

"Do you think maybe they might be waiting for us—wherever it is we are being taken?" she asks, her words pleading for an answer.

"Lu-lu, I don't know anything more than what you know. You must believe me." I won't dare tell her what I fear. The stories we've heard through whispers can't all be lies. Jewish people aren't wanted.

As the ride carries on, folks are becoming more lethargic and weaker. Taking in a full breath of air is nearly impossible and I'm sure everyone feels just as lightheaded as I do. Our bodies sway together like an airtight package of greased flesh—side to side and front to back with the waver of every curve the train takes.

I pinch myself every few minutes to keep as alert as possible. For all I know, the ride may not end for days, but it could also be over within minutes. The time to think is a punishment within itself as I wonder what I have done so wrongly in my eighteen years that I'm here, like this, trying to protect who is likely the last member standing of my family. Olivia has done nothing to deserve these atrocities, and to go through this without Mama or Papa adds insult to injury.

When I turned eighteen a few months back, I came to realize my youth was officially over and I had to accept that I would never get it back. If I make it through this—whatever this never-ending ride to hell is—I will always have a dark gaping hole between my childhood and whatever comes next. For Olivia, it's even worse: she was only ten when we arrived in Warsaw.

I fight against the exhaustion and desire to close my eyes, pulling me down to the wooden platform like an anchor. I can only imagine it's been over five hours now, and it must be well after midnight.

"We're slowing down," a man mutters.

"Can anyone see anything?" someone else asks.

"There are lights ahead," a woman replies. "There's also a sign in the distance, but I can't make out the words just yet."

Another long minute passes when the squeal of brakes shakes us all around like marbles in a bag.

"'Auschwitz.' That's what the sign says," the same woman speaks again.

No one says a word. I haven't heard of the location, and I doubt anyone else has either, but there's hope of being released from this crate soon.

I shake Olivia's arm, knowing she's probably half asleep, even while standing, somehow.

"I think we're getting off the train soon," I tell her.

"I don't think I want to get off. I might rather stay here forever," she says.

CHAPTER 16
MARCH 1943

ISAAC

A long platform, as much as I can see through the opaqueness of the night, sits before us with no sign of what's waiting for us.

SS officers are shouting from every direction, "*Aus!*" They want every person who was on the train out, and instantaneously.

With the sound of gunshots echoing in the distance, ferocious commanding shouts in German, and dogs that must be as large as their owners growling and barking, it feels as if we are walking straight to a cliff we will be forced to jump from.

As we make our way forward along with the others under a dark sky, crammed together as if we were still inside the cattle car, lights unfold over the distant horizon.

Olivia isn't asking questions now. She is silent and her hand is sweating in mine. I imagine her heart must be pounding against her ribcage like a fist thrashing on a locked door, like my own.

The wait feels endless, and maybe it's for the best, but we

seem to be moving just a step or two forward every minute we inch closer to dawn.

We listen to the same questions repeated by several more SS officers. "What is your age?" "Occupation?" "Ailments we should know about?" The soldier then points his thumb to the left or the right, splitting up the people into two different directions—neither path with a clear destination.

I watch mostly women, young children, and the elderly amble off to the left of the officer, finding the end of a long line that weaves around some brick buildings. Men and some younger women are the ones being sent to the right, down the path between a different set of blocks.

After hearing the questions, I realize Olivia won't have an occupation, not an official one. Without one, I fear we would be sent toward those who look ill and older than others. I don't think we want to go in the same direction as them.

"Lu-lu," I whisper, bending at my knees to lower myself closer to her height. "Your occupation is a seamstress. You have worked in Mama's dressmaker shop since you were old enough to sew."

"What about you?" she asks, clearly understanding why I've given her the story.

"Farming," I reply, knowing I have little knowledge of what farming entails. I'm not old enough to have had a profession as an accountant like Papa, and they may question my age.

"But—" Olivia argues.

"You go first. I'm right behind you." The thought of leaving her behind makes every organ in my body tense. I need to see where they send her.

I can only hear the questions, not Olivia's responses, but she is sent in the opposite direction to those who don't appear to be doing well. I pray that's a good sign.

I step up to the SS officer standing before me with papers in his hand. He doesn't look at me when he asks the three questions. He flicks his thumb over his shoulder toward the right—the same direction Olivia was sent in, and I walk as quickly as I can to try to catch up with her.

"Thank you, God. Thank you, for keeping us together," I whisper up to the sky as it awakens with the rising golden sun.

But I believe I showed my gratitude too soon as Olivia and I are immediately separated once we reach another stopping point. Women are sent one way and men the other. She looks up at me with eyes wider than coins. I can't think of what to say, I can only stare back with the same look.

I watch as her group is taken toward a long narrow building. There are wooden barrels just before the entrance, where women are dropping items. Olivia glances over at me as she drops Old-Bear into the barrel closest to her—her one and only belonging, now gone. I want to run across the dirt pit between us and rescue her cherished bear, but I'm no stranger to the sound of a gunshot, and I've heard far too many in the hours we've been here. We do as they say, or we do no more. It's clear.

There isn't much time to grieve the loss of Olivia's last connection to something outside of this hell. I'm ushered into a building with a similar look to the one she went into, finding a long table with female prisoners cloaked in striped uniforms, typing out the same information we were asked at the last checkpoint, with the addition of our names and country of origin.

A card with my minimal information is handed to me and I'm sent to a new line. It appears this is where they steal whatever it is I have left on my body. The men in front of me are emptying their pockets, forfeiting wallets, pocket watches, and jewelry. There are more prisoners doing the job of Nazis, collecting these items as if it is their idea to steal from their own kind.

Before I feel a sense of relief that I don't have anything on me, I spot the next order of business, where men are stripping their clothes off, from their hat down to their socks. Never mind the chill in the air, the Nazis are standing around, laughing, and pointing at each man who undresses. What is it we have differently than them, other than morals? What is there to laugh at? They are demoralizing us with every opportunity, even one as low as stealing our clothes. The thought of them doing this to Olivia makes me want to break through each wall of these barracks until I find her, but it's clear that any effort made to step out of line won't end well.

I peel the dirt-ridden layers off my body, knowing I've been wearing the same shirt, pants, shorts, socks, and coat for months. It takes everything I have to hand them over as if I'm offering them up without a fight. I don't remember the last time I have been without clothes or forced to look down at my ribcage protruding from my stomach. My knees stick out much farther than they ever have before, and my legs are skin and bone. There's nothing more I can hide about myself at this point. They will see how long I've been hungry and decide on their own whether I'm fit to continue moving.

The air against my bare skin prickles and the dirt beneath my feet feels like shards of metal. No one stalls long enough to find out what's waiting for us at the front of the next line. There's a metal stool, one where each man sits for no longer than two minutes as their hair is entirely cut off, then shaved down to the scalp. I'm nearly thrown off the stool upon completion and sent to the next corner of the building.

"You will all receive a number which we will track you by," an officer announces.

A fellow prisoner walks down the line of us, spraying each person with a horrible, pepper-scented mist. No one asks what they are covering us with—it's the least of our concerns now.

I strain to see several spots ahead, finding another stool where men are being shoved down to sit. Each man is told to lift his arm before a metal blade is taken to his skin.

There are no hints of pain to hear. Everyone must be biting their tongue or too used to pain by now to feel much of anything. All I notice is the ghostly complexion across each man's face.

It isn't long before my bare bottom is against the sticky metal seat. I lift my arm without being asked and stare over the shoulder of the man who is carving lines into my forearm. Each time the blade moves, blood trickles down the side of my arm. Numbness doesn't overcome the stitching burn. I look away, not wanting to remember the moment I became branded by a Jewish man forced to torture his fellow people.

Once I'm pulled from the stool and told I'm done, I'm given a striped uniform and sent out of the main building area. I don't see that the branding on my arm is in the form of a number—the one that essentially replaces my name until I slide my arm through the button-down top. These will likely be the last set of clothes I ever put on. We aren't here to live, and if we are, I'm sure they will do whatever is necessary to make sure we no longer want to survive.

I wish I could convince myself that they haven't taken the same measures for the women in the other building, but I doubt they are being any more courteous to them. The thought of anyone shaving Olivia's beautiful hair is more gut-wrenching than anything I see around me. She won't look like her when I see her next—I need to recognize her. It's the only thing I need right now.

At the exit of the building, the last working prisoner stands with a stack of papers. "Number," he requests.

I lift my sleeve and present my arm.

"Barrack eight," he says.

The wasteland outside of the building is filled with other Jewish people scattered around in their blue-and-white striped uniforms. I look in each direction, desperate to spot Olivia, but I don't see any of the females out here between the barracks.

They must have been taken to a different location or taken away from here altogether. I'm all Olivia has left, and I can't stop them from doing whatever they are doing to her. She's all I have left too...

It doesn't take long to find barrack eight. The interior is made up of wooden shelving, or beds, as men seem to be using them.

From behind me, an officer shouts, "Listen up. These numbers shall report to me immediately to be taken to the location of your assigned labor."

I push the sleeve of my shirt up again, trying my best to remember the six-digit number, but my mind can't seem to keep up with what's happening.

I shouldn't be surprised to hear my number called second on the list, but my exhaustion is making it hard to react fast. I'm not the slowest to line up, but not the quickest as I should be.

As hints of the sun begin to glow in the horizon, twelve of us are tossed into a wagon and carted away blindly for a slow twenty-minute rocky ride to wherever we are being put to work.

When the vehicle stops, we all tumble into each other like dominos under the attack of a tornado. An officer hands each man a tool upon clambering out of the dark vehicle. In front of us is a wide landscape of short grass that appears to roll out for miles. To the right is a barn nestled up against an edge of thick trees, to the left is a dirt road, and behind us is a pristine family home with two rocking chairs quaintly placed on the front porch. This doesn't seem like a place for laborers who've been hidden from common society for so long. Maybe the family home belongs to the Third Reich.

A guard stands before us, adorned with several weapons on display. He yells each word as if we are causing a commotion. None of us have the energy to speak. "Your only job is to dig within the outlined premises, finger- to elbow-length deep."

Deprived of water, food, and sleep, I feel separated from my body as I repeat the same motion of thrusting the tip of the metal shovel into the dirt and tossing the contents over my shoulder. I don't know how my body is still moving at all, but by some miracle I remain on my feet, tending to my chore, hour after hour without interruption.

But then the curtain of a top-floor window on the house swings back and forth as if moving with the wind. As far as I can see, the window isn't open. I continue to shovel but also keep an eye on the window, wondering if I might be losing my mind.

The SS officers do everything in their power to keep us hidden from Polish civilians, whether in Warsaw, or whatever town we might be in now. It seems it should be impossible to see a woman in a daytime dress with long dark curls staring down at us from the house's lonely window, facing the farm. She's looking directly at me as if we know each other. Do we? It only takes a moment to notice the yellow star sewn to the upper right side of her sweater.

She must notice when I spot her because, in the blink of an eye, the white curtains spill into each other once more, hiding the girl that was standing there just a second earlier.

CHAPTER 17
MARCH 1943

SOFIA

I knew it was only a matter of time before the laborers would begin working on the land. I could have avoided the scene if I had left my curtains closed, but there's no use in avoiding what I know is happening just outside my window.

They arrived early this morning, just a bit after Papa left for work—the workers were confined to a wagon attached to a truck driven by an SS officer. They were released to do nothing else but work for hours on end.

Each man is dressed in a blue-and-white striped uniform and was given a tool. A lot of them appear emaciated. Each one of them is nearly bald, and they are as pale as the clouds witnessing their work from above. It may be just March, but they are dripping in sweat from the work they are doing.

I wonder where they send the women to work, or what they do for labor. From the whispers I've overheard, the officers only keep young healthy women, and healthy men. The rest are sent to their "final destination," as the officers explain to Papa. The words are never spelled out, but I know they are killing the

Jewish people they have no use for. There isn't a doubt in my mind.

These poor men. They must be parched without a sip of water all day. Their bodies aren't oiled machines, and yet, it seems that's what's expected of them. The guards pace back and forth, holding their gloved fists behind their backs while inspecting each prisoner's quality of work—quality of digging dirt. The ground isn't fully thawed from the winter months. We're only a week into spring, but here, it won't warm up for several more weeks, which means they will be digging away at ice-covered dirt. But if the farmland isn't prepared before the end of April, we won't be able to use it properly for the upcoming season. Therefore, this is the only solution, according to the ordering officers.

If the guards weren't keeping such a watchful eye on them, I'd take them water, bandage their wounds, and offer them something to nibble on. My heart hurts just thinking about how they must feel.

One of the men, or rather, an older boy, glances up toward my window almost catching my gaze. I slink away, allowing the curtain to fall. I can't imagine how humiliated they must feel as it is. He looked so young—too young to be put through so much brutal labor.

Mama comes into my bedroom.

"Sofia, move away from the window. I told you to keep the curtains drawn now that there are—"

"Jewish men digging through frozen dirt on our property?"

"Don't you understand my heart is broken as much as yours?" my mother says.

"Have you looked at these men, Mama? Do you see their skeletal structures, the lack of color in their cheeks, their bald heads?"

"No, I'd rather not look," she replies.

"You'd rather avoid the truth, you mean?"

Mama's gaze drops to her intertwined fingers, her thumbs rolling around one another. "I'm not avoiding anything. I choose not to fill my mind with images I won't be able to unsee."

I take a few steps closer to her as she stands in the doorway. "You won't be able to unsee the sight of these poor men being treated like slaves, but you will sleep comfortably in your bed tonight? We should be next to them."

"We can only live in the moment, Sofia. You know this."

"They have the same stars sewn to their uniforms. How can you ignore the reality we're living above?"

Mama places her chapped hands on her chest, crossing her heart. "What am I supposed to do?"

"We should be helping any Jewish man or woman who steps foot on our property, and you know this. We are both aware the Nazis have no intentions of salvaging even one of their lives. I've listened to the radio enough to know the truth behind each piece of propagating tomfoolery downtown. I'm not sure who the SS thinks they are fooling, but surely every non-Jewish civilian sees right through the charades too. You can't tell me you haven't heard about the growing resistance in our country. What would they be resisting if innocent people weren't being tortured to death?"

Mama takes another step into my bedroom and closes the door behind her. "Enough, Sofia. I know what is happening at Auschwitz, and outside of our house, for God's sake."

"There's a boy outside, and he can't be much older than me. They don't care who they kill or push further into the ground. That boy could be—should be—me, and you should be beside me, and we should be forced to take part in hard labor from dawn until dusk. Taking note of what's really happening outside of my bedroom window seems to be the very least I can do at the moment. Personally, I'd much prefer to bring them food and water, but I suspect I'd be shot upon doing so, despite being the doctor's daughter. Am I right?"

Mama's chin dimples and quivers, then tears fall from the corners of her eyes, one by one until there are wet streaks lining her face. "You're going to get yourself killed—us, and there's nothing I can do about it, is there?"

I can't predict the future any better than she can, but if she's asking whether I plan to watch people die outside of my window every day, I can't tell her what she wants to hear.

"Has it dawned on you that we might have a responsibility to these poor people? We have been spared the atrocities they are trying to survive, and you think we should take the free ticket, hold it against our hearts and say a quick prayer for them?"

Mama gasps for air as if she can't find her next breath. "You are putting words in my mouth. I didn't say anything of the sort. I wish we could save everyone, too, but I don't know how to do so without endangering ourselves."

I spin around and walk back toward my window.

"The boy I just mentioned—I couldn't help but watch him throughout the day. He's been shoveling since the crack of dawn this morning and hasn't flinched with pain or fatigue. He just keeps going. I've imagined myself out there doing the same, and I don't think I'd survive. You tell me all the time, I'm just a child, and yet here he is, no more than a child himself, doing the work no grown man should have to do," I argue. "Nothing in this world makes sense, Mama. Not a single thing."

I pull the curtain away, making sure the sunlight pours in so she can catch a glimpse of what's happening outside. She would need to walk closer to see the full view, but I have a suspicion she won't be able to look away now.

Mama's eyebrows furrow and lines deepen along her forehead. She closes her eyes and tries to swallow against her tongue. With a couple more steps toward me, she's at the window, witnessing what I am. The men are becoming weaker now that it's been at least six hours since they began. One seems to be having trouble even lifting his shovel from the dirt.

The guard notices and approaches the tired man. We can't hear their conversation, only speculate at his condescending words.

"Do you see that other young man down there, working with a pitchfork that's taller than he is?" I say. "You would call him a child too, wouldn't you? The poor boy is working twice as fast as some of the others. It's because he's scared to die. I can see it, can't you?"

Mama watches the scene playing out, and neither of us are able to blink. I wish for just a second that we both blinked at the same instant the guard struck the poor man with a whipping stick. We heard the slash against the wind, striking the man's hollow body, and now he's falling to his knees in agony. His bottom jaw falls as he presses the palms of his hands against the cold dirt. The guard is yelling at him, but I can't make out what he's saying. The man doesn't react to the words. Instead, his elbows shake, threatening to release the weight of his body.

The guard takes the opportunity to whip the man once again. Blood splatters like a splash from a deep puddle. I cup my hand over my mouth, unable to take another breath. Then, between blinks, an explosive clap thunders against the glass on my window. I feel the blood drain from my face and my neck and chest become colder than ice. Mama's wide-eyed unblinking stare confirms what I suspect caused the noise.

"He knew he was going to kill him but tortured him first anyway," I choke out.

Mama cries out and pulls the curtain from my hand, dragging me down until we're seated beneath the window. With the sobs wrenching from her throat, I can't help but release my emotions as well. We can imagine the horrors of what's happening, but to see it—it changes everything.

"You're right, we have to help them," Mama says through

heavy breaths. "I don't know how, but we must. Whatever that might mean. I won't be able to go on unless I know we have done whatever we can to help."

I twist my head to peer through the blur of tears in my eyes. "I'm your daughter. My bravery doesn't exist without reason, and yours won't continue without purpose. We can help them, I know we can."

CHAPTER 18
MARCH 1943

OLIVIA

The sun is nowhere in sight when the first gong vibrates every wall and wooden beam within the barrack. It's hardly been more than a couple of hours since being assigned to this barrack, and in that time, I feel as though I've done nothing more than stand still, staring at the surrounding scene. Not all of us are new in this building. Some women look to have been here for quite a while. Others, like me, who are trying to find their bearings, seem to be in a state of shock. There are a few women crying, holding themselves, cowering in corners.

Every woman who has been here longer than me is scurrying around to prepare for whatever is next.

"Pardon me," I say, my voice so quiet I'm not sure the woman who looks to be around Mama's age hears me.

They assigned me to a cubbyhole-space, or a "buk" as they call it, to share with her and one other woman. It's where we will sleep. At least it's a bit of personal space. There's hardly space for one person, never mind three.

"What are we supposed to be preparing for?" I try to speak up louder, hoping to gain her attention this time.

She turns toward me but doesn't look down at first. Most people don't think to look down when searching for my voice. I'm so much shorter than the others, it's as if I stopped growing while living in Warsaw. "You look like you're already prepared to head outdoors for counting," she says, glancing at me quickly.

"Counting?" I question.

"We will stand in rows of five and wait for the German delegates to reach our barrack so they can confirm each of us is where we should be."

"They just sent us here, didn't they?" I ask, feeling confused.

The woman stares at me for a long moment. I try to find an emotion within her eyes, but there's nothing I can read about her. "Here," she says, pulling a piece of fabric out from beneath a straw-filled mattress. "For your head, so you won't be cold."

I glance around the barrack at everyone preparing them-selves to go outside for what I now know to be "counting." Most of them have their heads covered. I suppose I won't get used to a bald head. If I don't have to see myself, I can pretend that I still have hair. It's what I told myself a few hours ago after passing through the couple of queues.

I take the fabric and tie it around my head, my hands still shaking like when I first stepped off the train's cattle truck. "Thank you for being so kind," I say, offering my gratitude.

"You're quite young to be in here," she replies.

"I'm fourteen."

"I see. Well, the best advice I can offer is to keep your mouth shut and don't make a sound, no matter what happens. It will be your best chance."

"Best chance at what, if you don't mind me asking?"

The woman stares at me—I feel a chill from the lack of

response. "Just do as I say. When you step outside, there will be rows of five—only five before the next line begins. You must line up."

I nod my head, but she's already turned away, facing the exit to our barrack. I follow her outdoors, finding the lines she was speaking about. She ends a line of five women and I replay her words in my head: "only five." With panic, I do as I'm supposed to and start a new line behind them, hoping I've gone to the correct spot.

When others join me, I'm relieved, knowing I didn't make a mistake.

My legs tire after standing still for what must be over an hour. The woman beside me seems to be asleep with her eyes open. She hasn't moved so much as a muscle in the time we've been standing here.

I wonder how Isaac is getting along. He must be going through similar actions now, but there's no way for me to know. I haven't seen him since they sent us in different directions. All I can think about is the way he told me I'm fourteen now and I'm old enough to take care of myself. When Isaac was fourteen, we were still living in Krakow in our lovely family home. Mama took care of us both, so I don't recall him being old enough to take care of himself at such a young age. Of course, I know nothing is the same now that we are here.

If I were counting the minutes, I might know how long we have been standing outside. I can only decipher from the direction the sun is facing, and it's high in the sky at this point. My knees tremble like the railroad tracks beneath a train from the chill, nerves, and fatigue.

I have been staring at a beauty mark on the neck of the woman standing in front of me. She hasn't moved an inch, which has left me in her shadow and without a chance to feel warmth from the sun.

The sound of laughter carries through the distance,

bouncing off the walls between the barrack buildings. The surrounding women appear to straighten their shoulders, though I thought they were all standing perfectly upright to begin with. I do the same just as a group of Nazis in long black trench coats and caps walk toward us.

I continue to watch the woman in front of me, wondering if we're expected to do anything as the Nazis approach us. All I see is her hands gently falling by her sides before she clasps her right hand around her left wrist behind her back. She squeezes so tight it looks like blood isn't running through the veins in her hand. I notice bruising above and below where she's squeezing, wondering what happened to her.

The group of German soldiers stand before us, talking among each other first, before numbers are being shouted into the air, including mine—the one tattooed on the inside of my left arm, and marked on the white patch sewn to the upper left side of my uniform.

The soldier calling the numbers pauses and whistles, pointing at a woman in the front row. Without words, he instructs her to move out of the line and over to a new line of women preparing to go somewhere else. This process happens three more times during roll call. When the singled-out women leave, I watch the woman in front of me loosen her grip around her wrist.

"The following will report to the storefronts for labor duty," the soldier continues shouting. I hear my number again, so I follow the others who are on this list, too.

The women in front of me look young as well. Not as young as me, most likely, but young enough to handle labor. I want to ask where we're going, but I know not to speak.

Another one of the Nazis walks past, inspecting each one of us before dipping his head. "Walk," he shouts.

We follow him for what feels like miles until arriving at another set of barracks. Once inside, I can see this building holds piles of various materials, everything from shoes and glasses, to baby carriages, and toothbrushes. There are piles of clothes, stacked up toward the ceiling.

"You, you will sort through clothes, removing all objects from pockets, and preparing salvageable materials for fumigation," another new soldier says, approaching me from behind. "Over there. Watch and learn." He points to one of the largest piles of clothes. It's so tall, it's fallen over.

I make my way over to the pile and several other women sorting through clothes. "Welcome to Kanada," the one closest to me says.

Canada? "Are we safe here?" I ask.

"You are working in the one place that holds the richest of possessions of all the people brought here. It's kind of like the country of Canada—a country with an abundance of riches, right?" The woman shrugs as if she doesn't understand the context much more than I do. "No one is safe anywhere here. Just do your work and do it fast."

The woman looks to be around Isaac's age, but the loose skin beneath her eyes and to the sides of her lips makes her seem much older. She looks tired, worn, and lifeless by the extreme pale color of her skin. I suppose I must not look much better. She holds her stare on me while mindlessly sorting through the pile.

"You're lucky to be here." Her words sound more like mumbles, but the look in her eyes offers me a sense of sincerity. "Grab handfuls and search the pockets. If the clothing item is in one piece, fold it and place it in the bin to your left. If it's not in one piece, toss it into the bin over there to the right. We will then fumigate that bin."

"Thank you," I whisper, pulling the first item out of the pile, finding a floral frock designed for a little girl. There's a large bloodstain in the center of the fabric and I glance back over at the woman next to me.

"Who do these belong—"

"The people out there," she says, pointing toward the open door that faces a spout of steam funneling into the sky.

I don't see anyone.

"They're already dead," she explains.

CHAPTER 19

APRIL 1943

SOFIA

A week has come and gone since the prisoners of Auschwitz started tending to our farm from the early hours in the morning to late at night.

I managed to locate Papa's binoculars and have been watching the men from the window, trying to follow their every move, as well as the guards'. Once every few hours, there is a change of guards. It's typical for the pair of men to become chatty and distracted during their conversations, but I haven't come up with a solid plan on how I can help yet.

There has been some turnover, too. The man who was hit with a whipping stick the first day, he never came back. Three others who were scolded for not working hard enough, and none of them returned either. Second chances don't exist beneath the scrutiny of the Nazis.

The young one, the one I assume to be around my age, doesn't stall, pause, or lose his balance. For the life of me, I can't figure out where his continuous energy comes from, but he seems to have strength beyond what I can comprehend.

Twice, he has caught me looking out the window, and I wonder what he must think of me. From down there, my *Jude* patch must be a blur or unnoticeable. He must assume I'm clueless and lucky for not being Jewish like him—or worse, a Nazi sympathizer. What other kind of person would stand inside, watching the act of slavery?

The same as those who watched the poor Jewish people of Warsaw fall to their knees.

The thought of anyone assuming I am siding with a Nazi makes my stomach burn.

Nightfall is now crawling over the horizon, and I wonder how late they will keep the men here today.

"Sofia, I won't be home until late tonight, so I've come to say goodnight now," Papa says, entering my bedroom without so much as a knock on the door.

"Goodnight," I curtly reply without turning away from the window. He's asked me time and time again not to let anyone see me upstairs, but what does it matter?

"I asked you to stay away from the window," he says, his voice lacking his typical authority.

"I already know what's happening outside. What's the difference?"

There's no response from Papa. In fact, it's so quiet, I wonder if he's turned away to leave. Still, I keep my focus set outside, forcing myself to watch every second of the torturous slavery these men are still enduring after an entire day of relentless labor. It's easy to see they are all breaking down inside, but I can't see what keeps them going—what thoughts must be running through their weakened minds to encourage their efforts of inhuman endurance.

"Sofia," Papa says, breaking the silence after a long minute, "I must have a word with the *Wachmänner* outside. I will only take a few minutes of their time, but I ask that you please don't come downstairs until I'm gone."

"Are you inviting them inside?" I hiss as my stomach turns with disgust.

"Yes—for a moment into my office. I have to give them some paperwork," he says, straightening his tie while clearing his throat. I might feel strangled at this point too.

"I have no desire to share the same breathing space as those men. You have nothing to worry about," I assure him.

Papa leaves the room, only a lingering sigh from him remains. I rush to my nightstand and yank open the rickety drawer. I pull out the false bottom I slid into place a few weeks ago, knowing that a secret is no longer safe in my house. I slide out the envelope I stashed there and slip it into the pocket of my dress.

"You're home early," Mama says from outside of my bedroom to Papa.

"I—ah—have some business to tend to this evening and won't be home until late, so I was saying goodnight to our daughter."

"How splendid—well, don't let me get in your way, dear," she says with a scoff, questioning how he could be speaking so casually about his plans.

"Lena, would you mind preparing a pot of tea? I need to meet with the gentleman outside for a few brief moments."

Mama snickers. "I apologize. For a moment, I thought I misheard you, but by the serious glower on your face, it's clear I didn't."

"I don't understand what's humorous about my question."

"I'll be frank, then. Those men outside are not gentlemen. They are mongrels, and I don't make tea for their kind. However, if you feel the need to supply them with something that tastes better than the bacteria-ridden water they give the starving and dehydrated prisoners out back, then you can locate the teapot on your own, I'm sure. Goodnight, Friedrich."

I'm doing everything in my power to control myself from

dropping my bottom jaw in shock. Mama has become less and less concerned with her disapproval of Papa and his wrongdoings. It makes me proud of her, but at the same time, I know I've caused a great deal of stress in the house too.

Papa leaves and scurries down the stairwell, almost eager-like to greet those "gentlemen."

"Do you have the supplies?" I ask as Mama turns the corner into my bedroom.

"Yes, they are by the back door in the straw basket," she says, her eyes wide. "I should help you."

"I think it might be better if you keep an eye on Papa and those men in our house," I reply.

"You must be fast, Sofia. The risk—it's far greater than what you want to imagine."

"I'm aware of the risk. It's less of a risk than another one of them falling to their knees in weakness on our family's farm."

"Okay—"

"Mama, we don't have time to discuss this. Go downstairs. I'm taking the back stairwell." It's not so much a stairwell as it is a dormer window above a slightly angled awning which leads down to a lattice wall trellis that's older than me. I believe the ever-growing vines keep the ornamental decoration planted firmly to the ground. To Mama's dismay, I've used the escape route many times throughout my childhood but haven't had a need to use it in several years. Although the thought has crossed my mind many times over this past year while feeling like I might be stuck in this house forever.

I know I can get down quickly and do what I need to do.

Mama and I have had been trying our best to prepare a plan over the last six days while waiting for the opportune time to execute the idea.

My nerves fire through my arms and legs as I scale down the wall, careful not to snag my dress or sweater. The back door is only a few steps away from where I hit the ground, and I lift the straw basket Mama left here and move it behind the barn. The guards send the men behind the barn to relieve themselves twice a day. I hope they will have the opportunity to find what I'm leaving there for them. To be sure, though, I have written out a note for the boy whose attention I've already caught. There's something about him I can't move past—perhaps the mirroring image of a Jewish person my age, being forced to live in conditions I can't properly fathom.

With the goods stored in the basket, I run around the far side of the barn and call out with a bird whistle, hoping to attract his attention. I must sound like a poor excuse for a bird, seeing how quickly he turns toward me, continuing his repetitive digging motion. He has not taken a break from shoveling since the early hour he arrived here today.

He peers over his shoulder, but only slightly, afraid to look away from what he's doing.

"I have a note for you. I want to help."

I'm not sure he can read the words I'm mouthing or if I'm doing something so stupid it could cost him his life, but I've come this far.

I crane my neck, looking toward the front door of the house to make sure there's no guard in sight. My steps are as long and wide as they can be as I make my way over to the boy—the boy with pain written into his hazel-speckled green eyes. His cheeks are as red as the tip of the shovel he's using, and his lips are lacking color. He's breathing so hard, I'm afraid he might faint.

I tremble while reaching into my pocket for the note. "I don't side with them," I say, handing him the paper. His gaze lowers to the star on my chest, but I need to make sure he knows I'm just like him. "My mother and I have left food for all of you behind the barn. I'll do whatever I can to help. I just can't imagine enduring the amount of work you've been forced through each day. My heart aches for you. Do you have any family with you?"

The boy swallows hard, loud enough for me to hear. He stares deeply into my eyes for what feels like the longest minute.

"Uh—ye-yes," he stutters, "my little sister, Olivia. She's back at Auschwitz. It's just the two of us left now." He clears his throat, sounding as if he's trying to hide the pain laced through his words. Then he takes a quick glance around, and I can feel the panic radiating off his stiff body. "Well—thank you so very much for thinking of me—us, miss. Yo-you should go before they return."

"Yes, you're right. But first, tell me your name?"

"Isaac, miss."

"I'm Sofia."

A small smile tugs at the corner of his lips. "To me, you have been the beautiful girl in the window," he says. "Go, go on before anything happens. Thank you. Thank you, Sofia."

I place my hand on my cheek, feeling for the warmth rushing through my face. I can sense the stares of the others burning against my back as I run away toward the far end of the barn. With another quick check to make sure the guards won't see me pass by before reaching the back door, I see the laborers all looking for me, but with much subtlety. I believe Isaac was able to give them the message quickly, and I pray they can retrieve the food we left just as easily.

Once I'm back upstairs and safely in the confines of my bedroom, I return to the window to watch and wait. Upon the guards' return, each man is working harder and faster than when they left. There's a reward at stake and it seems to have given them each a slight boost. As the guards pass by one another, they stop to exchange a few words. Isaac takes the opportunity to peer up toward my window. I might be imagining it, but I think I see the corner of his lip curl into a smile. If I've given him just an ounce of hope today, I might be able to sleep tonight.

CHAPTER 20
APRIL 1943

ISAAC

There's only one explanation behind the reason I'm still alive, and I must assume my body is running off pure adrenaline. In science class, we learned it was the body's way of increasing heart rate and strengthening muscles to endure excitable situations—a natural reaction to "excitement" is the way it was taught. I realize now, excitement can also mean fear or panic. Science was never my favorite subject, and I don't know much about medicine, but I don't think anyone can live with a heart beating twice as fast as it should be, for hours and hours on end.

The man working beside me, David, said the act of labor must be completed by using mind over matter. I thought it was the best advice I've gotten in months. Early this morning, David collapsed, and one of the guards dragged him away. I'm not so sure anything can rely on mind over matter now. My reason for keeping my knees locked and my hands sewn to the pole of this shovel is simply for Olivia.

After a week of surviving life in Auschwitz, it's no secret what we are always one breath away from. They remove people and send them off to a far corner of the prison camp, never to be seen again. We aren't sure what's happening to them, but it's hard not to assume the worst.

David also told me not to become too chummy with anyone here because it will only lead to grief. One minor distraction could lead me in the path of David and a few others who have fallen to their knees this week. They weren't given a moment to stand back up before multiple bullets were shot through their heads. The Nazis call them worthless and tell one of the other laborers to move the body aside.

Since men and women have been assigned to different blocks, I'm only able to visit Olivia after labor hours, for a short time before the last gong of the day rumbles between the barracks. It's surprising we're allowed any time to roam between barracks, but for as long as it's allowed, I've promised her I would do whatever I can to visit her during that time of night. I can't fathom taking that promise away.

"Break!" a guard shouts across the field. "One minute. Numbers: 139564, 136792, 134871, 139124—go first."

In the seconds after receiving a note from the girl in the window, I made mention of the hidden food she left for us behind the barn. It will be tricky to allocate and hide within the fraction of time we have out of their sight, but we'll manage. We have to.

As usual, we run like overworked, tired derby horses, dragging our hoofs through the dirt with each step. My vision seems to blur and focus beyond my control as I spot the straw basket covered in dirt awaiting us. While relieving the little amount of fluid I have running through my body, I lean to the left to slip my hand inside the basket, feeling paper loosely wrapped around lumps. The others look over in my direction. Their eyes are all wide as if they are witnessing me take my last breath before someone puts the barrel of a pistol up to the back of my head. "In here," I whisper.

I grab one of the lumps and pull it out, tearing the paper off as quickly as possible between my raw fingers that burn with even the slightest of movements. There are four neatly stacked slices of bread cut into finger sandwiches, jam between each pair. I haven't seen this much food in longer than I can remember, never mind the sweet taste of jam I have caught myself dreaming about from time to time. I shove one into my mouth and rewrap the other before dropping it in my pocket for Olivia if I can find her tonight. I want to stop and allow the tart jam to dance along my tongue. I wish to take my time, to enjoy tasting something so delicious, but there's only time to chew the bread well enough that it makes it down my throat without becoming lodged. I've been so hungry for such a long time that I imagine the bread traveling down my esophagus, and falling into the hollow pit of my shrunken stomach. I'm back in my assigned position with the wood of my shovel against the raw skin on my palms before the bread has made it past my esophagus.

"Next group!"

The *Wachmann* shouts out another four numbers.

Now, I pray everyone has a share and disposes of it without being spotted. I can't imagine what the note in my pocket must say. The poor girl wanted to make sure I knew she wasn't one of them. Surely, I can tell the difference between a beautiful girl and a Nazi with black holes for eyes.

Mama always told Olivia and me that we can always depend on someone's eyes to tell us the truth. It's the only part of the human body that is incapable of hiding a lie. I remember staring at my teachers, trying to determine what they must be like outside of school by their eyes, but I couldn't figure out what Mama was talking about. Everyone's eyes looked the same, except for various colors.

It wasn't until we arrived in Warsaw that I understood precisely what she meant. There is good and evil, and nothing in between. No matter how light or dark their eyes appear, they all have one thing in common—a sinister glare. Unlike my own eyes which view the world with humanity and kindness—they somehow project a weakness these monsters can prey upon. I had just never come across someone capable of what these German soldiers are.

The sun has almost completely fallen behind the low stretch of mountains in the distance, but there's no way of knowing how long we'll be here tonight. Most nights we're allowed just a few hours of sleep before we are to report back to the wagon.

If we're lucky, we may be done with work earlier than normal. It seems the *Wachmänner* are a bit distracted tonight. One has stumbled a few times, and the other, his words are slurring as he yells out the groups of numbers for their break.

We aren't sure where they went when the owner of the house called for them, but they were inside for more than a few minutes and seemed to return in a different state of mind.

With the sunlight fading by the moment, the lights within the house flicker on one at a time. The warm glow against the curtains looks warm and inviting and I envy the girl, Sofia, upstairs.

Once more she appears as if checking on us, but this time her gaze seems to only find me. I do my best to avoid the distraction, knowing the *Wachmänner* are out of sorts on top of their normal cruel demeanor. With frustration for nothing I can pinpoint, I jab the point of the shovel deeper into the soil, pulling back more dirt than normal. The wooden shaft between my grip splinters into my flesh and I remember quickly why an even pace is necessary. I grit my teeth against the pain and I don't find any sort of relief upon releasing the wet dirt over my shoulder. There must be small shards of wood impaling my hand. I'll be lucky to escape an infection later.

I hear the *Wachmänner* mutter to one another, German slang I don't recognize. One man elbows the other and they both peer up at the window where Sofia is still standing. They aren't angered by her presence. Instead, they appear amused as one of them offers her a friendly wave.

Instantly, the curtain falls from her hand and she's out of sight, where I hope she stays for the rest of the night—for her own good.

"Gentlemen," a woman calls from the front of the house, "my husband asked that I send you on your way with these bags this evening."

"Ah yes, he mentioned you might have something for us," one responds. They've mentioned their names to each other, but seeing as we don't deserve names, I refuse to remember either of theirs.

The woman doesn't reveal herself from the front of the house. I assume she must be waiting for the guards to retrieve whatever she's holding.

A conversation ensues between the three of them and for a moment I slow the swing of my shovel and glance up toward a dancing light in the window. Sofia points to the barn then touches her fingers to her lips. I think she's asking if I found the food.

I nod ever so slightly and bow my head forward, hoping she understands my gesture of gratitude.

A choked laugh carries across the field. It's clear the woman speaking to the *Wachmänner* is very uncomfortable, but I don't think they care much about offering anyone comfort.

Sofia holds her hand up against the window for a split second, making the separation between the two of us incredibly evident. With more need for a distraction than ever before, I'm desperate to know what's inside the note—to know why she looks as scared as I feel.

.   .   .

Whatever the woman said or didn't say to the *Wachmänner* enticed them to end the evening of work earlier than usual and directed us to load into the wagon.

We sit like monkeys with our heads resting on our knees, desperately trying to find an even rhythm of breaths. There are two cracks of lights from streetlamps spilling into each side of the wagon's enclosure. It might be enough light to allow me a chance to read the note.

I struggle to pull it out of my pocket with how close we're sitting together, but I'm in the center of four others, their backs facing me. I unfold the paper over the top of my boots and wait for the right angle to catch more light from the passing lamps.

Each bump forces me to lose my place, but I'm able to read enough to understand why the girl in the window wanted to help us so much.

Dear sir,

I apologize if you've noticed me staring out the window at you. There are so many men working themselves to the bone on each side of you, but you've captured my attention, and I wonder about you—how you have the strength to endure what you are going through daily. You appear so brave and unfaltering, and yet, I feel fear down to my core just to imagine what it might be like to live in your shoes. There is so little I can do to help, but I wanted you to know I'm not staring down as if I'm above you. In fact, I should be beside you, and knowing this—I hope if I end up there, I have the same endurance you do.

I imagine your world must feel lonely, and while I'm living inside, safe for now, I feel like a no one, guilty, worthless, and wishing I could at least use my moments of freedom for good.

I know the food we left for you isn't much, but whatever I can do for you and the others, I promise to do.

I'm not sure if you have someone to tell you this, but what-
ever you do, don't give up. Please, stay strong. I am praying for
a future where we will all be free and happy once again.

Sincerely,

S~

My eyes strain against the aching muscles in my head, rereading the line about her being next to me. I'm grateful she has managed to avoid the torture. Even if there is just one of us out there who isn't suffering, there is hope. I hold the letter to my chest, wishing my heart could soak up the words and feel an ounce of something more than emptiness. There is still kindness left in the world. I needed to know this.

As the wagon slows down, I crumple it against my pounding heart then tear up her letter into as many pieces as I can to ensure no one can read the words, and I pile the small scraps into my mouth and force the soft paper down my throat.

We're dropped on the inside of the foreboding gates of hell, forced to walk across the prison grounds to our assigned barracks. This is the only time of day when we aren't escorted with a watchful eye, because once we are locked inside these cages, there is no way to escape. It's also my only hope of spotting Olivia for a moment. Her barrack is across the way from mine, about a two-minute walk, and as I walk by, she's staring out the door.

"Isaac," she says through her breath, "I wasn't sure you'd make it—we don't have long until the gong rings." She reaches for my hand. "I missed you so much."

"I know. I just arrived back from the farm where I've been shoveling all day. I'm so glad to see you. I hoped so badly that I would have just a minute to check on you at least. Are you all right?"

Olivia opens her two hands, flipping them over for me to see the tips of all her fingers. The skin is puckered and raw. "I spent the day pilfering through soiled fabrics." I thank God every day that they have her sorting clothes rather than doing what I'm doing. "How about you? Is everything okay?"

I remember the bread in my pocket. I pull her out of the block from within her row of barracks and off to the side of the structure where there is another row of barracks just a few feet away. For what feels like miles is only rows of barracks, housing blocks of prisoners. "Here," I say, unwrapping the bread and closing it into her small hand, "eat this, quick. It's bread and jam."

"Where did you get it?" she questions with an alarming look that bounces between my eyes and her closed grip.

"I will explain when I can. Just eat it. Please."

Olivia shoves the food into her mouth and her eyes roll back as she takes one second to enjoy the sweet taste on her tongue before swallowing it at once. She lunges for me and wraps her arms around me, burying her head into my chest. "You're the best brother a girl could ever wish for. I love you so much for loving me as much as you do."

"I'll keep you safe, Lu-lu, even if it's the last thing I do here on earth."

CHAPTER 21

APRIL 1943

ISAAC

I seem to have a little extra time between visiting Olivia and the sounding of the gong, which means I have a moment to check the *list*.

There's a list posted on a wall outside of the infirmary closest to my barrack block—it displays the names of those who are still alive and living within these gates. Mama and Papa's name aren't on the list, which means they were shot in Warsaw or died here or were taken elsewhere. I don't know if Olivia has seen these lists posted along various buildings, but I hope she hasn't been curious enough to scan through the names. To lose the last of her hope would be the worst possible thing for her.

Without an ounce of energy left, I shuffle through the dusty gravel back toward my barrack, spotting a dispute just a short way past where I'm heading. Prisoners are lined up along the wall of another block and an officer is shouting at them. "Where is he?" It's all I hear, over and over.

A shot fires into the air. It's a warning. Someone must speak up or they will all be punished. That is the unwavering rule here.

With dread, I step over the damp threshold into the wooden paneled block where more than five hundred sleep and call "home."

Our roll call must be soon, and we'll be given our evening bread with just enough time to swallow our food whole, wait in line for a turn to use the washroom and toilet before the last gong of the day will ring in the silence.

There isn't much chatter among the men in the barrack, especially considering how many of us there are. There's more commotion from coughs, groans, and angry stomach moans.

"They keep you later than they should there," one of the men says from his wooden bunk.

"We were released earlier than usual today. I'm grateful for that," I reply.

"Do they feed you at least?" he continues. There aren't very many of us who are taken away from the prison gates for our hours of labor, so there is a lot of curiosity surrounding the topic.

"Nothing more than the soup." I'm not sure if he wonders whether I'm receiving special treatment or if they are treating us worse than anyone here, but I can't blame him for wanting to know. Of course, I'll have to keep quiet about the extra bit of food I was graciously given. It wasn't from the Nazis well-doing, that's for sure.

It seems I might have been wrong about the labor job keeping us alive. It may drag out the inevitable, but they are working us to the bone and giving us less than our bodies require to function. It's only a matter of time before my body begins to feed off its stored fat contents—whatever I have left, anyway. I see it every day. Some of the others working on the farm are already emaciated and I've come to notice that if anyone appears beyond the point of repair, they're sent away and we don't see them again. It only looks like there are two paths through this torture, but they both lead to the very same spot.

Tonight, the gong rings before we have gotten through roll call or are given our meal. We move in silence, knowing we will no longer receive our rations. Yet, we continue rushing every step of the way as if it's our fault that the officers have fallen behind in their nightly schedule. Each person in our block will be punished for a missing person four barracks away. The longer roll call takes, the less time we all get. They do that on purpose too—to ensure we don't do anything reckless enough to hurt the others standing beside us.

We are lined up ten at a time outside of the block. Our numbers are called out, one by one, and we claim them as if we have won a prize, because if we are not loud enough, we will often start over from the beginning.

Another hour passes before I have a chance to use the washroom, but I should still end up with a few hours of sleep before it's time to report back out front. It helps to know there are only two more days until Sunday, the one day we aren't forced to do labor—for others anyway. We are forced to clean our living areas and repair whatever has torn or broken from the last week. That type of work is nothing compared to how tough the days of digging are.

I'm the last to enter my assigned buk along the row of other holes we're all to sleep within. There are four of us in a space—the size of one small mattress. We each must sleep on our side to fit, so we do our best to switch sides each night to make sure we don't end up with sores from being in the same position for too long. Like all the others I've seen, our barrack is made up of wooden structural beams and three levels of platforms to fit at least a couple of hundred people inside.

I share a space with Lev and Mathias, who are both from France, and Petr, who came from Prague. Lev and Petr are a little older than Mathias and me. They've been separated from their families without a hint of their whereabouts. They check the list as often as I do for the names they pray to see. Mathias is about a year older than me. His two brothers are also here in Auschwitz but in different barracks. Their parents were sent to another labor camp, but they aren't sure where, or whether they are still alive.

"How was your day, friend?" Mathias asks with his thick French accent. The only common language we all know is German. We were forced to learn it just to survive the Nazi rule. Not many countries in this hemisphere were spared from their undertakings.

"Very long," I reply. "You?"

"Same. But we're alive, right?"

"I question whether this is a fact," I reply, whispering my attempt at a small joke.

"What other choice is there? Us Jews don't believe in Hell. Therefore, we must still be alive." Mathias smiles and slaps the back of his hand against my shoulder. "Goodnight, friend."

"Someone was wrong about Hell," Petr chimes in. "They wanted us to believe there was no such place, but we're there, men."

"Hell, no, no," Lev says. "Hell is hot. We are freezing to our death."

We all snicker quietly, though Lev doesn't have much of a funny bone. If he does, he doesn't have the energy to laugh along with his hopeless statements.

I press my palms together and slip them beneath the side of my head, then search for the darkness behind my eyelids, knowing colorful memories of a blurry past can freely fill my mind until I fall asleep.

. . .

Violin lessons were my favorite part of the day. Uncle Lou used to play in a quartet for banquets and balls, and he wanted to make sure the talent was passed down to the next generation. He said I was a natural. Whether I was, I'll never truly know, but the confidence he gave me made me want to glide the bow back and forth across the strings for hours.

Mama and Papa wanted Olivia to learn when she was old enough to start reading notes, but she didn't take a liking to the instrument as I did. It was easy to tell after the third month of groaning scratches in every note except the correct ones. Mama didn't force her to continue. Olivia preferred tea parties and running her hands down every piece of fabric in Mama's closet, begging to try on all her dresses.

"You can come play for me and Talia during our tea party. It would be lovely to have some entertainment," she said, approaching me at merely eight years old with the most serious expression I had ever seen on her face.

"I don't think so, Lu-lu."

"Mama said you had to," she replied, folding her arms across her chest.

"Did she, now?" I questioned.

"See for yourself?" Olivia perfected the art of raising an eyebrow at the age of five, just in time to start school. She was often in trouble for giving her teachers a silent attitude. We were all aware of Olivia's ability to convey her feelings with just a look.

"I will save myself the trouble and just play for you and your little friend."

"Thank you very much. Here is a list of the music pieces we would like to hear." Olivia handed me a sheet of paper with pencil marks that looked more like chicken scratch.

"'Moonlight Sonata'? Olivia, that's a very difficult piece to play."

She didn't blink, which meant I could argue or just give up

the fight right then and there. The other songs were simple, so I decided to let it go.

Before I knew it, I was standing in the center of our sitting room with my bow in one hand and the violin in the other. Olivia and her friend were kneeling on each side of the tea table, holding their cups in the air with their pinkies stretched out. I had memorized most of the pieces I knew how to play so I preferred to close my eyes as I let the notes travel from my memory down to my fingertips. I would always lose myself within the music.

For the few moments the song would last, my mind would float along with what felt like the clouds; somehow feeling each note as if they had a different texture. The high e-note felt like a long unraveling piece of silk and the low c-note felt like wool, something warm to hold. I'm not sure anyone would have understood, but I could feel the music—each sensation, one right after another as if I could touch it all at the same moment. It was as colorful as it was sensational—a world meant just for me.

When the song ended and I opened my eyes, I found Mama standing in the arched entryway to the room, holding her hands over her heart and a tear rolling down her cheek. Talia's mama was standing beside her, holding a handkerchief beneath her nose. I couldn't understand what caused them to be so upset but also smile at the same time.

More than anything, I wish I could feel the notes running through me again, just once more.

CHAPTER 22

MAY 1943

SOFIA

"Do you think Papa is onto us at all?" I ask Mama, helping her in the kitchen, minutes after he leaves for work.

She's tossing flour onto the wooden board as if she's angry with the inanimate object. "I have no clue," she says. "He spends every night out in that cold barn, and I'm asleep by the time he comes indoors."

It's almost as if Papa doesn't want to talk to us just as much as we don't want to talk to him, but what reason does he have to avoid Mama and me when we are essentially the victims of this situation?

"Do you wonder if he would help us if he knew we were distracting the guards and sneaking the poor men food?" I ask.

Mama peels the heap of dough from the glass bowl and drops it down against the layer of flour with no concern about the small powder storm she's created. She wipes her nose on her shoulder and punches her fists into the center of the dough. "The man I married, he would help us. The man I'm currently married to, I'm not sure I know all that well."

"Are you going to invite the guards in for lunch again today?" I ask.

"Yes, yes, it's the only way the men receive a true break."

The few short moments I've managed to speak with Isaac, the more I've come to understand the purpose of their labor. The Nazis are working them until they are unfit to work and then they will be sent to a place where they are never seen again. For the first few days they were here, they weren't given a proper break to drink their broth, which was served from a rusty metal food container. They drink out of what looks like a dog bowl. Isaac said the others who work at different locations or within the gates of Auschwitz have an hour break at noon. I don't know why the guards here won't allow the same for them.

The guards come in waves about three times a day, and they hardly ever arrive in the same combination as the day before. Mama and I decided the only way to fix the situation is to distract the two men in charge. I would never go out on a limb and call Mama or me fine actresses, but we've done a good job of hiding who we are. At least, I hope so.

"We're doing the best we can," I tell Mama.

"Before the war, I could start a conversation with anyone, but now, I'm terrified to say the wrong word, wondering what they truly know about us. I fear they know what we're up to and they're toying with us too."

Mama has stopped speaking to me as if I am only her daughter. We talk more like friends now. There's nothing left she can hide from me, and it wouldn't do either of us any good. We're either on the same page, or we'll end up in trouble. Though at least, we have each other—allies fighting against the same side unlike Papa, it seems.

"You have always been able to read people well, Mama. I'm sure if they were playing with us, you would have an inkling," I assure her.

"I pray you're right. I do."

A knock on the front door makes us both freeze in place. Mama's hands are covered in flour, and I'm rinsing out the glass bowl beneath the running faucet. We look at each other with matching alarm, both of us likely assuming it's one of the guards—but for a reason we aren't expecting at this early hour.

"What could they want?" I ask, knowing Mama doesn't have a better answer than I do.

"Stay here."

Mama unties her apron and hangs it on the hook of the kitchen wall before making her way out to the foyer. I lean my back up against the wall, hoping to hear what's said.

The door creaks open, screaming a warning of hesitation. I imagine Mama is peeking through the opening, deciding whether it's safe.

"Good day, *Frau*. Might I be a bother and ask if you have a couple of aspirin to spare?"

Mama wouldn't be able to lie even if she wanted to, not with Papa being a physician. There's no doubt we have a stash of aspirin in the house. "Of course. Is everyone all right?"

I don't think Mama intended to inquire about everyone rather than just the two guards, but her nerves must be getting the better of her.

The pause in conversation makes my throat dry, wondering what look he might be giving her.

"*Herr?*" Mama prompts him to answer.

"I apologize. I have an awful pain in my head. The sun is quite bright today and I believe we all might have had too much to drink during a dinner party last night."

Everything inside of me wants to break through this wall and wring my hands around the man's neck. Do they even have a conscience left in their soul?

"Of course. Come in," Mama says. "I'll be just a minute."

I know Mama must be boiling inside. She turns redder than

a tomato when she keeps her anger silent. I wonder if the guard noticed.

She's running up the stairs to the washroom closet where we keep all medical supplies, and the man is pacing in the hall-way, on and off the oriental round rug. The loud clunks of his heels make my pulse race. In case he becomes daring enough to peek into the kitchen, I tend to the bread Mama was kneading and pick up where she left off.

"Something smells delectable," the man says. Without turning to look over my shoulder, I know he's in the doorway of the kitchen; I can tell by the way his voice is no longer muted as it was with a wall between us.

I swallow the lump in my throat and turn on my heels to face him.

"Thank you, *Herr*. It's just bread dough."

"Bread is somewhat of a high-end luxury these days, is it not?" he asks, his eyes skating down the length of my neck toward my yellow star.

I bite my tongue between my teeth, doing what I can to stop the words begging to pour out of my mouth. It's only a commodity to those they are starving to death.

"It is," I agree, feebly.

"Carry on, then. I didn't mean to disturb you."

I bow my head to show him the courtesy he must desire, though I'd rather slap him, and turn back toward the dough.

"I hope the men outside aren't bothering you. We've made it clear that they must always be silent. I can imagine it might be somewhat of a nuisance listening to the ruckus all day." The soldier chuckles silently as if taunting me.

The anger I feel inside forces the hairs at the back of my neck to rise and a flush of heat sprawls across my cheeks. "They aren't a bother. It's good to have more hands to help with the farming duties. There will be more crops this summer."

"Precisely," the SS guard says. Two more steps, each one

growing louder than the last, has me locking my gaze on the butcher block to the right of the sink. "I only ever see you working around this house. You don't get out much, do you, *Fräulein?*"

I choose not to answer, knowing nothing helpful will come out of my mouth.

"I've found you aspirin," Mama says, sneaking up behind us both. "Could I offer you a glass of water, perhaps?"

"That would be splendid, *Frau*. Thank you for being so gracious."

Mama silently skates by the man and tends to the cupboard. Her hand trembles while holding the glass beneath the faucet, so I take the glass from her hands and turn to face the man once more.

"Here you are."

Mama turns around and hides her hands behind her back, forcing a tight-lipped smile while the soldier takes the aspirin and a few gulps of water. He leans over and hands the glass back to me. "Again, thank you. And, *Fräulein*, if you are ever looking to escape for a bit, there are plenty of social activities we enjoy weekly, and I'd be honored to escort you to one. I'm sure the others would welcome such a pretty—" Again, there is eye contact with my yellow star. "Such a pretty young woman like yourself."

Bile rises from the pit of my stomach. The thought of attending a cheerful gathering with a roomful of Nazis would be my dying day, whether by choice or not.

"How kind," I reply.

"I don't believe I've gotten your name?"

"You haven't," I say. "I must get back to the dough before the flour dries up. Feel better, sir."

Disappointment sets in the man's eyes, which tells me that he is blind to the mass murder he has attached himself to.

"I'll have lunch prepared for you both shortly," Mama says, her voice wavering.

The guard checks his watch before glancing back up. "We're looking forward to it." Finally, the man bows his head and spins on his heels before leaving us in silence.

"What have we done?" Mama asks just as the door closes behind him.

"Everything we can to keep those men outside alive," I remind her.

I peek out through the kitchen curtains we keep closed. The men are all working in new areas on the land, scattered about, giving the guards less of an accurate view of each person at once. I search until I spot Isaac. He's puncturing holes into the freshened dirt, preparing them for seeds. The labor must be more brutal than usual today since they are all dripping in sweat, their skin glowing red.

"They're going to need more water today. They all look so parched and overheated from working so hard," I say to Mama.

"Sofia, what are we doing? Can't you see, we're walking a fine line between life and death?"

"So are they," I remind her, releasing the fabric of the curtains from my grip. "They aren't asking for what they are doing, though, Mama. They are doing whatever is necessary to stay alive. I found out more about the boy my age out there. His name is Isaac. It's just he and his little sister living in Auschwitz —he doesn't know what happened to his parents. Every time I look out at him, my heart hurts more than it did the time before. I only wish I could do something."

"Dear God, the poor boy! I can't even imagine a little girl living a life of slavery like these men outside. This world seems to have lost all respect for humanity, and I'm not sure how much longer this can continue. Furthermore, the guards are becoming too friendly with us. We should most certainly be questioning why this is the case."

"What are you suggesting?" I ask, knowing whatever it is must be atrocious since she has her head buried in her hands.

"I don't know what I'm suggesting. I'm speaking the facts—the reality of what's to come if we don't stop what's happening."

"If we stop, they all die. It's as simple as that. I am not going anywhere with that Nazi. We will continue to distract them with lunch and breaks for tea and do what we have been doing." I would hope someone would do the same for me if I was on the other side of these walls.

"You're right. I'm just terrified for us," Mama says.

"And as you've said to me many times throughout my life, 'That's how we know we're doing the right thing.'"

CHAPTER 23

MAY 1943

ISAAC

I worry what Sofia and her mother are doing to occupy the *Wachmänner* for a full hour, giving us a daily break, one we didn't have when we first began working on the farm. Whatever is happening inside, it changes Sofia's disposition. Though most of my speculation is from afar.

I've been stacking piles of hay since the sun rose over shallow hills in the distance. My arms feel sorer than usual from the change of motion from shoveling dirt, but the guards have been checking their watches, almost seeming more eager than we are for a break. I'm not sure what they need a break from, though—I wonder if it's exhausting to live as a miscreation of humanity.

One of the *Wachmann* elbows the other, signaling it's time for their break. They act like children waiting for the bell to ring before playtime.

The heels of their boots grind against the gravel toward the house. The wood of the front porch moans beneath their weight and the rap of knuckles against the door screams assertion, which is quite opposite from the way they seem to act toward the madam of the house.

Once the door opens and the greetings come and go, the door closes with a gentle motion. We tend to the metal container of soup on our own accord, hoping one of them doesn't return to remind us that we weren't formally dismissed: they enjoy these mind games they play with us.

I won't be the first to go for the soup, and most of us feel that way, which means we often wait a while before someone becomes hungry enough to risk the move.

A pebble bounces next to my foot and rolls against the side of my boot. I think it may have fallen from the stack of hay on the end of my pitchfork. I toss the stack into the pile and spin around to collect another heap. Before the metal prongs touch the hay, another small rock bounces off the side of my boot.

I glance around to find the source of flying rocks, spotting Sofia poking her head out from the back of her house. She waves me over, her eyes large. I'm nervous to move because no one else has stopped working yet.

"It's okay," she whispers. "I'm sure."

We've spoken less than a handful of times, but I suppose I trust her more than anyone else around me. Still, it wouldn't take much for a Nazi to force us to choose our lives over another.

I bring the pitchfork with me, imagining what could be done with it if I left it behind.

Sofia is casual in a royal blue day-dress, a black button-down sweater, her hair tidy and pinned back into a long braid, but barefoot, which disrupts her pristine attire. Then there's me, dark hair sprouting from my previously shaved scalp, and dirt-covered blue-and-white striped pants and top. The white isn't even white anymore. No matter how many times I try to rinse the dirt from the fabric, it still dries with a gray hue.

Before the walls closed in around us at Warsaw, Mama

would iron my shirts along with Papa's every day. The fresh scent of air-dried linen mixed with the heat of the iron made me feel polished regardless of whether I was going to school, Temple, or just out to play. I've almost forgotten what it feels like to be clean.

"Don't worry. Mama made them large sandwiches that should tie them up for a while," Sofia says.

"Are the *Wachmänner* bothering you when they come inside?"

Sofia's gaze falls between us, settling on a freshly sprouted patch of forget-me-nots growing along the side of the house. I don't remember the last time I saw a flower. It's hard to consider that I once took such beauty in this world for granted.

"I don't like them. To me, they are just nasty guards, and I won't see them as anything more," she says.

"I don't think anyone likes them aside from their counterparts."

"They're so bold and brash, though clownishly polite. I don't know how any of them could believe a word that comes out of each other's mouths, but, sadly, I must play along since I'm walking a fine line of being an exception to the Jewish rule."

"I understand quite well. I just— They haven't hurt you or your mother?" I ask, worried to know the answer.

"No, the opposite, in fact. One of them asked me to join them at a dinner of some sort, but I declined the offer. I'm sure it was a joke—something that would make all their friends laugh. Imagine one of them bringing a Jewish girl to a dinner..."

My jaw hurts from how hard I'm grinding my teeth together. Life is supposed to just continue as normal while part of the population is being tortured, starved, and murdered.

Sofia reaches forward and places her hand on my shoulder. Instinctively, I pull away, ashamed for her to have to touch something so dirty.

"They're scum," I mutter.

"I apologize if I offended you," she says, holding her hands up to her mouth.

I lunge forward, my hands outstretched toward her. "No, I — You're clean and I'm vile."

She tilts her head to the side with a look of confusion. "Don't be ridiculous, it's just dirt," she says. "I couldn't care less about dirt."

"Well, I do," I say, pointedly. "Sofia, why are you helping me—us?" I hold my hand out toward the others. "You're risking your life. You know this, don't you?"

"I'm a daughter of a 'Privileged Marriage' and a prominent doctor who has been asked to train the incoming SS doctors," she replies, shaking her head with disappointment. "He thinks by doing this distasteful job, he's saving us."

"My God, he is. If you don't act as one of their kind, you are indeed nothing to them, and that's the end of the story. There is nothing but black and white within their brainwashed minds."

Sofia's forehead wrinkles and she pulls her head back as if recoiling from an abhorrent statement. "My mother and I don't talk to him—Papa. We're incredibly angry with his decision to assist those men. We feel betrayed in every way, and I'm not sure either of us could know how to move past the fact of knowing what he's done."

I take a step closer to her. "Sofia, listen to me. I know you don't know me well, but I assure you—your papa has saved you from ... this."

Her gaze wanders as she sweeps loose strands of her long waves behind her ears. "I—I'm not sure I understand. Nothing makes much sense to me these days," she says. "I've left food for you behind the barn, but also, I have something extra for you, and one for your sister."

"My sister?" I ask. She remembers me mentioning Olivia. I hardly recall. I try not to say much about her, because the less anyone knows of her existence, the safer she will be. At least, I tell myself that.

"You mentioned the two of you were separated from your parents in Warsaw. Is she still there in Auschwitz with you?"

I peek around the side of the house, making sure no one is listening or watching. The others are filling their bowls with soup, chugging it so fast, some of it spills from their mouths. We tell ourselves to be careful, but when hunger ravages our brains, we lose control. Plus, the faster we drink the soap-tasting broth, the less we taste.

"She is, thankfully. They have her sorting through clothes every day. I pray her job will keep her safe."

"How old is she?"

"She turned fourteen in February."

"She's a child," Sofia counters, comprehending the reality of my sister's personal hell.

"Well, I'm not sure she remembers having a life as a normal child."

Sofia presses her lips together and her chin quivers. "She's all alone there while you're here all day?" Hearing the truth out loud hurts just as much as thinking the same thought repeatedly each day.

I'm left without a choice and yet, "I'm all she has."

"Your parents. Have you heard any information on their whereabouts?"

"Not a word." I feel somewhat numb inside, answering the questions I run through in my mind before bed every night.

Sofia seems as if she forgot her reason for even being outdoors. She spins around as if she's trying to find something, then dips her hands into the pockets of her dress. "Here... They're just some small pastries I made, but I don't want you to miss your lunch. I—ah, I wish there was a way we could bring your sister here somehow. I'm afraid I don't know how it would be possible though."

I take the wrapped pastries from her hands, feeling the dried scabs on my fingers scrape against her silk-like skin. "Thank you for this. I don't know how I will ever repay you, but I will." I drop the small bundle into my pocket to divvy up later in between meals. "And thank you for asking about my sister—it was very thoughtful of you. I appreciate the momentary distraction from the—"

"Hyenas," Sofia sighs.

I haven't heard anyone refer to a Nazi as a hyena, and the thought of one letting out a loud cackle brings a smile to my face as I choke back the threat of laughter. "I'd love nothing more than to steal their last laugh, trust me."

"It's nice to see you smile," she says, reaching for my face. It takes everything I have not to back away from her touch, but she sweeps her thumb across my cheek. "Hopefully that's just dirt and not manure."

The laugh I was holding back a minute earlier rumbles out of me without warning. The feeling in my stomach, and in my chest, it's so unfamiliar, but incredible at the same time. I wish I could keep laughing. I would laugh until I passed out. To feel that instead every other emotion in the world could save me from losing my mind.

Sofia's laughing along with me, but we both stop when we hear heavy footsteps against the wooden floor inside of the house. "Thankfully, we have thick walls. You might still have a minute or two. I'll stall them so you can have some soup."

"You're a gift to this world," I tell her. "Remember that."

Sofia smiles shyly and turns around on her toes, her dress swishing as she tiptoes in through the back door.

"Mama, the linens are all folded upstairs," she shouts. It's her way of making it sound as if she's just come down the back stairwell rather than in from the back door. "My apologies; I lost track of time and didn't realize we had company."

I can't bear to listen to any more of the chatter, knowing

Sofia must cower to those monsters, putting herself in grave danger, so I set off to claim my allowance of soup if there's any left.

Feeling as though I only have a few seconds to spare, I fill my bowl with what's left at the bottom of the metal container and pour cold broth into my mouth, emptying the contents with just a few sips. Within a minute, I return to the pile of hay with the pitchfork in hand. I have one more heap piled onto the prongs before the *Wachmänner* step out of the house, chirping with laughter, their uniform coats unbuttoned and informal as they rub their hands against their overfilled bellies. "Hyenas," I mutter under my breath.

CHAPTER 24

MAY 1943

OLIVIA

The pile of clothing never seems to grow any smaller, no matter how many items we get through in a day. It seems for every heap we separate, they dump another twice the size.

"The *Wachmann* keeps looking at you," Beatriz whispers without moving her lips. "Did you do something wrong?"

Her question makes my stomach hurt because I've been wondering the same thing. There are *Wachmänner* guarding every corner, but this one has been staring over here all morning. Maybe he knows I stole some scraps of fabric and thread. I was very careful when taking those few items. No one was in sight.

"I didn't do anything," I reply to Beatriz. The two of us have been working side by side since they assigned me to this building, this place she and the others refer to as *Kanada*. It's called *Kanada* because it's one of the safest labor jobs to have in the camp. Beatriz has been here a few months longer than me, which means she has seen a great deal more and her insight, while valuable, is terrifying. I no longer need to wonder why there are lines of people waiting to walk through an iron gate just across the way from this building. Beatriz told me they are the people who are being sent to the right rather than the left upon arrival, and they are unaware that they are walking toward their death.

When I see other girls my age in that line, I wonder why they spared me or found me fit to work when others aren't. I don't know if I'm here on an account of luck or on some merit of which I'm unaware. The thoughts haunt me day and night, wondering if or when they will realize they made a mistake by keeping me.

"Move around the pile so you aren't in his view," Beatriz says, continuing her machine-like movements of taking an article of clothing and tossing it to the right or left.

With slow, subtle movements, I shuffle to the side. I reach for pieces of clothing so I don't seem suspicious to the watchful eyes.

It only takes a minute to realize my attempt to slip out of sight was useless. The *Wachmann* has also taken steps to the side, keeping me in his line of sight. My throat tightens upon the realization. He's watching me, and I'm terrified to know why. Maybe I'm not working fast enough. I try to move at the same speed as Beatriz, to take a handful of the clothing, sort through each piece, sweep my hand through all the pockets, and toss the items into the proper pile.

"You've made him smile," Beatriz mumbles.

Her words don't settle my nerves. There's nothing funny or uplifting about what we are doing with these bloodstained, torn, and soiled clothes. "What should I do?"

"Ignore him," she says.

Her advice is simple to follow until I notice him taking steps in my direction. I'm up against a wall with no one else behind me. There's no one else to look at: it's me he's watching.

My heart races when the clicks from his heels cause the

floor to vibrate, and when his shadow creeps over me, I find it hard to breathe.

"*Aufstehen!*" he says, his word full of authority. I do as he says and stand up, keeping my gaze locked on the pile of clothes rather than on him. *Please don't hurt me. Please, God, keep me safe.*

"You look bored. Are you not having any fun?" he teases.

"I'm not bored, sir."

"Very well. There is another pile of clothing I need you to take into your inventory. Follow me." The *Wachmann* twists on his heels and takes a long step past me.

Panic lodges in my throat as I spot the frantic look within Beatriz's eyes. I follow the man, feeling a weakness in each step, my ankles threatening to break beneath my weight.

The walk is short and within the building. There's an open door the guard is pointing to, waiting for me to step inside. There is a pile of clothes within the confines of the closet-size room. I walk in front of him and lean in toward the pile to scoop as much of it up into my arms as I can, but no sooner than I have curled an armful against my chest, do I hear the door close behind me.

"You're a very beautiful *Jude*," he says, his statement causing a cold sweat to break out across my body. "I will reward you for this."

My heart plunders, and I bite my lip to stop my chin from quivering. I want to plead with him to leave, but it will only make things worse.

I'm trapped.

CHAPTER 25
MAY 1943

ISAAC

I'm not sure if hope is a good thing or a bad, knowing the most likely ending to my story. When I was younger, Mama would tell me not to get my hopes up if something was unlikely to happen, like a friend being able to join us for supper, or Papa having the weekend off so we could visit our cousins in Krakow. Many times, my hopes were filled with pleasant surprises, so I tried to only "get my hopes up" on occasion.

It's been quite some time since I've considered relying on hope, but maybe it's been long enough that some good fortune is due.

All through the night, my dreams are filled with a life I thought I could no longer imagine. There are endless fields of grass, wildflowers, roaming horses, and cattle. Hunger isn't on my mind, and I feel clean, content, and free. Olivia is with me, and her long auburn curls bounce along with the leaps she takes through the blooming flowers. Her cheeks are rosy and slightly plump, and her eyes are full of sunlight and radiate happiness. In the dream, I consider searching for Mama and Papa, but the field seems endless, as if we could run for miles and miles. I try to turn around, curious of what is behind me, but I can only move forward. There is some kind of force blocking me from looking back. If only dreams were a sign of the future instead of a reflection of the past, I might consider the thought of making it through this imprisonment.

Though it's Sunday morning and we aren't tending to our typical labor jobs, we must clean our living quarters, our clothes, and tend to any other personal matters that can't be dealt with during the week, like visiting family and friends who live within these iron gates.

Today's the only day I get to spend more than a few minutes at a time with Olivia. It's almost like the reward for all the moments I long to spend with my sister during the relentless week.

In lines, we all walk together like an inchworm, slowly, but evenly paced until we reach the washroom and stand in silence, weak in the knees, and impatient for our turn to feel water against our skin.

We are expected to always move, never stopping for a moment to rest, yet we are also forced to wait for anything that keeps us alive and well. There are obstacles in front of me, blocking the way until I can see Olivia, and the minutes feel like hours by the time I've finally finished my hot water with a few coffee grains floating along the rim. I didn't save my extra portion from dinner last night because Lev wasn't given anything upon returning from his labor job. A man was late for transportation, so they were all punished. His stomach was growling so loudly, he was curled up in pain last night. The three of us in the bunk shared what we had left over with him. It was easier to part with the food, knowing we wouldn't be working like dogs today, and helping him felt better than the measly crumbs would feel in the pit of my stomach.

I finally make my way to Olivia's barrack. The doors are

usually propped open during the day, which makes it easier for me to find her without having to walk into the women's building. Many of them are skittish and would rather not have any visitors, understandably so.

Olivia isn't where she would normally be, in her bunk that she shares with three others. I know quite well she could be in a few different places and I try hard to convince myself she is safe.

I stop in front of the open door, peering around, but I hear whispers growing from behind the open door.

With a step inside, the boards beneath my feet creak, and as if a record was yanked away from the needle, there is nothing but silence surrounding me.

I poke my head around the door, searching for Olivia, finding her curled up with her knees and head buried against her chest. Her entire body begins to tremble and she's whispering, "Please, no. Please, no." Next to her, I see a striped pajama coat, crumpled in a ball, but it isn't hers as she's wearing her uniform.

"Lu-lu," I whisper, "it's me."

She slowly lifts her head from her knees and stares up at me through her dark, wet lashes. "Isaac," she utters, "I thought you were... one of the *Wachmann*."

I kneel in front of her and pull her in against me, holding her as tightly as I can to make her stop shaking. Her bones prod against her skin and she feels fragile and unsure of my presence. Something is different today and I can't help but feel like it's more than just the fact of us wasting away a little more with each passing hour. "Why are you hiding behind the door?"

"She was fixing my coat," a woman says from two buk columns down. "She's our seamstress here. None of us have had to walk around with holes in our clothes, thanks to your sister. She's our little miracle." While the woman attempts to force a smile along her pale, thin lips, I notice a despondent look in her eyes.

My heart breaks, but unlike the quick record scratch, the pain is like being stuck as the needle trips, scraping the vinyl again and again in the same spot. How many times can my heart bear this pain?

Her body is weak in my arms as she releases all of her silent tears at once.

"It's okay," I say, running my fingers over her head. It's the first time I've seen her without a scarf on her head and I feel the need to cry, to know she's been stripped of another thing she loved—her hair. "Can I see what you've been sewing? Where did you find the needle and thread?"

She sniffles back a few tears. "I found them in a dress pocket from the pile of clothes I was separating. I—" Olivia looks around guiltily. "I kept it."

I should lecture her and tell her never to step out of line here, but what we do is a matter of survival, and there are worse items she could have pocketed.

"I'm sure it will come in handy," I say.

"Yes, it already has. I was just about done with what I'm fixing," she says, a breath catching in her throat. "There was a hole just below the front pocket. It wasn't a very nice place to have a hole, if you know what I mean." Olivia's cheeks blush with a red tint.

I close my eyes for a moment, feeling euphoric to have seen the smallest of smiles on my sister's face. She's still able to conjure a joke—she isn't completely shattered like so many others, and I'm grateful for this small gift. "I suppose the chill might not be too pleasant," I reply.

"No, not at all," the woman from the buk calls out. "It was quite awful, in fact."

"I don't see any hint of a hole in the fabric now," I say to Olivia.

"She's a miracle, like I said," the woman repeats.

"Mama, Papa, and I always knew that about you. We just didn't want you to be too sure of yourself, so we kept that to ourselves," I say, giving her a quick wink.

She slaps my arm as she always has and sticks her tongue out at me. "Maybe someday I'll still get to make beautiful clothes. Do you think that could happen?" Her question feels like a knife slicing through my chest, recognizing the look of naivety laced through her tired eyes.

"Absolutely," I assure her, wishing with everything in my soul that I'm not giving her the same false hope I slept with last night. "You're making quite a name for yourself around here." My voice is almost inaudible, making sure she's the only one who can hear me. "You're doing exactly what you should be."

"I miss them, Isaac. It's so hard to sleep at night, wondering where they are or if they'll find us. Do you think they're looking?"

I'm not sure I can look Olivia in the eyes and honestly say there's a chance we'll see Mama and Papa again. There's always a possibility, but we can smell the foul odor of death. The odors change by the day, depending on the temperature, wind, humidity, and quantity of those being incinerated. It didn't take long for us to find out what was happening on the other side of the camp. With each living person working a job that supports the Third Reich in some way, men have witnessed the reality of what they are doing to the living and dead bodies. It's become apparent that Auschwitz is, in fact, the last stop for all who arrive here. If there's a chance Mama and Papa are still alive, we haven't seen them within these gates, which may be a good thing or a bad thing.

"I'm sure they're looking for us," is all I can say, still running my hand against her head.

Olivia pulls my hand down, holding it in front of her face.

"Your wounds are infected," she says, with worry lacing each word.

Whatever part of my hand that hasn't scabbed over is raw, red, and not healing. The pain has become familiar and I've been able to ignore it. "I'll be okay."

The likelihood of the open sores healing throughout today is slim, which means I'll be working against them again first thing tomorrow morning.

"Isaac, no, you can't leave that infected. You know better."

"What am I supposed to do?" There is no answer. If I go to the medical building, my name will be put on some list, and I'll be on their radar. My days will be numbered.

"At least clean it and wrap it up," Olivia scolds me.

"It *is* clean."

Olivia wriggles her way out of my embrace and reaches beneath the closest wooden tower of bunks. The sound of wood creaking makes me wonder what she's doing, but she pulls out a small piece of white fabric.

"I've managed to save a few scraps from going into the incinerator too." She wraps the material around my hand and knots it at my wrist. "Keep your jacket hanging low, to your fingertips when you're walking around. No one will see."

For the first time in our lives, Olivia has taken care of me, and while I hate that she has had to grow up so quickly, my faith in her gives me a sense of pride. I plant my hands on both sides of her cheeks and kiss the top of her head. "You never cease to amaze me."

I can't help but wonder if this moment will be her life's greatest accomplishment—learning to take care of others at fourteen years old. Mama and Papa would be proud of who she has become.

CHAPTER 26

MAY 1943

SOFIA

Sunday nights seem to be the only time the three of us are in the same room at the same time. Dinner is quiet as usual, and with nothing left to do between supper and bedtime, our parlor is the only place to go, unless Mama and I lock ourselves in our bedrooms.

"What are you reading, *mały myszka?*" Papa asks, sweetly. He has been trying harder than usual, perhaps to make me hate him a little less. In truth, Isaac's words stung me the other day when he defended my father. I wanted to tell him he didn't understand, but he of all people would.

"*The Grapes of Wrath,*" I say with a raised brow.

"Where on earth did you find a copy to read?"

"The library has one copy and I had been waiting," I reply, simply.

"Haven't you read the book before?"

"I have, but I suspect there are parts I might not have understood as much last time."

Papa clears his throat. We've all read the book.

"Sofia," he says, placing the newspaper he has been reading on his lap, "I understand your motivation to be a hero in times like these, but it isn't as simple as saving a person from starvation. Surely, you understand this."

I reposition myself on my chair and hold the book up higher. "You asked me what I was reading, not what I was thinking. Besides, isn't that your purpose in life? To be a hero to others?"

Papa slaps his hands on top of the newspaper, crinkling the pages. "My purpose in life is to care for you. How can I make it clearer? I don't want to live in this miserable silence with both of you, knowing how unwanted I am in my own house. Imagine being in a place where no one wants you?"

He can't be serious. We have a front-row view of that very scene out on the farm. "I suspect it's hard for you to imagine anything at all."

With a huff of aggravation, he says, "For your information, I am not the enemy. In fact, I'm very much the opposite. I have hurt no one, but apparently my own daughter and wife. I'm a doctor—a profession I worked toward my entire life—and now I'm being scrutinized for my accomplishments, but only by the two of you. Do you think I side with those mongrels in uniform? Do you think I've become one of them?"

"Haven't you?" Mama asks, without lifting her eyes from the magazine she is thumbing through.

Papa sweeps the newspaper off his lap and onto the ground, the sheets splaying out toward the fireplace. "I took the position because they told me doing so would keep my 'Jewish wife and daughter safe.'"

"Yes, but I thought Jewish people in mixed marriages and families aren't being affected by the laws like the other families? We aren't safe at all then, are we?" I ask, dropping my book down onto my lap.

"Sofia, we have raised you to be Jewish. You were not

baptized like me. Unfortunately, we are at a greater disadvantage for that reason."

"But your parents were Aryan. That was what kept us truly 'privileged,' I thought," I add.

"You both wear a *Jude* patch because the SS know you are Jewish. It was never something any of us could hide. You know this. It's practically in front of their noses every day. If I don't adhere to their requests, which are truly silent demands, I will give them a reason—one hardly needed—to remove the 'privilege' you two receive. I would be putting the two of you at risk of—"

"Being worked to the bone, tortured, starved..." I offer.

He stands and the blood red of his neck rushes up his cheeks. "Do you think I'm unaware of what you do during the day? Feeding these soldiers our food, sharing our tea and coffee, entertaining them with smiles. You are working against me. You must think you are punishing me in some way, but, in truth, you are walking closer toward the enemy. They know you are Jewish. What do you think is going through their minds while sitting with you?"

We didn't think Papa knew anything about what happens here during the day, which makes me pause.

"This isn't about you, Friedrich. It's the only way those poor men working on our farm receive a break in the afternoon. Don't talk to us like we're the ones falling for their propagating manners and gratitude."

But, have we?

"I'm not ignorant or blind," he argues. "Every person in this war is trying to survive, regardless of how that looks from the other side."

"That makes you a man who ignores the truth of what is happening on the land we own," Mama counters.

"With all due respect, dear, you are very much in the dark as well. In fact, neither of you have a clue what is happening on the land we own." Papa turns to look toward the curtain-covered window, the one that overlooks the farm. "If you both would have a little more faith in me, you might have more understanding of why I do what I do."

Mama takes a stiff inhale through her nose and tosses her magazine down onto the side table. "By all means, Friedrich, enlighten us."

Papa's nostrils flare and he pins his hands against his hips. "Very well. Follow me."

Mama and I give each other an unsuspecting look of shock. We follow him out the front door, down the porch steps. He scoops up the handle to the lantern we leave out front and continues down the path between a set of bushes that lead to the farmland. Mama and I are both in our robes, pulling them tighter across our bodies to fend off the cool spring breeze.

"Where are you taking us?" Mama calls out ahead to him.

"To the barn," he replies, walking at a much faster pace than the two of us can keep up with.

The barn—just as I suspected before searching every corner of those wooden walls. I found nothing, so I can't imagine what he's planning to show us.

Once we're all under the barn's roof, Papa places the lantern down on an empty wooden work bench. "I have a plan," he says.

"Here in the barn?" I ask.

"Beneath the barn."

"I don't understand," Mama says, folding her arms tightly across her chest.

"We inherited this property from your family, yes?"

"Clearly, I'm aware," Mama responds.

"None of us would have known that the foundation of this barn is much deeper than we could have assumed. Whoever first built the barn must have had the need for a bomb shelter underground."

"My great-grandfather built this barn with his two hands. That's what my parents told me," Mama says.

"War is not new, and most people do not want to be a part of it. Maybe your great-grandfather wanted to have a safe place for the family if ever needed."

"What are you saying?" I ask, feeling as though I've missed part of the conversation. "What does the foundation of the barn have to do with keeping someone safe?"

Papa leans down and sweeps his fingers along the dirt-covered ground until he finds whatever he's looking for. He reaches under the wooden workbench and retrieves a long, flat metal tool and shoves it into the ground. The sound of metal scraping against wood confuses me, but when Papa steps on the flat tool, a wooden hatch lifts, exposing a dark hole beneath.

"For months, I have spent every night digging out the dirt that filled up a third of the foundation. Considering we weren't aware of the space beneath the barn, I thought it was a good solution for those who we can help. I've also been storing as much canned food as I could get my hands on. There are two areas in the back end of the space, one for food storage and the other for any various necessities."

My heart thunders along with wild thoughts flying in every direction. We can help people. Papa has been trying to help people all along, despite what we thought. I can't be angry with him, knowing what he's been working so hard to accomplish here.

I run over to him and wrap my arms around his neck, feeling an abundance of relief, knowing I don't have to hate my father.

"You've created a place to hide?" Mama questions. "That's what you've been doing every night?"

"Yes, darling. I'm not this person who you see me to be. I'm a doctor because I love helping others. There is no part of me that wants to see a person suffer, and we are surrounded by this unrelenting reality without much we can do to stop it. This isn't a world I want to be a part of—it's a world I fear, for you, me, and all the others trying to survive."

Mama's eyes become glossy as she stares at Papa with what seems like a loss for words.

"May I see?" I ask.

"There's only a ladder and no lighting." Papa reaches over to grab the lantern and hands it to me.

They both follow me underground, where we see a shell of space concealed from the world above us.

Papa looks at me with a familiar gaze of compassion, one I thought he may no longer be capable of showing. "Sofia, we can't be reckless. I've put a plan in place so we can begin carefully saving at least some of those who work here on the farm, but if we act too bullish, the SS will speculate and we will then be responsible for many deaths, including, likely, our own."

"I want to help," I say. "Please. Let me help."

"I need to discuss a few things with your *matka* tonight, and tomorrow we will talk more about this. It goes without saying, I'm sure, this cannot be mentioned to anyone, under any circumstances. Am I clear?"

My first thought was to tell Isaac that I could save him and his sister. Papa would surely agree when he learns they are without their parents and being worked to death. Of course, I realize there are hundreds of thousands of others in the same situation. How will any of us be expected to play God?

"I'm not sure what to say," Mama follows. "But I'm interested to hear your plan."

Papa looks proud from the little I can see in the glowing light of the lamp, but the pride will only last so long when he comes to understand what I have just come to terms with. It will be our job to choose who lives and who dies.

CHAPTER 27
MAY 1943

SOFIA

I've been sitting by my door for the last half-hour, waiting for the thud of Papa's shoes to descend the stairs. He leaves before the two of us are awake most days. After a sleepless night with relentless thoughts stirring around my head, I'm desperate to know what they talked about last night after we went to bed.

The sun begins to rise as I continue to wait and I'm wondering why I didn't hear Papa walk by. I pull myself up to my feet and make my way over to the window to see if the men are already beginning their workday. They're beginning to plant the crops in the endless rows of soil they've been preparing. They're utilizing at least five times the amount of land we originally were.

Sometimes I choose the very wrong time to look out the window and I wish I had waited just a minute or two longer. One of the guards has been switched out for a new one and this man has no soul left. It's clear as he strikes one of the men with a baton, over and over, screaming at him for whatever it is he's done wrong. The prisoner falls to his knees.

Everything happens in slow motion when a scene plays out like this. I can't turn away, just as the prisoner can't run. It's a truth I need to face. The Nazi is so angry, his face is inflamed. The prisoner mouths something to him, and it looks like a plea escaping along with the tears from his eyes. The curtain to my window has become the quilt concealing the monsters I used to think lived beneath my bed. Truth be told, the monsters live outside, not in the dark, and not hidden in any way.

The Nazi seems to run out of breath and pulls a pistol from the holster on his waist. I want to wish that he will have a change of heart, but if there's anything the Nazis have proven to be good at, it's making a decision and sticking with it.

My window ricochets from the blast. The prisoner's face is buried in the dirt and blood saturates the fabric of his striped coat like a sponge in water. The Nazi yells at another prisoner and points to the unmoving body, then juts his thumb toward the wagon they arrived in.

I watch as the other prisoner drags his fellow comrade away, his feet scuffing through the grass, his head hanging to the side like a rag doll.

What's his name?

Does he have a family?

Will they ever know how he died?

Why are tears not falling from my eyes after witnessing yet another death? Am I dead inside too?

The urge to find the weapons Papa keeps hidden in this house is bursting through me. I believe they are beneath their bed in a locked metal container.

I can't watch another death take place on our property. With anger boiling my blood, I rush out of my bedroom and barge into Mama and Papa's room without knocking, something I've always had the courtesy of doing—we've run out of time for upholding manners.

They are both standing at their window, likely watching the aftermath of what I witnessed.

"We have to do something now. We don't have time to wait on a plan. Can't you see, Papa?"

Papa turns around. His eyes are red and glassy, and his cheeks are white, colorless. "I helped that young man last week," he says.

"The one just killed?" I ask.

"No."

He doesn't have to explain any further. He helped the man who just took another life for no good reason.

I grit my teeth and clench my fists by my side, trying my best to control my growing anger. "How did you help him?"

"He had an infected wound on his hand. If I hadn't treated him with penicillin, he might have—" Papa chokes on his last word, cradling his hands around his mouth. "What have I done?"

I look at Mama. Her eyes are also red, and her eyelids look heavy as if she didn't sleep last night. She stares back at me, but her gaze feels like it's going right through me.

"There's something I need to handle outside and then I'll be back up to explain what we're going to do," Papa says.

"No, you shouldn't go out there," I say, reaching for his arm.

Mama grabs my hand and pulls me back. "Let him go," she says.

Papa leaves the bedroom, and we listen to his footsteps fading as he makes his way downstairs.

"What is he going to do?"

"I'm not sure," Mama says. "The plan he has is still quite dangerous, and there are no guarantees it will work. The risk is greater than hope."

I want to say I don't understand, but I do: to help anyone is a risk to everyone involved.

Within a long minute, Papa is outside, walking casually

toward the murderous Nazi. My father's hands are in his pockets, his shoulders are back, and there's a smile on his face. He's greeting the man as if he deserves something more than a bullet to his head. It's suddenly clear that Papa can act just as fake and pretentious as them—he's becoming a stranger.

The Nazi holds up his hand with a simple bandage wrapped diagonally across his palm and grins before placing his other hand on Papa's shoulder. Papa looks pleased and nods his head to the side as if he wants the man to follow him.

I race down the hall to the washroom so I can peek out the window on the other side of the house.

"Sofia," Mama calls out, "don't let them see you. This is what your father is concerned about. If we act obvious, they will smell a rat." Yet she's standing behind me, just as curious.

"Why is Papa showing him our empty garden shed?" We hardly use the space for anything other than storing old tools. Vines have grown up every side of the gray wooden panels, making it almost unnoticeable in the spring and summer seasons.

Papa lifts the rusted latch on the door and pulls on the wooden slab. The Nazi pokes his head inside, then steps back and nods his head in agreement. He shakes Papa's hand and says something to make himself laugh, but Papa just smiles in return, then bows his head, and leaves the man to continue studying the shed.

Mama and I both scamper back to her bedroom so Papa doesn't know we were watching, and we wait for him to come back upstairs.

We're both out of breath, and I'm sure Mama is as confused as I am. It feels like several minutes have gone by before Papa re-enters the bedroom, quietly closing the door behind him.

"Please tell us what's going on, Friedrich," Mama says.

"I gave them a place to put bodies," Papa replies. "They've

been storing them in the wagon all day, and they're running out of space."

I've been avoiding the thought of how many men have perished on our land. Whether from punishment, starvation, or heat exhaustion, it seems that out of the thirty who arrive each day, at least two or three of them are falling to their death by dusk. They are quickly replaced with new workers, so it may go unnoticed to a person who isn't paying as close attention as I am. At least Isaac is still standing, still working—surviving another day.

"You gave them an excuse to kill more people?" I ask.

"They can't kill the men who have already 'fallen' to their death. If we can somehow tell the laborers to forge a couple of deaths a day—perhaps the weakest of the bunch first—we can begin saving them after the *Wachmänner* leave for the night," Papa says, tilting his head to the side as if I'm supposed to understand what he means.

"That's not true, Papa. I've seen them shoot men who have already fallen to their death."

Papa stares at me for a long moment. I'm hoping he is listening. "Well then, we need to distract them upon disposal of the bodies, so they aren't focused on their identity, or ensuring a man is truly dead. It will be in our favor that they aren't the ones who carry the dead away. They force the other prisoners to do so. I told the man outside that I would let him know when the shed becomes full so he can coordinate the extra transportation needed." I don't see how this will go unnoticed or unquestioned by superior SS officers.

Papa doesn't understand how quickly the guards move when a man has fallen to his knees. It's an easy target and another notch in their belt, so they make sure the dead are truly dead.

My mind is racing. The plan will work against us and the laborers.

Mama has been quiet since Papa returned to the bedroom. I assume they discussed most of this last night and she's not surprised by anything he's saying. She said it would be dangerous.

"We must watch who is in the greatest danger of falling victim to the Nazis on guard and make sure we help them first," Mama says, ignoring my concerns.

This means Isaac will likely be last. He's one of a few who have stayed upright since the beginning; he's fitter and younger than most of the other men. I could argue with Papa, but it makes the most sense. However, I selfishly want to save Isaac, which seems impossible with this plan.

"Papa, why aren't you at work right now?" I ask.

"I'm late, and I need to get going," he says. "I informed the administration that I would be late today, taking care of some personal matters this morning. I needed to have a better idea of what the setup was here with the *Wachmänner*, then take care of the storage space for the bodies."

"You don't think they will go on a killing spree today with all the extra space they have for bodies now?" I question again, this time with more wrath.

Papa checks his watch, then lifts his coat off the tall metal rack next to the door. "It looks like it may rain in about an hour. The two *Wachmann* outside will be happy to accept shelter, which will leave time for one of you to inform the men outside of our plan."

"Our plan is unfinished, Papa. We can't tell them to do something for a chance of hope, but also inform them that there is a chance they will be shot." Each of my words comes out with a harsh snap.

"We are in this together, Sofia. I can only carry out one of the three parts of this plan. If this is not something you want to partake, I must have misunderstood the reason for your silence over the last several months. But this is not something I can handle alone. Either we all agree on a plan, or life outside will have to remain as is."

"We'll handle the coordination," Mama says, walking up behind me and placing her hands on my shoulders. She squeezes, something she does when she is silently trying to warn me.

CHAPTER 28

MAY 1943

ISAAC

It's hardly the middle of May, and the sun is relentless. I don't remember it ever feeling this hot at this time of year. We've hardly had any rain, which we desperately need for these crops to grow. Maybe the sky ran out of tears while watching us suffer down here.

I've begun counting the seconds to check off how much time is left until my body earns a break. I've been arched over for days, and my back is starting to feel as though it has a question mark bent into my spine.

There have been so many men here giving up the fight to live. I think some may have fallen to appear dead so that they are dragged away and left somewhere to lie in silence, but the Nazis must know what's happening because they shoot each man—there is no escape.

I run my finger through the dirt next to the pile of seedlings I'm planting. It's the ninth line, marking the ninth hour I've been working today. Our last break should be soon, assuming

Sofia and her mother can still stomach the thought of afternoon tea with those two hyenas.

Without much to look at, I've found myself staring up at Sofia's window far more often than I should, enough that could get me in trouble if I'm spotted, but I can't stop myself. She's the first beautiful thing I've seen in years, and I could probably stare at her all day if I had the chance. The thought of Sofia smiling at me or laughing at a joke along with me makes me wonder if the girls in school would have liked me. I suppose I was always on the quieter side and didn't have much luck making friends easily, but by the time I was old enough to care about who I sat next to, I was already forced out of the common public school and sent to a small private school for Jewish boys. It was no more than a homeschool but with a few extra children in attendance, and none of us were at the same academic learning level, which made it impossible to be taught properly.

The *Wachmänner* have settled themselves in a position where they can see when the front door of the house opens, and when Sofia's mother's warm smile invites them inside. I'm puzzled by the fact that the guards know Sofia and her mother are Jewish women, yet still act courteously. I can only assume someone has instructed them to be tolerant since her father is responsible for training their doctors. I'm not sure Sofia understands the gift her father has been to her family by giving himself to the Third Reich, which in turn became Sofia and her mother's saving grace. When we spoke of him, she seemed so angry toward him, which I understand on one level, but I wouldn't wish for her to know the other level I've been left to face.

I've been lost in thought for so long, I didn't notice the *Wachmänner* had been called in for afternoon tea. The back door of the house creaks, a sound that would be hard to hear if I wasn't listening for it.

Sofia's hands wrap around the corner of the house before

she peeks out to check for the guards. "Isaac," she whispers, "come over here, quick." She waves me over as she often does, afraid of too many of the others spotting her.

She looks tired today. Her hair isn't pulled back into a braid as usual. It's loosely splayed over her shoulders. Her cheeks are red and splotchy, and she has a look of concern running through her eyes.

"What is it?" I ask, running over to her without enough breaths to keep me standing. I rest my hand against the wooden shingles of the house to hold up my weight. "Are you all right?" It's so hard not to worry about her after knowing what she has gone through to keep me alive with the extra food she's shared. I doubt I'd still be standing here now.

"No, no, Isaac, I need you to listen carefully. Papa—my father—fixed a shelter beneath the barn. It's large enough to hide some of you. But I'm afraid it will end badly. He wants me to let you know that the weakest out here should pretend to die, in the hope that they are taken to a shed he has offered to the guards. My father thinks we will be able to hide those who are still alive in there, then move them into the barn's shelter during the night."

The breaths I thought I were missing are suddenly back, coming and going faster than they should. No one can fool the Nazis. It's as if there are thousands of eyes watching all of us at once, even if there are only two *Wachmänner* present. If we ask anyone to act dead, they will be shot before being brought to the shed, and if not, they may rat us out in the hope of getting on the guards' good side.

"It won't work," I say. "The *Wachmänner* will shoot them to make sure they're dead. No one will make it into the shelter alive, I can promise you that."

"But—" Sofia says, with a disheartening sigh. "I want to save you and your sister, of course."

My gaze falls to the patches of grass between us. "That's impossible. She won't ever be coming here."

"I know," Sofia sighs.

"The thought of shelter is a dream, but the kind that's merely an illusion, I'm afraid." My heart aches, knowing there is safety just a few steps away. The fact that I won't be able to make it there alive is almost hard to comprehend.

"I will think of something. Have faith, I will."

I place my hand on her cheek. My hand warms upon touching her and she stares up at me with a look that's searching for a solution. It's all part of the plan—keeping the dangling fruit just within sight to torture us more. "Are you losing sleep over this?" I ask.

"I need to save you, at least you and Olivia, if not others, as many others as I can. I can't live inside of that house knowing what is happening out here," she says.

She grabs my bad hand and squeezes it between hers. I clench my teeth and swallow hard, wishing to ignore the pain. When I open my eyes, she's staring at me. She pulls my hand up and forces my fingers to unclamp.

"Your hand," she whispers, "it's infected."

"I'll be okay," I assure her, though I likely won't be.

"No, I'm going to find something in Papa's medical storage bin. I'll be fast."

I'm shaking my head. "Sofia," I say, with nothing to follow.

She holds a finger up, telling me to wait, and disappears into the house.

I retreat to the dirt holes, placing as many seedlings in their spot as fast as I can.

Sofia returns as quickly as she promised. I glance toward the front of the house, making sure there's no sign of tea ending, then make my way back over to her. She grabs my hand with haste and pours antiseptic over my entire palm. It burns, but the pain is nothing in comparison to the other agony I'm in. Sofia places the bottle of antiseptic down on the step behind her and pulls a loose piece of cotton fabric from her pocket. She wraps my hand and tucks the material beneath the tightest section, just as Olivia did the day before.

"One more thing," she says, poking her head out to check the area. "Turn around and lift your arms."

"What? Why?"

"Do it," she snaps. "There isn't much time left."

I twist around, keeping my head turned over my shoulder to watch what she's doing.

She bends back down for the bottle of antiseptic then reaches into her pocket and pulls out a small wrap made of thick canvas. Sofia undoes it just enough to retrieve a syringe, flips the cap and yanks at the waistband of my pants, pulling the fabric down a few inches on the right side.

"Hey, hey, what's—"

She spills some antiseptic over the exposed skin, then jabs me with the needle, so I bite my tongue to stop myself from letting out a groan.

"A shot of penicillin," she says. She gently releases her grip on the waistband of my pants, allowing the fabric to fall back into its original place.

I turn back to face her, feeling foolish for the groan I let out. In the same amount of time it takes me to turn around, she has already concealed the needle and replaced everything in her pocket. "Could you give me a little warning next time you want to jab my behind with a needle?"

"You're welcome," she says, trying to hide a smirk. Sofia shoves her hand into another one of her pockets and I question whether I should take a step back, but she retrieves a small paper-wrapped package. "Here, this is for you and your sister— it's a couple of servings of sunflower seeds. They will give you protein and energy. Mama and I froze them in our ice box last fall after our final harvest." She places the bundle in my hand

and leans forward to place a quick kiss on my cheek. Without warning, my stomach twists into a knot as heat blooms through my cheeks. The touch of her lips—so smooth and tender, ignited foreign sensations I want to keep with me forever. "I'll keep thinking of other ways to help you. I won't give up, I promise you that."

I blink and she's gone. It's as if I just imagined everything, except for the throbbing ache in my behind. That part is most definitely real.

The barn taunts me on my walk back to the soil. I wish more than anything there could be a way to save Olivia and me, but I've seen people shot for just looking suspicious. The walls even seem to listen to us.

Just weeks ago, they caught three people trying to escape from Auschwitz. They shot them dead, stripped them of their clothes, and hung their bodies along the wall of a building. It was a warning to the rest of us not to be tempted by the idea of escaping. There is no way out—at least no way out alive.

CHAPTER 29

MAY 1943

SOFIA

I've been pacing the hallway in front of my bedroom, waiting for the hyenas to leave the house. Mama doesn't want me downstairs anymore after the third invitation to join one of them at a glorious dinner party. It's hard to hide the truth of my feelings and the conversation ended with an eruption of laughter, laughter I wasn't taking part in. They are playing me as a foolish Jewish girl just as I'm sure they do to many others.

When the front door closes, Mama's heels echo loudly as she charges across the house and stomps up the stairs, finding me at the top.

"Mama, what's wrong?" She looks like she did something terrible.

"You were right about that plan not working. Did you tell the boy?"

"He agreed it wouldn't work, but I wanted him to know we were going to find a way. He needs hope, they all do."

"Good, good. I've seen them shooting dead bodies too. You were right to tell your Papa that yesterday."

"What does that have to do with the terrified look on your face?" I ask.

"There's only one way I can think of that might work—" Mama's forehead wrinkles with worry. "When I was going through the icebox earlier, I found something your father made me keep in there in case of emergency."

"I don't understand?"

"Have you heard of something called Nightshade?"

The name doesn't sound familiar. "No."

"What about *Atropa belladonna*?" she continues. "You know what that is, don't you?"

"The plant?" I say.

I vaguely recall a conversation a couple of years ago about removing the plant because it could make the horses and cattle sick. It hasn't been mentioned since, but I assume it's because we had to sell our livestock to the Nazis.

"Yes. The berries that grow on the plants are toxic," Mama says, biting down on the tip of her fingernail.

"What does this have to do with rescuing Isaac?" The muscles in my chest tighten as I try to follow her train of thought.

"Well, if the toxic berries are consumed, perhaps, it would cause a person to become ill—possibly so ill they—"

"You want to kill the guards?" I question, clutching at the pleated fabric hanging from my hips.

Mama stares at me with a look of perplexity. "Does it make me less of a person that I would prefer to see them all buried underground?"

I shrug, feeling the same. "No, it makes you human."

"Well, one less of them would be very helpful at the moment," Mama says without faltering. "Every day, they have the same tea, and it would be too obvious if they both became ill or—"

"Die? Mama, who else will the SS have to blame?" My head

is reeling with panic.

"The guards come and go so often, and there are several periods throughout the day that one is here alone."

"What if he isn't alone when he becomes sick?" I question. I'm not sure if Mama has thought this all through. It isn't like her to act on a whim.

Her hands are shaking as she clasps them together. "He'll come to the house if he isn't feeling well. They seem to think we will help them every time they have a slight headache, never mind the effects from poison. Once we tend to him inside, it will be easier to conceal what's happening. Once he's—"

"Mama, how do you know the Nightshade will do anything at all, or at the very least give us the type of opportunity we need?" My throat tightens and I can hardly swallow through my nerves.

"The serving size was enough assurance for me to know this will work."

"Then what? I don't see a purpose to this aside from revenge."

"I've been thinking about this day and night. I've hardly slept. There's only one way to fool those men, and it's to look like one of them. I'm afraid nothing else will work."

"How will a sick or dead guard inside of our house help?"

"We'll be in possession of a uniform—anyone wearing that uniform can do whatever they want. If we can't fight them, we can become one of them, even if just by looking the part. It will allow us to save people," Mama says, proving how much she has, in fact, thought about this plan.

"And what about the dead body?" I can't stop myself from pacing back and forth. "We're going to get caught," I mutter. "Why didn't you warn me first?"

"I had a sudden moment of courage and knew if I didn't act on it then, I might never," she says, now sounding unsure of herself as she takes ragged breaths.

"We have to keep an eye out. We must watch their every move. This is so dangerous. What if he doesn't die? He could live to tell someone that he became suddenly ill, and there will be questions."

"I know, I know. I've considered this outcome too. The guard I gave the nightshade to has been helping himself to the honeyberry bushes outside. Some sprouted berries a little early this year. If, somehow, he manages to pull through and questions arise, there is reasonable cause."

"Unless someone comes to check the honeyberry bush. It won't take long to realize honeyberries are not poisonous," I say.

"If he doesn't die, I will forage for some nightshade plants to place alongside the honeyberries." The look in Mama's eyes is dark. This plan is far more detailed than I expected and it's obvious it didn't come out of nowhere. I just don't understand why she never mentioned the idea.

"What will we tell Papa?"

My mother looks toward the nearest window. The sun illuminates her frozen glare and without much time to think, she says, "The truth. What matters right now is that we save that young man. No one should be out there being treated like slaves, but a child—we must help him first."

"What about the others?" I ask, trying to hide the fact that I've placed him ahead of all of the others, unfairly so.

"I'm your mother, Sofia. I see the way you look at that boy, Isaac—the way you've spoken of him. Plus, he and his sister are without parents. They need us. Then we'll tend to whoever else we can help too."

"So many of them need us."

"It would be impossible to choose one person over another," Mama says. "Your heart chose for us, so we'll start there." She places her hand on my shoulder and tries to force a small smile. "We'll be okay. I have faith in us."

CHAPTER 30

MAY 1943

SOFIA

Mama and I have been peeking through the kitchen window, looking for signs of illness in the guard. It's been just over a half-hour. Between staring outside and glancing back at the clock, my heart feels like it's beating twice as fast. I know the guards typically switch shifts over the next hour and if they leave the premises, the efforts will have been for nothing.

"Something should have happened by now. I chopped up the leaf along with the berries. The leaf is the most potent part. It's supposed to work quickly," Mama says, staring as if she can't afford to blink and miss something.

I've been on my tiptoes, looking over the windowsill for so long, my legs are starting to shake, but, like Mama, I can't look away. *Please God, help us. Help us so we can help others.*

I don't expect prayers to work. Too many people must be praying at this exact same moment, begging God to spare their lives. It's all we've known, though: a prayer is the only way to ask for help.

"He just put his hand on his stomach," Mama says, sounding breathless.

"I'm not sure that means much."

"Hush. We need to watch for the signs. Anything can mean something," she argues.

I blink for the first time in what feels like minutes and take in a deep inhale, trying to slow my pulse.

"There. There. He's curling over, he must be in pain."

My eyes flash open. "He's saying something to the other guard."

"Go upstairs right now," Mama tells me. "Go, now!"

Before obeying her, I see the guard walking in our direction. As I leave, Mama ties her apron around her neck and shoves her hands into the canister of baking flour—I assume to make it look like she was doing something other than waiting and watching for the man to get sick.

I stop halfway up the stairwell where I'm out of sight but can still hear what's happening.

The knock on the door is weak, almost hard to hear. Mama stalls before making a show of how loud her heels are on the wooden floor as she makes her way to the foyer. "Can I help you?" Mama asks after opening the front door.

"Yes, *Frau*. Do you mind if I use your toilet?"

"Oh—yes, of course. It's just down here," she says. Her heels click against the floor as she walks toward the washroom beneath the stairwell.

"Thank you," he says, his voice weak and hoarse.

While the guard is busy, I make my way up the stairs and into my bedroom to watch out the window.

Within minutes, the other guard is glancing over toward the house, then checking his watch. He seems impatient as he switches the weight from one foot to the other, over and over. The guards each come and go separately. It seems they all have different schedules throughout the day. By the looks of it, the guard outside has somewhere he has to be, but I'm sure he won't leave the laborers unattended.

I'm pulling a thread from the hem of the curtain, winding it around my finger, waiting, watching, listening, not knowing what will happen next. Then there's Isaac, unknowing, still shoveling with every ounce of strength left in his body.

A heavy thud from below startles me into releasing my grip on the curtain. I run to the stairwell and make it halfway down when Mama knocks on the door of the toilet room. "Is everything all right, *Herr*?"

I take a few more steps down, unable to hear a response.

Mama knocks again and asks the same question, but there is still no answer.

She twists the doorknob and shakes it against what I assume to be resistance.

Quietly, I descend the remaining stairs, finding Mama trying to push against the door. I push my sleeves up to my elbows and step in beside her to help. "He must have fallen in this direction," Mama says. It takes two of us several shoves to move the door enough that we can peek inside. "Are you all right, *Herr*?"

"Is his chest moving?" I whisper.

"No," she says.

I shove my shoulder into the door as hard as I can, forcing it open several more inches.

"Sofia, you're going to snap his neck!"

I consider stating the obvious, but this is not the right time. "Do you have enough space to get inside?" I ask.

Mama squeezes through the opening, barely making it through.

"Check his pulse?"

"I know, I know," she hisses.

The seconds between Mama disappearing into the small room and waiting for her to respond feel like hours.

"There's no pulse."

"Back up so I can push the door open more," I say.

"Hold on. When I say to, push. I'll pull his legs."

"Okay, ready when you are."

"Push," Mama says.

With less effort than before, I'm able to push the door open wide enough to catch a glimpse of the guard lying dead in the middle of the toilet room floor.

"Now what?" I ask, my heart hammering.

Mama looks up at me from where she is knelt on the ground next to the guard. She clasps her hands together tightly, showing flour caked between her knuckles. "When it's safe, bring Isaac inside. Make sure the other guard doesn't see."

"What if there isn't a break between guards? They overlap sometimes."

"One won't leave unless another is present," she says. She's been paying attention as well as I to what happens outside.

"Okay."

I run toward the back door, cracking it open just enough so it won't creak from the rusty hinges. It's only a few steps to the corner of the house where I can usually capture Isaac's attention.

It takes a minute before Isaac notices me. The sun is sinking lower in the sky and this area already has a lot of shade. I poke my head out just enough to look for the guard's whereabouts, spotting him walking out to the dirt road in front of the house while checking his watch.

"Isaac," I call out in a whisper.

His gaze shifts toward me, but his head doesn't move from the direction he's facing.

"Come here quickly. It's urgent." I wave him over with a swift hand gesture.

He looks over to where the guard was and back at me. Then looks again to be sure. He moves with smooth, long steps, making his way over to where I am.

"What's wrong?" he asks between uneven breaths.

"The guard, one of them. He's—" I sweep my hand along my throat, afraid to say the word out loud. "We can help you now."

Isaac takes a step backward. "What? No, no. Sofia... Please... I can't make such a rash decision, not without Olivia. I can't leave her."

"This is the only way you have a chance of saving her," I spit out, knowing I haven't come up with a plan, but thinking there must be a chance if we have a soldier's uniform to use.

Isaac runs his hands down the side of his face. "Sofia, why— I don't know—"

"Please, let me help you. Please, Isaac. You can trust me."

Isaac drops his head and squeezes the back of his neck. "I won't be able to live with myself if I don't save her. You must understand."

"I promise you, I understand." I spot the guard returning, his gaze still fixated on his watch. "The other guard—he's returning. Isaac, you must come now."

He doesn't question me again, instead following me into the house. I lock the door behind us.

"Come on, upstairs. Hurry," I tell him.

We're halfway up the stairs when a hard, hollow knock on the door startles us. Neither of us can help but pause at the sound.

"Go all the way upstairs. The first room on the left is mine. Stay low and away from the window. Hide." I squeeze my hands around Isaac's arms, feeling the bones through his skin. "I'll protect you."

"I want to protect you," he says.

"Then hide, please."

Isaac releases a shuddering breath and I release my hands from his arms.

"Don't worry." I have no right to say that. This might be a mistake that will cost us all everything we have.

The door of my bedroom sweeps against the floor, then the slow release of the doorknob sputters into silence.

Mama closes the toilet room door just as it was before we pushed our way inside.

"The front door," I say.

"I know, I'll handle it. Go upstairs. Stay out of sight."

With reluctance, fearing the thought of being trapped with no place to run, I make my way back upstairs, but just out of sight so I can hear what's happening below.

"Back so soon," Mama says after opening the door.

"*Frau*, did Wachmann Borg come inside?"

"Oh yes, he needed to use the toilet, but he was only here for a moment or so. He left several minutes ago. I assumed he was returning to the farm."

"*Nein*. I haven't seen him return."

"Oh, he did say he was going to do one last round before leaving. I just didn't know what he meant, of course."

"Ah. Good."

"Good day, *Herr*," Mama says, her voice calm, sweet, and charming—nothing like what I'm sure she's feeling.

The sound of the door closing allows me to take in more air. The lock settling into place gives me momentary peace.

Mama and I meet at the bottom of the stairwell.

"Go into my bedroom and find your father's clothes—something Isaac can wear. Give him the means to wash up and bring me his uniform so I can dress the man in there," she says, pointing to the closed door.

"What are we going to do with the body? Or worse, what are we going to say when an SS officer comes looking for him?"

"We'll place him outside the back door before the last

perimeter check. A dead man in a prisoner's uniform will be taken away just like the others who have perished here."

CHAPTER 31
MAY 1943

SOFIA

I continue watching, noticing a new guard arrive almost immediately after the other left. There are only minutes before the second one arrives for his duty as well. Neither seems any wiser about a missing guard from the previous shift. I thought the soldiers were vigilantly aware of everything happening at every second of the day, but perhaps we got lucky this time. One can only hope.

Just as I hear the water faucet run dry from the washroom next to my bedroom, I step out into the hall, waiting to help Isaac. He steps out, his cheeks and neck red from what I assume to be a harsh scrubbing, and hands me his striped uniform.

"I'll take these to my mother. I'll be back in just a minute, make yourself comfortable," I tell him, noticing how much more handsome he looks in clean clothes. Everything is loose and baggy on him, but I don't think he cares since it's clean.

Isaac offers a small smile before returning to my bedroom. He has said little since he's been inside, and I can only imagine the thoughts going through his head.

I hurry down the stairs toward the bathroom where Mama is standing guard, almost as if she's waiting for the man to come back to life. "I have the uniform."

"Good. Come help me change the man's clothes."

We squeeze back into the toilet room, each of us standing on one side of the body. I should feel something other than relief when being so close to a corpse. My stomach should ache, my heart should race. But I don't feel any of that.

As we undress the man down to his skivvies, I come to notice how heavy each limb is and I'm worried about how we will be inconspicuous when moving him out back. It takes several minutes to re-clothe him in Isaac's uniform. Even though he's dead, he still looks far too healthy to be in these clothes. His cheeks are plump. It's clear he has not been hungry, and he has a full head of hair, unlike the bald slave laborers.

"We need to remove his hair. And he's too clean," I say to Mama.

She's crouched down in her dress and heels, glancing at her watch. "You're right, and I've also noticed the numbers from their uniforms inked on their forearms too. Your father has a pair of clippers I can use, and I'll find a pen with ink," she says.

With the amount of dirt that has flaked off from Isaac's uniform, I brush it together to form a pile on the floor and coat my hands to smear the man's face, neck, and hands. I even shove some of the dirt beneath his trimmed fingernails.

Mama returns before I take more than a few short breaths and doesn't hesitate before taking the razor to the man's head. "Write the numbers from the patch on his chest down on his forearm," she says, handing me the pen with a bottle of ink.

I do as she says, carefully marking each number as the man's shaven hair storms around us. Within minutes, Mama has removed all the hair, and I have cleaned up every strand. The cut isn't clean, but it's about as short as Isaac's.

"How are we going to move him?" I ask.

"If you can lift his feet, I can pull from under his arms. We can slide him across the floor."

I do as she said and take the man's feet that don't quite fit into Isaac's worn shoes. "Let's twist him around first so we can open the door," Mama says.

It takes a lot of strength to move the man, even just the bit we did to turn him sideways. I'm worried this will be too difficult or we'll make too much of a racket when bringing him outdoors.

The front door of the house opens, then closes without warning. Mama and I stare at each other from our hunched positions, each holding a different end of the man's body. We're frozen, not knowing what to do. Papa rarely comes home this early.

"Lena, Sofia?"

"It's Papa," I whisper, stating what is already obvious.

Mama's look of worry doesn't ease though.

Papa's hand brushes against the cracked door, nudging it open a little wider. The door is free to open now that we've twisted the man around.

Papa takes a step back, recoiling from the sight. He presses his fingers to his forehead as his eyes bulge. "Oh my— Dear God! What on earth is going on here?" he says louder than I wish. "Why—Lena, why—just why is there a laborer in this house?"

Mama doesn't respond right away. I'm assuming she didn't expect Papa to come home amid this plan. "Friedrich, calm down, please. Please, keep your voice down. I just need to move him out back and then we can talk," she says.

"No, no. No!" he shouts. "Stop. I'll call for a *Wachmann* to move him. I can't believe he came inside. How could you let this happen?"

I reach out for Papa's arm. "Papa, it's not what you think," I speak up. "Stop talking that way, like those men outside aren't being treated like slaves."

Papa pulls his arm away from me. "That is not what I meant. I took part in an agreement with the SS." He removes a handkerchief from his pocket and dabs his forehead. "Did this man just pass out in here?"

"He's dead, and he's not a laborer," Mama says. "Now please, we're out of time. Either help or just run along and turn me into the gestapo, Friedrich."

"What?" Papa mutters. "This is a *Wachmann*? He's dead. And he's in our house? How? Why?"

"Friedrich, just help me," Mama repeats through gritted teeth.

"What am I supposed to help you with? It looks like you've already done a fine job at whatever you were trying to accomplish. Dear God, how will I explain this? This is it. We're all going to pay a severe consequence. You realize the likelihood, don't you?" Papa's veins are pulsating, he's seething.

"We need to move him out back," I repeat Mama's words from a minute ago.

Papa's face becomes inflamed, burning with anger as fury flashes through his eyes. "This was not the plan," he says, taking Mama's place by the man's head. "Help Sofia with his feet."

The three of us move the guard to the back door. I clutch the doorknob, twist, and push it open. I'm the first outside, so I lean back to make sure there is no one in sight. "It's clear," I whisper.

We place his body far enough away and out of sight from the back door, not too far from the side of the barn, but out of sight from the others. No sooner than we drop his body are we back inside, locking the door behind us.

"Are you both out of your minds?" Papa growls, baring his teeth. "What was the point of this? Tell me how this man died, and in our house, of all places."

"Come sit down in the kitchen and we'll start at the beginning." Mama lifts the wooden spoon next to the simmering pot of stew. "Your daughter made stew for tonight." Mama always tells me food will take the anger out of any man, but I'm not sure there is any meal in the world that will help now.

"Lena, tell me what you've done," Papa demands.

CHAPTER 32
MAY 1943

ISAAC

I can't blame Sofia's father for his anger at everything he's come home to today. In fact, I might be more than a bit angry about finding a dead man in my house, despite who he may be. I hold little hope for his understanding once Sofia and her mother confess to hiding a Jewish man upstairs, but I'd like to think they wouldn't have taken the chance on helping me if I was going to cause their family trouble.

I know the three of them are arguing somewhere downstairs, but it's far enough away that I can't make out what they're saying. Maybe they have already informed Sofia's father of my whereabouts. Between the family's futile words and the Nazis' shouts growing louder from out the window, I feel like I'm standing on the wrong side of a mirror. I should be outside, being scolded, along with every other prisoner. I shouldn't be sitting on Sofia's bed near the window she has been watching me from for the last couple of months. I suppose she's likely felt the same way, given her faith.

I'm not sure how long I'll be up here, but I take a moment to look around, curious to learn more about who Sofia was before the war. We were all different before, and since then, we've been morphing into unrecognizable beings.

The stack of books on her writing desk catches my attention first.

Charlotte Brontë's *Jane Eyre*, Ann Radcliffe's *The Italian*, William Faulkner's *Light in August*, and—I stand from her bed to get a closer look at the book on top—Jeffrey Pulver's *Paganini, the Romantic Virtuoso*.

I'm taken aback by the selection. It's clear I know little about her, especially from just admiring her in the window, but these books speak of her character and the fact that she isn't afraid to face darkness.

The door to Sofia's bedroom swings open, stealing my every breath.

"Isaac," she says with urgency.

"Yes, I was just looking at your books. I hope—" The pause between us makes me feel like I've been caught trying to steal something.

"My father would like to meet you."

"Sofia, if me being here is a problem, I can—"

"You can what?" she asks, tilting her head to the side. "Walk out there with your arms up?"

"I just mean, I can take care of myself."

"Well, of course. You wouldn't be here right now if you couldn't," a man's voice interrupts our conversation before turning the corner into the room.

He's middle-aged, several inches taller than Sofia, but with matching dimples and eyebrows, and stands behind his daughter. He places his hands on her shoulders. "Sofia, a moment, please."

"Papa, you said you wouldn't—"

"Sofia, now," he demands.

Though she's trying hard not to react, I see the muscles

flexing in her jaw. I'm sure she must be grinding her teeth together. She steps to the side but doesn't go too far.

"I'm Friedrich," her father says, taking a couple of steps closer to me. "You have nothing to worry about. If you heard anything I said downstairs, I was taken by surprise when I arrived home from work. My anger was not toward you. I didn't know you were upstairs. While I don't agree with the way my wife handled matters today, our common agenda was to save whomever possible."

"I don't want to cause problems," I say, my pulse racing.

Friedrich is looking at me with sympathy, something I dislike very much. I was born into this life, and I will take the days as they come, but if luck finds a way in, I will take that too. "I know you won't cause problems, but we need to do whatever is necessary to keep you safe. The SS are in and out of this house far too often for you to be in here during the day. The SS recruited me to train their doctors, and while I don't condone the Third Reich or any part of Germany's power over Poland, I saw the position as an opportunity to keep Sofia and my wife safe for the time being."

"You're a noble man," I say, clasping my hands behind my back. "My father was the same way in the face of our family, but I fear he might have lost the battle." I don't want the same to happen to Sofia's father. "Which is why I know it's important that I help by staying out of sight and out of mind."

Friedrich clears his throat. "I'm sorry you are in the dark about your father. I can't imagine—but, for tonight, please make yourself comfortable. We have a spare bedroom across the hall. Before the *Wachmänner* arrive with the laborers tomorrow, I'll show you to the bunker beneath the barn. You'll be safe there."

It's too soon to tell him about Olivia, but I can't spend a day in peace knowing I haven't attempted to save her too somehow. The thought of what she'll be thinking tonight when she doesn't see me makes a scolding heat burn through my blood. I don't know if I made the right choice.

I push the sleeves up to my elbows and clutch my left hand over my right wrist. "I'm very grateful for your hospitality."

Friedrich's stare falls to my arm, the numbers branded along my pale skin. "They will think you're dead. The deceased *Wachmann* clothed in your uniform has the same number sewn to the jacket, correct?"

The thought of my uniform matching up to my number didn't enter my mind until now. If Olivia knows anyone working for administration, she could find out that they have marked my number for dead. She'll think I'm gone and give up hope. This was a mistake.

"Yes, and now I see the consequences of my actions. I shouldn't stay here."

Friedrich gestures at me to hush. "That wasn't what I was insinuating. There isn't a missing prisoner they are looking for. It's better off that way."

"Not for my sister," I reply.

Friedrich takes in a deep lungful of air, puffing his chest out. "Perhaps we can help her too."

I'm aware of the unlikelihood, and yet, in the heat of the moment, I believed there was a chance when I shouldn't have. I've abandoned the one person I vowed to stand by, but for now, I don't know what to do. "Thank you," I say.

Friedrich replies with a stiff nod. "Lena is setting out supper now. I'm sure you're quite hungry. Come on downstairs and join us."

When I step out of the bedroom, I spot Sofia to my left. She looks downcast, just the same as I feel inside. Maybe she's able to see the mistake I made, too.

CHAPTER 33

MAY 1943

OLIVIA

"Are you all right?" Zoe, one of the two women I share a buk with, asks. "You aren't sick, are you?"

"No, it's just that my brother hasn't been by tonight," I say.

"Maybe he had to work later than usual," she replies.

It's such a simple answer, one I could presume to be true, but then I become lost, wondering if that isn't the case—wondering if something bad has happened to Isaac.

"I'm sure you're right," I reply.

All labor is meant to end at a particular time, returning to the encampment earlier than seven at night before they hand out our evening bread. It's almost nine, which means the gong will chime soon to announce the nighttime silence. Then I'll have to wait until tomorrow night to see if Isaac is okay. I know I won't be able to sleep tonight.

"What happened to your arm?" Zoe changes the subject, but not to one that I prefer to talk about.

I peer down at the sore spot on my forearm, just above my

wrist. A bruise in the shape of a thumb tells a story I want to forget—one I want to stop reliving almost every day.

Once again, I didn't fight the *Wachmann* off—I knew the pain would only be worse if I tried. His need for what he is taking from me might be all that is keeping me from being sent to my death.

I didn't notice the bruises from the unnecessary tight grip. The pain in my chest surpasses everything on the surface. My mind is scarred, my body ravaged, yet I'm alive, and for that, I'm supposed to be thankful.

I tug on my sleeve to hide the evidence. The thought of Isaac asking the question instead of Zoe makes my stomach churn. "I tripped earlier," I say, staring down at the torn lace of my black boot.

"You just need to make a knot so it won't fray any further and the knot will keep your boot from loosening," she says, believing my story.

"I forgot, but I'll do that in the morning. Thank you," I say.

I walk to the open door, where others are returning from the washroom and glance around, trying my best to see between the sparse lights. The only thing I see are lines of people waiting for their turn to wash up or use the toilet and *Wachmänner* strolling by as if they're enjoying a casual night out through a quaint downtown area, rather than manning innocent people they are holding captive as prisoners.

Please, Isaac, please be okay. I can't go on without you. I need you.

CHAPTER 34
MAY 1943

SOFIA

I'll never be able to erase Isaac's pain from my mind, witnessing each wince and expression. I want to make it better, cure every ailment he is suffering from, and give him hope for a future, but I can't.

The four of us take a seat at the kitchen table. The hollow clunks and thuds from the chairs fumbling around isn't nearly as loud as the uncomfortable silence between us all, but that's insignificant now because I feel like I can breathe, knowing Isaac is about to have a hot meal.

While watching Isaac spoon steaming stew into his mouth, I have the opportunity to sit and gaze at him. I'm able to take in more of his features: mysterious eyes that radiate with various hues of browns. His thick black brows cast shadows over his deep-set eyelids. With lips slightly wider than average, I imagine he must have a radiant smile that would light up a room, though I have only seen hints of happiness thus far. His arms and hands are covered with scars; some look ages old, leaving me to wonder if he was an adventurous child. An active youth might explain his ability to conquer the hours of physical labor, but no one is prepared for what he has survived. The strength of his physical structure is apparent by the way he holds himself up—with pride that was intended to be stolen from him long ago.

Isaac doesn't speak between mouthfuls. I can't blame him. Lost in a trance while watching him, I'm trying so hard to understand a smidgen of what he has been through, but it's as if he's keeping that reality locked inside.

Mama is standing in the doorway. She has her finger resting on her lips and her eyes are glossy and unfocused—a telltale sign she's lost in her mind somewhere.

"As Friedrich might have mentioned, I'm going to go make up the spare bedroom for you, the one across the hall from Sofia's room. We'll make sure you're up early enough to move down into the bunker before work hours begin on the farm," she says.

This situation is playing out as a surprise to me, unraveling by the moment. I didn't think Mama or Papa would allow him to stay here. I assumed they would move him down to the bunker right away, but I'm glad he will be able to sleep in a warm bed for the night.

Isaac lifts his hand and presses it against his mouth. "I'm ever so grateful for the offer, but I'm not sure it's a safe idea. I would be putting you all in a great deal of danger," he says.

The brightness of Isaac's eyes dims like the sun fading behind a dark cloud. He must be thinking what I am—how dangerous everything is now. If we loosen the reins on our plan, we could be responsible for many deaths, as well as our own.

"We will be fine for this evening," Papa intervenes, stepping into the kitchen. He disappeared after speaking to Isaac, and I'm not sure what he was tending to, but I can't help wondering if he was checking to see if the body out back had been carried away. I'm also curious about how long it will take the SS to notice they have a missing guard.

Isaac doesn't argue, but instead focuses on finishing every drop of the stew in his bowl. "I'm not sure I have words for how delicious this meal has been," he says.

"There's more where that came from—you won't go hungry on my watch," Mama says, holding her hand up to her chest as a gesture of promise.

"Your hand—your skin is quite raw," Papa says, lifting his head to get a better look across the table.

Isaac closes his fingers into a fist, hiding the wound.

"I gave him a shot of penicillin before," I mumble, assuming Papa will now have another reason to be furious.

"You did?" he questions.

"It looked like it was becoming infected, and I know how quickly an infection can spread throughout the body. I wanted to make sure that didn't happen." I'm confident I did the right thing. Over the last couple of years, I've read all of Papa's books on medicine and practice. Of course, I'm not trained, but saving a life is saving a life.

"May I see?" Papa asks Isaac.

Isaac holds his hand out and uncurls his fingers from the angry, red and raw skin on his palm.

"You should heal up just fine. I have some ointment for that and bandages that I'll leave in the washroom upstairs for you. Yes, I would have given you a penicillin shot as well." Papa looks at me with a raised brow. "Thank you, Sofia."

Despite the pride I feel, I keep my expression neutral, knowing one wrong move could aggravate Papa more than he already is.

Isaac stands from the chair and takes his bowl over to the sink, twisting the faucet to begin rinsing.

"No, no, I'll clean those," I say. "Please, don't worry about that."

"It's nice to use warm water to clean a bowl. It's no problem," he argues.

I make my way over to the sink and take the bowl from his hand. "You are our guest, and you won't be doing any of the cleaning."

Isaac smiles, wider than he has before, proving my theory of the way his expression could make a room light up.

"Sofia," says Mama, "your father and I are going to put clean linens on the bed in the guest room. You can both take your time down here and come up when you're ready." She stands up and tries to catch Papa's eye as he's the one who seems to be staring through the wall in front of him. I wish I knew what they were both thinking—their concerns, fears, and long-term plan. Maybe they don't know yet. I'm not sure which is worse—knowing or walking around dangerous dark corners. Papa rises from his seat and follows Mama out of the kitchen.

With one last rinse of Isaac's bowl, I take the dishrag hanging over the waterspout.

"I feel useless," he says. "Allow me to at least dry the spoon."

I twist my lips, debating whether to give in, but it's just a spoon, so I cave and toss the towel at him and hand over the silver.

He's thorough while running the dishrag over the spoon, which offers me a short moment to notice the numbers on his forearm. The puckered skin is angrily scarred with ink. I run my fingertip over the numbers I penned onto the dead guard's arm, wondering if there is any significance or if they are chosen at random.

Isaac's hands stop moving, as if my touch has frozen him stiff.

I yank my hand away, feeling remorseful. "I'm sorry— I—"

"Don't be sorry," he says. "The number only reminds me that Olivia could find out there is no life attached to these digits now. I've abandoned her and my heart is so very heavy now. Please don't confuse my feelings for how grateful I am to you and your family, but I'm having trouble coming to terms with the pain I might cause her."

I take a moment to understand what he's saying. The thought of a number representing a life didn't register in my head before now. "Are you privy to information regarding the status of numbers?"

"Not usually, but Olivia's barrack comprises all women laborers, most of whom tend to onsite physical labor or administration work. It would be much easier for her to find out information about a prisoner's number than it would have been for me, and I fear she knows this well."

I take the spoon and dishrag from Isaac's hand and place them down on the counter. "Isaac," I say, reaching for his hands, "I'll do whatever I can to help save her. There must be a way."

Isaac shakes his head without a moment to hesitate. "Escaping from Auschwitz is almost impossible. The SS have caught most of the people who have attempted to do so, and then killed them. The few who might have made it didn't leave a map to follow their lead. The likelihood of surviving an attempt is very rare. I knew this earlier when you said you'd help me save her, and for a moment I thought it may be possible, but as the fog lifts from everything that has happened over the last few hours, I realize how foolish I was."

Though it guilts me to offer optimism, he needs something to motivate him to keep going. "We mustn't give up hope. We have a guard's uniform in possession, too. There might be a way we can reach her."

Isaac tries to force a smile, but he struggles to move his lips. "Maybe you're right. The SS assigned her to a job within the prison camp. She's tending to the items that have been taken from or left behind by Jewish victims, working in a location the other women refer to as 'Kanada.' It's said to be one of the safest labor jobs to have because it's indoors and not as strenuous as other jobs."

I walk Isaac back over to the kitchen table and wait for him to take the seat before joining him in mine. "If Olivia has a job in a safe area, she would have likely outlived you at the rate you were being worked. It isn't even summer yet, and I fear how many will die from extraneous labor in the heat without enough water or food. Come wintertime, there would be no work left on the farm. What would happen then?" I ask.

Isaac lifts his gaze from the tabletop and looks into my eyes. "I didn't think of it that way."

"You've both made it this far. Try not to lose faith yet," I say, realizing I should be following the advice too.

He leans back in his chair and wraps his hands around the back of his neck. "You're right. The guilt I feel, though, it's heavy on my chest."

"If she had the chance to escape, knowing you had a better chance of survival, would you be angry with her for passing up the offer?"

"Of course, but I'm her older brother—all she has left in the world—or so I think," he says with a downcast grimace.

"We won't give up trying, you know that. No one could ask for more of you," I say.

Isaac stands back up and dips his hands into his pockets. "I should get some rest."

"Of course. You must be beyond tired. I'll walk you up to the guest room."

Once I stand, we both tuck our chairs in and he follows me out of the kitchen and up the steps—a slow, painful walk during which I lack the ability to find consoling words.

"I can't thank you enough for what you've risked for me," he says, stopping in the hallway just before reaching the two bedrooms.

"You would have done the same if given the chance." I don't

mean to sound as if I know him better than I do, but from the way he speaks of his sister, I know he has a heart of gold and a type of strength I didn't know existed.

With his shoulders low and bent forward, Isaac looks as if he has so much more to say but can't find the words. I wish I could comfort him more, but all I can do is say goodnight and hope he finds enough peace to sleep tonight.

He takes a step toward the guest room but stops once more and turns to face me. "I saw you were reading about Niccolò Paganini."

"Are you a fan of his music?" I ask, knowing people either love him for his talent or are mesmerized by his mysterious personality and unique lifestyle.

"Yes, very much so. I used to be a violinist, and I find him to be quite inspiring. His music is both soul-rending and uplifting, but I'm not sure I know many people who would read his life's story."

My cheeks fill with heat. "I think it's the unique people of the world who we should learn something from. Everything else is just black and white."

"I couldn't agree more," he says, a smile outshining his emotional fatigue.

CHAPTER 35
MAY 1943

ISAAC

A neatly folded pair of blue cotton pajamas sits on top of the teak bureau across from the four-poster bed. I've never slept on such a large platform, or one that is cloaked with bright white linens and a complementary navy-blue quilt. The drapes are lush, silk trimmed with lace, and a nightstand with an antique mantel clock sets the scene for the most perfect night of sleep I could have dreamed of over the last four years.

The pajamas feel like feathers skating down my ragged skin as I pull the pants up and button the shirt over my chest.

I shouldn't be relishing this luxury, not when Olivia is wondering where I am and sharing a tight buk with others.

Aside from tearing my heart out of my chest, I'm left with no other option but to climb into the bed and close my eyes. The linen smells like ivory mixed with fresh mountain air and the warmth of the quilt makes me feel like I'm sinking into a cloud.

The last time I climbed into a bed—a real bed, not scraps of fabric filled with hay, newspaper, or softened wood chips—was the last night in our family's home. I can still picture every detail of my bedroom, as if I was just there yesterday. My rosewood bed frame had been hand-carved and passed down two generations. The light-colored walls made the room look bigger, but the worn wooden floors offered comfort and they matched the exposed beams along my angled ceiling. The pattern among the beams would pull me into a trance, allowing me to fall asleep wondering what it might be like to walk along the beams as if it was the floor—how much more interesting life would be if gravity didn't keep us down.

The urge to walk across the ceiling and experience the world from an upside-down view kept me awake some nights. I remember thinking that an upside-down world might make more sense than the one right side up. If I had to be different, I wanted to be as different as possible with the ability to break the laws of physics. If I could walk along the ceilings, being Jewish wouldn't seem like such a big deal in comparison.

No one could prevent me from seeing life in that light while I was dreaming.

I didn't know it would be our last night there. Mama and Papa didn't want to worry Olivia or me, not until it came to giving up our home.

The heaviness of my eyelids pulls me away from my memories and my regrets.

The grounds in Auschwitz are covered in loose dirt that kicks up with each step we take. It isn't so bad when walking alone compared to when we must follow a line of others. It's quiet here. There aren't others around, not that I can see. I don't see Wachmänner *or officers. There isn't smoke piping into the sky from the buildings in the distance, and the air doesn't smell like manure.*

With the abundance of silence, I notice a faint sound from a nearby block. Someone is playing the violin. I've heard others playing string instruments here before. The Nazis force a select group of people to play in a small orchestra as the new prisoners depart the cattle cars. It's a cruel trick to offer the incoming people a false sense of hope.

Just as I know the truth behind the beautiful sounds, I fall into the trance like everyone else and follow the haunting chords, finding Niccolò Paganini standing in the center of an empty block, his eyes closed, his fingers moving like electrical currents along the strings; they are blurry from where I'm standing. The sound echoes off each buk, wooden post, and wall, making my heart race with hope. Though the music doesn't stop, he removes his bow from the strings and points toward the door I entered.

I turn to leave, but the music follows me, the notes grow closer together; the pitch becomes higher, and it forces me to walk faster toward Olivia's block. I can save her now that no one is here. My feet carry me as if I'm walking across the wind, right in through the door to her dark abode. The notes growing from the hollow spruce drop several measures, vibrating against my bones as I search around for my sister.

"Olivia," I try to call out. I can't hear my voice.

The tones fall into a minor, foreboding heaviness as I spot her hiding behind the door once again, shaking, crying, bruised, and battered. She lifts her head and stares at me.

The horse hairs of the bow moan against the lowest of notes as Olivia's lip quivers. "Why did you leave me? You promised you'd never leave. I can't live without you, Isaac. You know this," she says, her voice as jarring as the melody.

I try to step toward her, but I can't move. Instead, the notes from Paganini's violin skip across the musical staff, hitting the most tormenting pitch, so high it can pierce a soul. Human fingers shouldn't be long enough to reach a note so deafening— we shouldn't hear something so powerful, but the pain it causes —it disappears. As does Olivia.

. . .

I'm out of breath as I snap upright, sweating, peering around in the dark, but I can't see anything. "Olivia," I call out before remembering I'm in a foreign bed, one I don't belong in, one too far away from my beloved sister. She's going to die because of me.

Tears form in the corners of my eyes, then fall one by one until my face is damp. The pain is reeling through me. I want to believe I followed the right path, but there's no way to convince myself of this.

I sit, hunched over in shame, until a light tap on the door startles me.

Friedrich appears in the doorway. "It's time to go into the bunker before the laborers arrive."

"Yes, of course," I reply, trying to speak through the dryness in my throat.

"I'll give you a moment to get dressed," he says.

I change my clothes as quickly as I can and meet Friedrich in the hallway. He's partly dressed for work in a white dress shirt and slacks, almost ready to start his day at the same time I would start mine. Yet he's here, helping me as if I deserve to be helped. I deserve nothing more than the others out there or in Auschwitz.

We're silent as I follow him out the back through cool, damp grass that tickles my ankles. The horizon teases us with the hint of grapefruit spilling out over the distant mountains. The view is something I have avoided for a long time, since the rising sun is only an indication of another day in this life. The world is not a beautiful place, but nature is like a mirage—one I keep blindly reaching for.

Like a light switch, one step in through the door of the barn, and the mirage is gone again. I watch as he lights a lantern, then searches beneath a pile of loose hay. A hatch separates from the floor and Friedrich hands me the lantern.

"Sofia and Lena have left you the necessities for getting

through the day. Once the *Wachmänner* leave with the laborers this evening, we'll bring you back inside."

"I'm very grateful for your hospitality," I say, taking the lantern from his hand.

"Please, don't thank me. Helping one person is the very least I can do."

I bow my head and lower myself down the dark ladder hanging from the edge of the hatch. It's cool and musty, but I see they've left me blankets, books, paper, a pen, newspapers, and canned food.

The sound of the hatch sealing feels like the start to a long day, but a day I should feel relief in knowing I'll survive. Instead, I know it will be a day I spend thinking about Olivia suffering.

CHAPTER 36
MAY 1943

SOFIA

I couldn't sleep right now even if my mind was free of worry. I'm afraid I'll be watching the minute hand on the clock tick by all day until the guards who have just arrived with their slew of prisoners leave tonight.

There has been a lot of shouting outside. I can't quite make out what the guards are yelling about, but I'm also afraid to peek out. I've come to see that their moods reflect their behavior toward the Jewish men and it's hard to predict how they will feel each day. After last night, with a guard gone missing, I imagine there is a lot of anger spilling down from the top command.

I've also heard Mama and Papa arguing in their bedroom in low voices. It's around the time Papa would leave for work, but it doesn't sound like he's even close to walking out the front door.

I slip my arms through my robe and tighten the ribbon around my waist. I can't just sit around, wondering what's happening. I walk toward their room, holding my ear up to Mama and Papa's door. They've gone quiet, though.

After a couple of terse knocks against the door, Papa snaps, "Come in, Sofia."

I let myself in, finding their room to be dimly lit due to the closed curtains.

Papa is dressed for the day, his shirt is neatly tucked into his dress pants, but his suspenders are not over his shoulders. They are dangling by his sides and the collar of his shirt is unbuttoned down to his undershirt.

Mama is still in bed, resting beneath their pear-colored feather quilt. She doesn't look as forlorn as she did last night, but her shoulders are stiff.

"You should have included me in your plan," Papa says to me. "This will not just fall on your *matka*. You are an adult now and you know what you did last night could have caused irreparable damage. It still can."

"You won't listen to us," I argue. "You haven't seen what goes on here during the day. Your plan would have gotten innocent people killed."

He thinks he knows more than us, and he does in many cases, but we are the ones who have been watching the horrific acts of abuse every day.

"I'm not allowed an opinion on your plan, and yet yours could end up being no better than mine. Now there is a missing *Wachmann* and our farm is the last place he was seen."

Mama sits up a bit straighter, leaning against the satin puckered headboard. "That doesn't mean we had anything to do with him going missing. I'm sure soldiers and guards snap to their senses sometimes and take off when they realize the life they are surrounded by."

Papa slaps his hands against his hips and tosses his head back. "It's always so simple with you. If the SS officers believed every word from every commoner, don't you think this country would be in a much different situation right now? Those men only listen to what Hitler and the other Generals of the Waffen-SS tell them."

"I'm starting to question if you were being truthful about wanting to help those poor men, or were you trying to keep us quiet?" Mama asks.

Papa combs his fingers through his dark hair and grits his teeth. "I'm trying to keep you two alive. How can I make this any clearer?"

I have nothing to respond with, and the flat line of Mama's lips tells me she feels the same.

Papa shakes his head and secures his suspenders over his shoulders. "I have to go. I'd ask you both to stay indoors and avoid contact with anyone outside, but I'm sure it won't make a difference what I say. You should know you are now walking across very thin ice and one wrong step will be the end for us all."

As if punctuating Papa's statement, the doorbell chimes. He takes his coat from the edge of the bed and tosses it over his shoulders. "I'll tend to the door," Papa says, stepping out into the hallway and closing us inside. The back of the bedroom door is another reminder of the separate worlds we are living in.

Our doorbell doesn't often ring. We've found that the guards tend to knock if they need something, and we haven't had guests or friends over in years.

Mama sweeps her legs out from under the quilt and begins pacing around the room with a sudden spark of concern.

"What's wrong?" I ask, watching her move back and forth like a ping-pong ball.

"What if he's right?" Mama asks.

"About which part?"

"All of them, Sofia. There are no rules to this war. The Nazis do as they please, and if they choose to hold us accountable for what happened to the guard yesterday, they will blame us."

"Why yesterday of all days? Wouldn't we have done something like this weeks ago?"

"If they need blame, they will find it."

The loud click of a man's heels interrupts our quiet argument.

"One of them is in the house," I whisper.

Mama opens the door a crack.

"We are searching for Wachmann Borg. Could you or your wife tell us when you saw him last? No one has seen him since he was on duty at your farm yesterday."

They must be close to the stairwell if we can hear them so clearly but I know Papa wouldn't lead anyone that far through the house.

"Wachmann Borg?" Papa questions.

"Yes, *Herr*. I take it you might not have been acquainted with him. Perhaps if you check with your wife and daughter, they might have more information."

"I can certainly question them when they return from their morning errands, but they haven't mentioned the name around me. I've asked that they stay out of any business going on outside the house."

"I see."

I feel the heat rushing through my cheeks as I pull away from the door.

When we hear the footsteps disappearing into silence, Mama closes the bedroom door.

Papa's heavy footsteps warn us he's on his way upstairs. I assume he's only angrier now.

Mama sits on the edge of their bed, awaiting the wrath.

Papa walks in and closes the door gently behind him, a distinct contrast to his heavy footsteps. He dips his hands into his pockets and inhales sharply through his nose.

"Well, I'm not sure what they suspect, but he questioned when the two of you saw Wachmann Borg last," he says. "I'll let him know later on that it was early on in the day yesterday that you saw him last. I would like to think that will be the last of the questions about him. Let's just hope. After all, the man could be anywhere, I suppose."

"It wouldn't kill you to have a little faith in us, Friedrich," Mama says.

A loud, pain-filled groan echoes against the bedroom window. Mama and I look down toward our feet, both knowing what is likely happening out there.

Papa peeks through a small opening between the curtains and recoils from whatever he witnesses.

"They aren't animals," he mutters. "Why strike them with steel bars? What's the purpose?" Papa is asking himself the very questions we've been wondering this entire time.

OLIVIA

It's hardly been two days since I last saw Isaac. It's also been the longest day while wondering if he's okay, and I'm terrified of finding out why he didn't come by last night. I'm sure there could be a logical explanation for why he didn't show up, but I know he wouldn't let anything get in the way of checking in on me. Something or someone kept him away. I know many Jewish people are deported here from other locations, but from the stories I've heard, none of the prisoners go elsewhere once they are here.

If the war ever ends...

If I survive...

If I'm in one piece...

There's no saying what will happen to me. I'm fourteen, without parents and now my brother too. If they are alive, any of them, I don't see how I'll ever find them. I'm an orphan whether I live or die.

"Olivia, if you keep staring at the pile of clothes, you know what's going to happen," Beatriz whispers.

"It's going to happen regardless of whether I stare at the clothes," I reply, my voice unwavering.

She can't tell me I'm wrong. I think we tell ourselves lies to help us survive longer—longer until...

The *Wachmann*, the guard I despise the most, leaves the barrack likely for his lunch break. As soon as he's out of sight, Beatriz stands up and stretches out her back, then rubs her palms against her sore knees. "The death line is long today," she says.

I join her, standing in the open doorway where we overlook the line of people leading to the gas chambers.

None of them know what they are smelling in the air.

No one knows what awaits them on the other side of the gates.

No one knows why they were told to go right instead of left.

"Where are they taking us?"

"Please, tell us where we're going."

"They separated me from my husband and son. Do you know where I would find them?"

"Have you seen my mom?"

The questions from people in the line are endless and all we can do is stare. At first, when I would watch the queue move past our barrack, I would want to fall to my knees and scream with confusion about how the world has become a word Mama and Papa told me I wasn't old enough to use. It isn't ironic that I'm not old enough to say Hell, but I'm living at its gates.

When I watch now, there's a numbness that takes over me and coats my heart with what feels like tar. The heaviness I feel makes me want to revolt, but I don't have the strength. I would save all the poor people in the line, but I'd become one of them. Instead, I feel envious. Tomorrow, they will no longer know of the horrors that exist. They'll be in a better place, along with everyone I love. I'll still be here. I'll still have nothing left, and yet, I will still have more taken from me, like I do every single day.

Beatriz wraps her hand around my arm and pulls me away from the door. "You have that look in your eyes again," she says.

"It's the same look I see in yours," I reply.

The question we all ask ourselves is how long can this last? Is our work worth the suffering? Will we all end up in that line at some point? No one knows.

"Do you want me to ask my buk-mate about your brother? Would it be easier to know if he's on the list?"

Beatriz's buk-mate works as a *kapo* tasked with leading several other laborers with administration work. She compiles lists of arrivals, departures, and daily deaths. If Beatriz's buk-mate agreed, I imagine the answer would be easy enough to gain. I know Isaac's prisoner number because I memorized it along with my own when we first arrived here. The fear of the truth is too much, knowing I will lose the motivation to live. Though, to know he's not suffering would also give me some peace of mind. I miss him so much and the thought of never seeing him again, never receiving a hug that's always a little too tight, never hearing him say everything will be okay, even if it's said in vain, it's unbearable. I'm not ready to say goodbye.

"No, please. I don't want to know. The slim chance that he's somewhere—it's all I have. I don't want that taken from me."

When the day ends, and there's a short bit of time before the last gong rings, I stare toward the open door of my barrack, waiting for Isaac to poke his head in. The minutes feel like short seconds, the time disappears and then the low guttural clang from a mallet clashing against metal feels like a fist against my chest. Another night without Isaac has come and gone.

I climb into the buk, settle onto my side, and stare at the skeletal woman's back next to me. Images of the *Wachmann* who locks me in a small room every day for several minutes make me want to purge the bread in my stomach. I wish I could burn the memories—something like that should be easy to do here—but I'm forced to relive them again and again.

Between the thoughts of what I want to avoid and the prayers I want to believe in, the only thing I find are tears burning my cheeks, my body singeing like it's on fire, and memories I wish would go away. The foul odor of waste, corpses, eroding living bodies, and the sickly moist air that sticks to my skin with the slightest breeze. A cough lingers in the air, making me wonder when I'll become ill. A cry that speaks of impending death, and the symphony of groans rumbling from my empty stomach—I want to make it all stop.

I want to block my nose, clench my eyes, cover my ears, and tell it to stop.

CHAPTER 38

MAY 1943

ISAAC

To sit in solitude is a different type of poison. Being alone with only my thoughts feels like a punishment, even though I know that this seclusion is for safety. I've done nothing more than pace the perimeter of the bunker hundreds of times, trying to focus on counting steps versus the immeasurable amount of guilt burning through every fiber of my body.

I tried to read the book Sofia left for me, Edgar Allan Poe's *Tales of Mystery & Imagination*. If I had to guess at the reason she left me this to read, it was a tool for distraction, to take my imagination elsewhere. But nothing could distract me from my guilt.

It's hard to know what time of day it is. There's no form of natural light in here and I'm no stranger to minutes feeling like hours. If I measure the time I take to walk past each wall down here, plus the time I took to eat some of the canned perishables, the moments spent flipping through pages of a book, and sitting on a bucket to relieve myself of all the foreign food I've ingested over the past day, I would have to say at least eight hours have passed—if not longer.

The moment I hear footsteps trailing along the wooden floors above my head, my heart stalls—wondering if a Nazi can smell the blood of a Jewish man, or if the *Wachmänner* and laborers have left for the day, and it's Sofia or one of her parents. With quiet movements, I make my way to the farthest corner, blockaded with piles of non-perishable foods, and slide down against the cement wall to hide in case all has gone wrong.

"Isaac," Sofia sweetly whispers my name. Her voice is something I've thought about many times today between the bitter moments.

"I'm here," I reply, making my way toward the dangling ladder.

"It's safe to come up now."

I grab Sofia's book before scaling up the swaying ladder, finding her waiting with a lantern in her hand.

"Was it awful being down there alone all day?" she asks, her brows knitted together.

"I'm alive. I can't complain," I say, brushing the hay off my clothes.

"Mama and I made a hot supper. I hope you'll enjoy it. We wanted to make you something nice."

"You don't have to do so much for me," I say. "You've already done so much."

She stares at me with wonder, as if I shouldn't be turning away such an offer. "We've done so little."

"You may see it that way, but I don't."

Sofia turns around, leading us out of the barn and toward the back door of the house. Once inside, she removes her laced-up boots and leaves them by the door but doesn't skip a moment to speak. "I'm not sure what type of books you like to read, but I've found myself lost within Edgar Allan Poe's words many times, so I thought it might—"

"Distract me?" I question.

"Allow your mind to go somewhere else other than a musty bunker beneath the barn."

I was right, I guess. Sofia seems like someone I've known for much longer, yet we're strangers at the same time.

"Poe is brilliant and a favorite of mine, too. Maybe I'm speculating about the books I saw in your bedroom yesterday and the one you lent me today, but you seem to have a lot of dark stories. We live in such a dismal world right now, what is it about them that intrigues you?"

Sofia clasps her hands and tilts her head to the side. "Someone always has it worse than us. Reading others' nightmares, whether true or not, can only make our current situation feel lighter. At least, that's how I feel. I couldn't speak for you after what you've been through—what you're going through." She tucks a couple of long, dangling curls behind her ears. "I'm sorry if I made you feel worse."

"No, no, of course not. The thought you put into choosing a book for me means more than I could explain."

Sofia's cheeks flourish into a warm shade of pink. I didn't mean to make her blush, but I'm not ashamed for doing so either. She seems so tough on the outside, but I think she displays most of her strength like the rest of us—a form of armor to shield off the meekness we feel.

"Supper will get cold. We should join Mama and Papa at the table now."

I nod, offering a small smile. The closer we walk toward the kitchen, the more heavenly the scents become—fresh bread, the mouthwatering aroma of cooked tomatoes, and spices I've forgotten about throughout the years.

Sofia pulls a chair out from the table; a seat facing a steaming plate of food.

"Mama and I have made *Lazanki,* but we left the sausage

out because we weren't sure if you prefer kosher meats. Mama and I don't keep kosher like we used to."

I don't remember the last time we've seen kosher meat available—it feels like a lifetime ago.

"Any form of food is a gift today," I reply. "Thank you all for allowing me to join you for supper."

"Was everything all right for you in the bunker today?" Friedrich asks, placing a napkin on his lap. The man looks tired, with heavy bags lining the bottom of his eyes. I hope I'm not a source of apprehension.

"Of course. It was more than I could ask for—wonderful, really."

"How wonderful can a chilly bunker be for ten hours?" Lena follows. "I'm so sorry we have to keep you hidden. It's cruel."

"It's a luxury compared to others like me," I assure her.

"Please, start eating," she says, gesturing to the plate.

I don't think any of them are allowing their pity to show upon their faces, but I sense them all looking at me as I take the first few bites of food. I must stop my eyes from rolling backward, while enjoying every second that a warm, savory bite of food touches my tongue. Each time I lift my gaze from my plate, I find them darting their eyes elsewhere.

"Has anyone come looking for the *Wachmann* who disappeared yesterday?" I ask. I've been worrying that the missing *Wachmann's Kommandant* will question the family.

Lena and Sofia set their focus on Friedrich, who is slowly working through a large mouthful. Once he's swallowed the food, he clears his throat. "Yes, in fact, someone was at the door this morning, asking if we had seen him. I was firm that none of us had seen him since his duty yesterday. We'll see if there is any further follow-up, but it's nothing you should concern yourself with."

Friedrich's confirmation of my concern causes a lump of

crushed tomatoes to catch in my throat. I place my napkin over my mouth and cough to force the bite down. The family is all staring at me with concern, but I should only be grateful it was so easy for Friedrich to dissuade them from further questioning.

"If you don't mind me asking, how old is your sister, Isaac?" Lena questions.

The mention of Olivia makes it impossible to swallow the food in my mouth, so I take a drink from my water glass. My heart flutters, but I wash the mouthful down. "Fourteen," I reply, grinding my teeth.

"You must be seventeen or eighteen?" she continues.

"Yes, I'm eighteen."

"Sofia, as well," she says.

Once our plates are all clean, Sofia stands as if in a rush. "I'll be right back. I have to go get something," she says.

Friedrich glances at Lena, seemingly in the dark about whatever Sofia is up to, but Lena has a slight grin across her lips.

Before Sofia returns, Lena is on her feet, collecting the plates.

"Please allow me to help with the dishes," I insist.

"No, dear," she says, cupping her hand around my chin before taking my plate. The warmth of her hand reminds me of Mama's, the way she would always grab me by the chin to tell me not to worry. I've needed someone to tell me that, but I've had to convince myself, which feels impossible most of the time. "You're so thoughtful to offer. Your mama did a fine job raising such a gentleman."

Friedrich clears his throat again, a cue of some sort to tell Lena to stop talking.

"Anyhow, Sofia will have you occupied in a moment, I'm sure, and I don't mind cleaning up here."

"Come into the parlor," Sofia says, poking her head into the kitchen. She disappears as quickly as she spouted off the demand, so I look over at Lena to gauge her reaction.

She nudges her head to the left. "Go on."

I press my napkin against my mouth and place it down before excusing myself from the table. I haven't been in the parlor, but by the direction Lena seemed to point, I assume it's on the other side of the kitchen.

It is an open room with a sofa, smoking chairs, and a round coffee table, but the beautiful hearth above the fireplace draws my attention. It looks like the one we had in our home, a stone façade, hand-built centuries ago.

"What is the next distraction you have for me?" I ask Sofia.

The mischievous look in her eyes tells me she's nervous but also excited, maybe unsure of which to feel more.

She reaches behind one of the tall smoking chairs and retrieves a hard, black case with a handle. The shape is familiar, telling me what's inside.

"My grandfather played the violin. He left it to me before he died, telling me I would someday find someone who could make it sound the way it should. We had a small joke between us that the person would never be me, because I'm not always very coordinated, not in the way it takes to play such a chal- lenging instrument. He was, though. He would play for us at every Shabbat dinner and all the holidays. It was the only time our entire family would stop talking to allow for complete silence—while in the presence of the beautiful music he would play."

I haven't touched a violin in years, and I'm not sure I remember the notes or where to place my fingers. I might embarrass myself and let her down. "This is a lovely idea, but I'm not sure I can."

"You should try," she says, opening the case as if this isn't a request. Sofia doesn't intend to let me leave this room without playing a few notes.

"You mustn't judge me. I might have forgotten how to play," I warn her.

"How could I judge you when I don't know what those four knobs on the neck even do?"

"Those are to tune the strings," I say, taking the violin from her hand.

I pluck each string to see if it's in or out of tune. As I expected, they are each loose from lack of use. I wonder if anyone has touched the instrument since her grandfather passed away. I take a minute to match the string's notes up to what sounds right in my head. I take the bow from her hand next, inspecting it, finding it in need of rosin.

"Is there anything else in the carrying case?" I ask.

Sofia lifts the case and places it on the coffee table, inspecting the few compartments inside. She passes over a block of rosin, so I reach down and help myself to it. "What's that?" she asks.

"Your grandfather didn't teach you how to play?"

She shakes her head and scrunches her nose. "I tried a few notes once and everyone covered their ears, so I decided I'd be better off leaving the instrument to someone who might be less tone-deaf," she says, along with a shy laugh.

I chuckle along with her. "Believe me, everyone sounds that way the first time they pull the bow over the strings."

I hold the violin beneath my chin while running the amber bar of rosin across the tightly wound bow made from silky horse hairs. Once I return the rosin to its compartment in the case, I place my fingers on the neck of the violin and close my eyes, hoping my fingers remember what to do.

The first pull of the bow releases the most beautiful sound, and the wood vibrates against my neck, giving me a familiar sense of calm.

"I used to play Chopin a lot. Maybe I can recall one of his pieces."

My memory doesn't serve me much use, but it seems to be programmed into my fingertips as they move along the strings as if I just played *Mazurkas* yesterday. I keep my eyes closed, afraid of noticing a look on Sofia's face—whatever she might think of the music. I continue playing, feeling the warmth of the honeyed notes flow through my veins. The sound masks the darkness behind my eyes, replacing all thoughts by painting millions of stars surrounding a brilliant farmer's moon. Dust from the rosin wafts around me, reminding me of the scent of wildflowers just after a rain shower. Sound ripples from the strings, and blocks out the rest—just for a moment.

When I pull the bow away from the strings, I open my eyes, wanting nothing more than to begin another piece.

Sofia's eyes are filling with tears. A smile wider than I've ever seen on her face is stretching from ear to ear, and Friedrich and Lena are beneath the arched opening of the room, staring as if they just witnessed something unearthly.

"That was marvelous," Lena says. "Bravo! Goodness, I'm at a loss for words. I've never heard something so beautiful between these walls."

"She's right. My grandfather's jaw would have hit the floor. He was great, but you—you have talent like I've never seen before," Sofia says. "You're like Niccolò Paganini—that's how talented you are."

I choke through an uncomfortable laugh, trying to digest the compliments. "I appreciate your enthusiasm, but I don't think I could compare myself to Paganini, of all people."

"You aren't giving yourself much credit, young man," Friedrich says. "Talent is talent, and you have something more than that."

Their words make me want to cry, something I have avoided until last night when thinking about Olivia—Olivia who would dance around like a princess in a long dress whenever I played the violin. She would pretend she was at a ball. Papa would dance with her, and Mama would hold her hands over her heart, smiling at the scene in our tearoom. I would give anything for one of those evenings back.

"I think we might need to make this a nightly occurrence," Friedrich says. "It will give us all something to look forward to each day."

I try to bite down on the smile forming across my cheeks. "I would love that."

"So would I," Sofia says, her cheeks rosy.

"Are you all right?" I ask her.

Lena and Friedrich seem to take my question as a hint to leave, which I didn't intend, but I won't mind having a moment alone with Sofia.

I ease the violin into the case and secure the bow within its grips. She's still staring at the spot where I was standing. "I just feel so much right now," she says.

"What do you mean?" I ask.

"My heart felt as if it was lodged in my throat while you were playing. Those sounds—I've never felt like that before listening to music."

"Some music runs through our veins," I explain.

She breaks her stare at the fireplace and turns to face me. "You are miraculous—to create something that sounds so dreamlike."

"It's just the violin."

"No, it was everything inside of you pouring out through each movement of your fingers."

Her words sink in, knowing how much I just felt and how badly I want to release that pain through music again and again. "I'm sorry if I upset you," I offer.

She stares up at me, her eyes large as saucers, sparkling beneath the large candelabra. "You didn't upset me. I don't know what I'm feeling, but it isn't bad—it's a lot all at once, I suppose."

"You don't have to explain. I understand." It's hard to stop myself from staring into her eyes, because I want to know what she's feeling more than anything else.

"What do you feel inside when you're playing like that?" she asks.

There's no way to explain it, but when I look at her glossy lips, my heart swells, and my pulse races. I know I would see all the stars in the sky if—

Without another thought, I lean forward and place my hand on her cheek. Her cheek leans into my palm and she closes her eyes. It's an invitation I hope I'm reading properly. I press the tip of my nose to hers before reaching in a bit more, allowing our noses to brush side to side as our lips graze one another's. I close my eyes, finding those stars just as they were when I was playing. The moon might even be larger than it was. The fragrance of wildflowers is now a warm vanilla from the sweetness of her lips. I place my other hand on her other cheek and hold her tightly, feeling a warmth I never knew I needed. I'm not sure I'll ever want anything as much as this ever again.

When I pull away, her breath shudders. "I—Oh my," she says. "I think I understand what I was feeling now."

"It was the only way for me to show you how I was feeling, too." I wrap my arms around her, embracing her slight body against mine. "Thank you for everything you've given me, especially the ability to forget about the world for just a few minutes."

CHAPTER 39
JULY 1943

OLIVIA

The air is as stale as it could possibly be within the four walls of this barrack. The piles of clothes are damp from the recent days of rain, which makes the humid area smell more putrid than usual. The *Wachmänner* are holding handkerchiefs up to their noses while they stand and carry on with their private conversation per usual. It seems the longer we are here, the lazier the guards become. Often, they seem more interested in chatting with one another than supervising us here so intently. The break from their cunning glares is always a welcoming feeling.

"What do you think?" Beatriz has pointed her toe to the side.

"Where did your shoes go?" I ask, looking around her as if the answer would be in sight.

"I traded mine for a pair I found in their pile over there," she says, pointing down the row at the other toppling piles of various items.

"What if someone saw you?" I mutter, gritting my teeth. I know many of the women help themselves to items from within this goldmine of belongings, but the consequence of being caught is far worse than the effort of trying to get away with anything.

"Those two hens are too busy talking about whatever women they must have paid to give them attention last night."

I glance toward the center of the barrack, finding the two guards deep in a humorous conversation. I want to tell her one of the two she is calling a hen has no reason to pay for attention when he takes what he wants for free, but she knows this. Her bodily rights have been stolen from her like mine, but not as frequently. She told me it doesn't happen as often because she makes it easy for them, and they don't like that. She suggested I try the same. Except I don't understand what she means by making it "easy." I don't fight or speak, what more can I do?

I glance down at my shoes, the gray tips where my toes are scrunched up against the ends. My boots don't fit, and they haven't for quite some time.

"I'll find you a pair."

"No," I argue. "They'll notice."

"They don't care," she hisses.

I continue to separate clothes, ignoring Beatriz, knowing she won't listen to me, no matter what I say. I'm not sure when she lost the ability to feel fear, but she seems to be free of it now, and I wish I could feel the same. Maybe I'm living in a state of terror because I haven't had the nerve to seek out an answer about Isaac's whereabouts. If I had nothing else to live for, I might be more like Beatriz.

While I've been trying to block out the sight of Beatriz rummaging through a pile she hasn't been assigned to, the heavy sound of clomping heels growing in volume makes my heart thud like an echo to their approach.

"Where is the other *Jude* brut?" the *Wachmann* I am all too familiar with asks, referring to Beatriz.

"I'm not sure," I say, keeping my head down.

"*Aufstehen*," he says.

I do as he commands and stand, but keep my focus on the pile of clothes, staring at a perfectly circular splotch of blood on a white undershirt.

The other guard steps up to the side. "Today, is my turn, yes?"

"*Nein*. I don't share."

From the corner of my eye, I notice the two men face each other almost as if in a standoff.

"Comrade, be a friend," the unfamiliar guard pleas with a sinuous grin.

"*Nein*. Where is the other *Jude* brut?" the familiar *Wachmann* shouts at me again.

Beatriz must have seen or heard the commotion because she appears out of nowhere.

"I'm right here," she says. "I was moving a barrel." Her voice doesn't even waver like the rest of ours do. She's come to terms with life here. I can't do such a thing.

"Take her," the familiar *Wachmann* says.

The other *Wachmann* inspects Beatrice, starting from her forehead and slowly skates his dirty gaze down to her new shoe-covered feet. "I'd rather the young one."

"*Nein*. Take her or go elsewhere," he says, pointing to Beatriz.

"You can take me," she offers. "I don't mind."

I can only assume this is what she means by making it easy for them.

The unfamiliar guard clears his throat.

A cold sweat spreads throughout the upper half of my body. The numbness follows—a feeling I have learned to fight through to keep myself upright.

"You are my *Jude, ja*?"

I swallow against the bile rising to my throat and glance over at him—the stormy-cloud-colored eyes that haunt me in my sleep. He thinks I'm his, as if he owns me. I don't understand.

"*Ja?*" Again, he tries to confirm the answer he is expecting.

"*Ja, Herr.*"

He winks and tips his head. "I'll be back in a bit, my *Jude.*"

He walks away, leaving me in the despair of wondering how I ended up here—why me instead of the other women within several steps from me.

Beatriz takes my hand and squeezes. "I'm sorry for leaving you. I won't do it again."

"I can't do this, I think I'm dying inside," I tell her. I'm so scared of everything, and without Isaac, I feel like I've lost whatever strength I thought I had.

"You are going to survive, Olivia. You hear me? Just listen to me, okay? I made it easy for him, that's why he left. Don't you see?"

I don't think she's right. If I said what she said, I think the man would have taken me. He said he wanted the younger one. That's me.

CHAPTER 40
SEPTEMBER 1943

ISAAC

The very moment the hairs of the bow strike the taut strings, my soul leaves my body to feel the sound from the outside. The nightly occurrence of playing the violin for Sofia and her parents feels like a blessing I don't deserve, and I likely wouldn't feel right doing anything of enjoyment if it wasn't for their requests. The guilt seeps away when the vibration moves through me, but it's only gone for the time I'm playing.

Which happens far sooner than I was expecting tonight. I halt the movement of both hands upon noticing the look of shock and dread in Sofia's eyes as she stares at me from across the room. She stands from her seat, as do Friedrich and Lena.

I'm perplexed as to what's happening, but it's something that has the three of them winded.

Friedrich takes the violin from my clenched fist, then the bow. "Go," he whispers.

Sofia takes my hand and Lena follows us as we make our way up the stairs and into the master bedroom. Lena locks the door, spins around and falls against the wooden slab, holding her palms up flat against the door on each side of her face. She's listening for something outside of the bedroom.

"What's going on?" I whisper to Sofia.

"The doorbell. You didn't hear it?"

I shake my head, knowing how lost in the music I become. The notes overwhelm me, and I can't hear anything above them. More importantly, I've become too complacent. I feel safe when I shouldn't. I have let my guard down so many times over the last few months while thinking I'm protected from the world outside, but I'm not. None of us are. How could I be so ignorant?

Lena's nails press into the wood like a paw with claws. "I can hardly make out what's happening." She whispers so softly I question if I'm imagining her words.

Sofia takes my hand and holds it against her chest. Her heart is pounding like mine.

"Someone is inside," she utters.

I hear multiple footsteps too.

Lena lifts one hand from the door and places it over her chest, clenching the fabric of her dress. She closes her eyes and swallows hard. "Please leave," she mouths.

The faint sound of laughter carries up the stairwell, offering a moment of relief that the visit isn't with malice or anger. The succession of footsteps occurs again, the hollow thuds dimming to a silence.

The minutes carry on as we seem to hold our breath. I shouldn't be in this house causing the family so much extra distress. They don't need more on top of what they already must endure. I should be in the bunker.

The front door opens and closes again, and Sofia loosens her grip around my hand but doesn't release me. Her heart continues racing at the speed it was at. Maybe we shouldn't feel relief until Friedrich finds us.

A single set of footsteps carries up the stairs and Lena steps away from the door. Her suddenly calm demeanor tells me she recognizes the weight of her husband's steps.

It isn't much of a surprise when he walks through the door. He's pale and his forehead is glistening. He drops onto the edge of the bed, between the three of us. His head falls into his hands and he releases a deep sigh. "A new doctor is starting in the morning, but they needed the training materials for him tonight. Someone didn't do their job today, hence the lack of warning and phone call," Friedrich explains.

A groan rumbles in Lena's throat. "I thought they were back to ask more questions about their missing guard. I don't know how many times they can ask the same questions."

"It's only been twice, Mama," Sofia says.

"Two times too many." It's been at least two months without a question from the SS. Though I question daily how long this safety will last, the quiet nights have given me a false sense of protection.

"We're lucky that's all it is," Friedrich says.

"I shouldn't be up here at night," I interrupt their argument. I'm the reason they are living in this sort of terror.

"Don't say that," Sofia scolds me. "You're not sleeping in a cave every night."

"I've slept in a sewer. Trust me when I tell you the bunker is a palace in comparison."

Sofia gives me the look I hate, the one where she feels sorry for me. It's the last thing I want from her.

"Stop looking at me that way. I'm fine, and happy to sleep down there so you can all sleep soundly."

"No, don't say it again," Sofia argues. "I refuse to go along with the idea."

Lena and Friedrich don't argue with their daughter, but there is a questionable look in their eyes, making me wonder if they wished Sofia wouldn't fight me for insisting on their safety.

CHAPTER 41

DECEMBER 1943

SOFIA

It's hard not to wonder if a war can last forever. There are no signs of the end. We see a couple of small wins against Germany, but they are so few and far between. Yet I'd like to think there are forces out there greater than Germany's.

Mama and I sit in the house all day with every curtain drawn, preparing food with the small number of rations we often end up with. For a while, Papa was being given extras directly from the Third Reich, but the extras tapered, and we aren't sure why, nor are we in a position to ask. For now, we have enough for ourselves and Isaac, and with the insulation Papa lined the walls of the bunker with, it's been warm enough for Isaac to be comfortable down there during the day.

Though there are no more laborers on the farm for the winter months, we have all agreed it's dangerous for Isaac to remain inside during the day. Nazis have become more aggressive with house raids and if they decide to barge in, there is nothing we can do to stop them. Isaac still sleeps in the house, and we've come up with an escape plan if the doorbell was to ring after dark. I'm not sure the plan is foolproof, but Papa feels he can hold off whomever might be at the door long enough for Isaac to make his way out the back door and into the barn. The bunker is not a place I imagine anyone would be comfortable sleeping, especially after sitting there all day long. For now, the risk of keeping him indoors is one we're taking.

Mama and I work in silence during the afternoon hours, storing what we can and preparing the rest. As of a few weeks ago, there are no more prisoners working on the farm due to the snow and frozen grounds. The fear of running out of food, supplies, and safety feels never-ending. All we can do is prepare for the unknown and the unexpected.

"I've noticed you and Isaac have been coming upstairs later than usual at night," Mama says, grinding her palms into a lump of dough.

My mind reels like a film, recalling the stolen late-night moments of whispers, secrets, his lips touching mine—us longing for more. I don't think I've ever known another person as well as I know him, and though there's no promise of what will happen in the future, I don't feel as alone as I once did. I shrug to delay my response, the one I feel heating my cheeks. "Sometimes we just lose track of time, I guess."

"You must know all there is to know about each other by now," Mama says, a small grin forming along her lips.

"Mama," I hiss. "I'm sure there's plenty I still have left to learn about him, but our conversations are riveting and engaging. He paints pictures with his words, and his violin playing, and I feel like I have a window into the life he once lived."

Mama chortles and shakes her head. "Well, he is such a lovely gentleman, and with a heart of gold. I've overheard the ideas he's come up with to save his sister, and while I know none of them have been safe enough to attempt, it shows how strong he is—the way he never gives up hope."

"He is a wonderful person," I agree.

"That's all?" Mama asks.

I'm aware of her speculations. Nothing goes unnoticed with a Jewish mother, not one who so desperately wants grandchildren someday. Lately she speaks of a future neither of us thought we'd have, and as much as I try not to play into the hope, it's hard to ignore the possibilities.

"What do you mean?" I ask, delaying the inevitable she's always hinting at.

"You're in love, Sofia. I'm not blind." She isn't asking me the question, but rather making a statement.

Her words make my face warm, and I become clumsy, dropping the bowl of flour I was mixing with seasoning. It falls onto the counter and only a little of the mixture spills out. "Look what you made me do," I scold her.

She chuckles softly. "Love makes a person lose their grip on reality—and mixing bowls in your situation. You can't blame me for that."

I can't help but sigh. "How could I not love him, Mama? I admire his strength, courage, and endurance. His determination is sometimes otherworldly. Being around him makes me feel like I'm making a difference, and I've never wanted anything more."

Mama rinses her flour-covered hands under the tap. "You don't give yourself much credit, but I believe he thinks the very same way about you."

"I'm just the girl in the window, I didn't have to survive the unthinkable like he has."

Mama whips a dishrag from a cabinet knob and dries her hands. "Just the girl in the window?" She questions my statement. "You saved Isaac's life, and he does not see you as anything less."

Mama's words bring a smile to my face. I would hope anyone would take a chance to save another. Then again, there are far fewer good people than bad left in the world. Or so it seems.

"I'll feel a sense of pride when he can be free," I say. It's the truth, but I don't feel like I've accomplished enough. The extra food we continuously left for the prisoners who were working on the farm never felt like enough, especially while continuing to watch them from my window—witnessing one fall one after another as the colder temperatures crept in. The guards stopped replacing the fallen men, and when there were only a few left, they were taken to work elsewhere. At least I hope that's what happened to them. I wanted to save them all, but after Papa was questioned about the missing guard, there was no way to safely help any more of them. What's worse is I still don't know if I'll be able to reunite with his sister.

"We'll get there. We will," she says.

It's a mother's job to give us the confidence needed to push through hard times. I'm old enough to see my mother's truth. The world is not a friendly place, and there are far less chances at happily-ever-afters than I once believed.

"Shh, do you hear that?" I ask, wondering if it was the squawk of a bird or the brakes of a car.

Mama rushes out of the kitchen, walking toward the front door. "Your father is home."

I turn to look at the clock on the wall, noting it's only noon. I brush the last of the spilled flour from the counter and follow Mama.

The door blows open as if the most powerful gust of wind were to have hands. "Friedrich, what is the urgency?"

Papa spins around and slams the door closed, twisting the locks into place.

"Come away from the door," he says, pulling us both by the arms up the staircase.

"What in the world has wound you up?" Mama asks, her voice trembling.

Papa doesn't say a word until we are in their bedroom with the door closed. "We need to leave."

His words steal the air from my lungs, leaving me clutching my chest. "What for?"

"Have you listened to the radio today?"

"No, we've been baking and cooking," Mama says, fear rippling deep lines down her forehead.

"The Nazis are going to begin taking the Jewish family members of 'Privileged Marriages' into protective custody."

"Protective custody?" Mama questions.

Papa shakes his head. "It's what they're saying to prevent chaos. We need to leave. You and Sofia are no longer an exception or a 'privilege' to society, according to the Nuremberg Laws."

"Where will we go?" Mama cries out.

"I'm not sure how long we have, but we should assume hours rather than days."

The three of us are silent, all staring into different directions. There doesn't seem to be an option aside from the bunker beneath the barn.

"What is your plan?" Mama asks.

"You'll need to go down there with Isaac, and I will stay up here and stand guard. I will tell them you were gone when I got home from work—that you left me when you heard the announcement on the radio."

"Papa, they won't believe you," I say. All the fears I've had all along are coming to a narrow, sharp peak.

"It's our only option."

"Come down there with us. Let them think you disappeared as well," Mama says, reaching out for Papa's hand. It's the first sign of affection I've seen shared between the two of them in longer than I can remember.

"They'll ransack our house, then the barn, and—we know the risks. These risks aren't ones I'm willing to take. From the very start of this, my only objective was to keep the both of you safe, and it's my job until the end."

"Papa, no, you can't just stay behind. They could punish you with motives of treason." Hot tears pierce the corners of my eyes and I heave in the air I was refusing to inhale. "Please, Papa. We're a family, we must stay together."

"This is my final decision," he says, holding his hand over his eyes. "Please don't make this any harder than it already is. The last thing I want is to be away from you, but I'll be up here, and I'll bring you food and continue to keep the three of you alive."

"Then why does this feel like a goodbye?" I whimper.

Papa steps forward and places his heavy hands on my shoulders. "This is not goodbye, Sofia. We are a family of unwavering strength, and I won't let anything come between us. But you must let me handle this in the safest way. Otherwise, all of our efforts will have been in vain." Mama and Papa are both red in the face, tears are flowing like streams, and I know I look the same. The war has finally caught up with us, and just like everyone else, we are no bigger or stronger than the force that will inevitably take us down. All we can do is go out with a fight. "You must have faith in me. Let's gather whatever you need for the time being and get you down there before it's too late."

Mama and I spring to action, working against the hitches in our sobs as we gather belongings to take to the bunker.

"There's food in the icebox, and some loaves of bread in the oven. We were about to make some dumplings, but—"

"You will not go hungry," he says.

All we can do is listen and trust him, following him out of the house and across the farm.

The barn seems foreign now—the opening behind us and the enclosure in front. I imagined having to stay down here like Isaac, trying to understand every part of the horror he endures, but I didn't sense the walls caving in on me when I thought of how it might feel.

Papa lifts the hatch just like he did the first time he showed us the space below. He was filled with pride that day. Today, I can only see sorrow written across his face. He hands Mama and I both lanterns.

I inhale as much fresh air as my lungs will withstand and hold it inside as I prepare to descend into the cavernous space below the barn floor.

It all happens so quickly, the transition from living above ground to the bunker where we will now be confined. We no longer have a choice. As we were always meant to be—we are now prisoners of this war too.

We stand in a proverbial separation between two worlds: underground, where Hitler wants all Jewish people to be, versus above for all those who aren't hated. This is where we kiss Papa goodbye and thank him for doing everything humanly possible to save us, including the labor of making the bunker habitable. If I could take back every bit of wrath I've tormented him with over the last couple of years, I would do so in a heartbeat, but it's too late to undo what I've done—what Mama has done to him.

Mama goes first, reaching the tip of her toes down to the top rung of the ladder, staring up at us both as she climbs down. I follow, taking the first few steps before I stop and stare up at Papa hovering above my head. All I see is the grief etched into the deep lines along his face.

"Papa," I cry out, knowing there's no time for more words.

"I love you, *mały myszka*. Always."

All we are left with is a fallen tear from Papa's eye as the floor panel closes.

CHAPTER 42
DECEMBER 1943

ISAAC

Sofia told me to bring the mantel clock down into the bunker, hoping it would spare my mind of wondering how much time has passed. Today, I've been thumbing through the pages of Shakespeare, deciphering the difference between musical notes and iambic pentameter, wondering what it might sound like if a composer were to write music in the same way. While it has been a wonderful distraction, I know I haven't been down here over five hours today, yet there are heavy footsteps above my head. Someone is in the barn, something that never happens in the daytime.

I close the cover of the book and place it down before making my way over to the corner of the bunker that has a barrier to hide behind. Whispers from above force my heart to race like it hasn't raced in quite some time. I've grown complacent about my safety down here, but I know now I should never let my guard down.

The hatch above the ladder lifts from the ceiling, and a

blinding glow from the sunlight fills the room before whoever follows.

I peek around the edge of the wooden pallet, finding the sight of black-laced black boots descending. The material of the dress is familiar, one I've seen several times. It's her favorite daytime dress because of the navy-blue hue. Lena follows Sofia down and there is panic written on both of their expressions as they stare up through the open hatch, their faces lit like they are beneath a spotlight.

The hatch closes quicker than I'm able to understand what's happening, but I make my way over to them, both silent, still staring toward the closed hatch as if they are waiting for it to reopen.

"What's happening?" I ask.

"There has been a new Nuremberg Law instated," Lena says, her voice breathless.

"I don't understand," I reply, wondering what else they could add to the already absurd list of laws the German-occupied countries must follow.

"Mixed marriages—'Privileged Marriages'—are no longer an exception to the eradication of Jewish people. Papa must tell the men he works for that we have fled upon hearing this change. We can't go back up there now," Sofia says, staring past me to the bleak wall she will now have to find comfort in somehow.

"He said he will continue to care for us," Lena follows. "He won't let anything bad happen to us. We must have faith," she says, wrapping her arms around Sofia and pressing her daughter's cheek to her shoulder. The bravery Lena is struggling to show for Sofia's sake is an evident façade—one that can't mask a pale complexion or bloodshot eyes. It's impossible to accept an endless sentence of entrapment.

If Friedrich is about to tell the SS that his wife and daughter fled, it will put him in as much danger as the two of them—the three of us—are in.

"He shouldn't say you two left by choice—no one would do so at a time like this. There's nowhere to go," I mutter, afraid of being too harsh for the fragile state she's in. "He should tell them he left you and sent you to turn yourselves in. It will keep his hands cleaner."

Sofia and Lena share a look, a broken look of despair. "He's right. Should I go and tell him?"

"Mama, no. We need to wait until he returns with supplies."

"I agree," I add.

Sofia is pacing back and forth from one end of the bunker to the other, clutching the buttons at the top of her dress.

I stop her mid-step and wrap my arms around her. "It's okay," I say, trying to soothe the thoughts likely running through her head.

"No, it's not okay. There's no end in sight to this war. If something happens to Papa now, how will we survive?"

"Your father is a smart man, Sofia. You know he will let nothing stop him from taking care of you and Lena."

Sofia sniffles. "You, as well. He said he will continue to do whatever he can to care for the three of us."

Guilt strikes me as I realize that there is no longer any hope of saving Olivia. I should have done so when I had the chance, even if it meant risking our lives. The quicker we all realize there is no way out, perhaps it will end sooner. It must be what the Third Reich wants from each of us. The stubborn may last longer, but Sofia was right—there is no visible end to our suffering.

"Listen, we have each other. You two aren't alone. We can't give in to what they want us to feel. If we are hopeless, there is nothing left." My words are the exact opposite of what I'm feeling inside, but they are words for her sake, not my own.

Lena is still staring up toward the hatch with a look of shock —it must have all happened so fast.

"How long can time stand still?" Sofia asks.

"I believe Shakespeare described a situation like this. He said something along the lines of: *Time is what we can depend on to untangle this—it isn't up to us.* I believe the man was wise with his words. We must wait for the storm to pass before we become part of it, right?"

"I should have left you with a different book," Sofia says, her shoulders falling forward.

I press my finger beneath her chin, forcing her to look up into my eyes. "We have to stay strong, especially now." I brush my lips softly against hers, hoping to remove some of the uncertainty that I have had to push away for so long.

When I pull away, Sofia touches her fingers to her lips and spins around, wondering if Lena saw our moment of affection. The poor woman hasn't moved her stare from the ceiling, though.

Sofia makes her way over to her and wraps her arm around her shoulders. "Mama, come away from the hatch. We'll be okay." She looks at me while speaking these words, needing reassurance.

Every second between now and whenever Friedrich returns will be full of questions, and plans for scenarios we may have to face. But for their sake, I know I must keep the thoughts to myself.

OLIVIA

I can't take the wonder of not knowing if Isaac is alive or dead any longer. Living in this nightmare leads nowhere, and I can only continue walking through the tundra of bone-chilling winds, through the snow, toward the endless wall of clouds for so many days in a row before I feel the need to fall to my knees and beg for forgiveness. Surely, I've done something wrong in my life to be here, other than being born into the Jewish faith. I wish I knew what it was so I could repent for those sins, but until I figure it out, I will continue to suffer every day. Maybe my wrongdoing was being born into this world. I'm not wanted here—not for the reasons a person wants to be wanted.

I've avoided asking about Isaac's number even though I know someone who can find out. There's only a few more minutes until the second gong rings tonight and I fight against the combative snow, stinging every inch of exposed skin. Ruth, a woman around Mama's age, works in administration, but makes frequent visits to the Kanada barrack to collect or deliver information to the *Wachmänner*. Many of the others have gone to her with questions about family members, but I've held off, hoping Isaac would return. I needed to believe he was still alive, but I'm not sure I can convince myself I'm still alive. I need to know.

I poke my head into the block she lives in, finding her straightening up her few belongings. My arms are woven around my chest as dread sparks every nerve in my body.

"Ruth," I call out quietly. "I was wondering if I might ask a favor?"

She turns in response to her name, and I notice she looks much more frail than the last time I saw her. I suppose we are all decomposing in that way.

Ruth is very kind and softly-spoken. She places her hand on my shoulder and forces a small smile. "What can I help you with, dear?"

I can't stare into her tired, hazel eyes. The empathy hurts, probably for both she and I. I drop my stare down to my boots. "I was wondering if you could look up a number for me if you have a chance—it's my brother. I haven't seen him, and I'm afraid the worst has happened."

Ruth squeezes my shoulder, and I wonder how she can still feel for others when she must continuously scan the list of numbers that represent all the deaths this prison is responsible for. "Poor dear. Of course, I'll look as soon as I'm able to. Here —" Ruth turns around and lifts the straw-filled flimsy mattress and retrieves a small notepad. "Write down your brother's number and your name. You're in the block next door, right?"

"Yes, that's right."

"Hold onto your faith. Don't let go," she says.

I'm able to glance back up at her, but I'm trying my hardest to ignore the burning sensation behind my eyes. "Thank you. I'm very grateful for your help," I say as I pass back the notepad on which I have just written the number that has been burned into my memory. I can only imagine how many other numbers representing people have been written in here, and how many of them heralded good news.

"Have a good night, dear," she says, squeezing my shoulder once more.

The wind and snow are both colder and more brutal on my short walk back to the barrack. Thick snowflakes fall on my eyelashes, blurring the view ahead. If only a couple of droplets of watercolors could filter out what lies ahead, I might survive this.

CHAPTER 44
JANUARY 1944

ISAAC

Even after three long weeks of stepping foot outside of this bunker, there's no way to tell someone everything will be okay when I've already accepted that half of my family has likely fallen victim to this unbalanced war where the Germans are fighting with knives and the Jewish have been left with nothing but broken spoons.

Sofia doesn't believe she has suffered enough to deserve my empathy. She still calls herself lucky for making it through the last few years unscathed even though she's trapped now.

"This war isn't about who has more muscles, or who has a higher level of intelligence, more money, or power—it's about hatred, and the repercussions of such a feeling are more powerful than any weapon in the world," I explain. "You have endured the same amount of hatred as any other Jewish person in Europe."

Sofia only looks at me with her sad eyes when I remind her of these facts. "You're wise beyond your years," she says, resting her head against my shoulder.

We sit like this most of the day, our backs against the cold walls, our fingers intertwined, and endless thoughts floating along with our slow, heavy breaths.

Her father brought us a portable radio a couple of weeks ago, along with a supply of batteries so we could listen to daily broadcasts that may or may not contain updates about the state of our country and the war. The broadcasts seem to repeat throughout the day, so we tune in around the same time every evening, keeping the volume at a minimum. There hasn't been much news to hear, but we know that doesn't necessarily mean things haven't progressed.

Lena sits to the side of the hanging ladder, waiting for the moment Friedrich returns. She tries to spend her time reading from the stack of books we have, but I'm not sure she's looking at the words more than she stares at the blank spaces between them. She's become a hollow shell of the person she was, and despite our efforts to help her, she insists on staying in the one spot and waiting for the nightmare to end. It often feels as though Sofia and I are down here alone.

"I wish you could play the violin down here," Sofia says.

"As do I."

"When I would watch you play in the house, you would get this look on your face—I could only describe it as passion or love, pure happiness. I've never had something that makes me feel that way, and I'm afraid I won't ever have the chance to find what that is," she says.

"You make me happier than whatever look you've seen on my face while playing."

"How is that possible? I've done nothing but make your life harder and caused your sister heartbreak. I don't deserve your kindness, Isaac—I don't."

I pull Sofia onto my lap and wrap my arms around her. "You committed the most selfless act. I don't blame you for the chain of events, or the pain I feel for my family. You were right when you said my job would be eradicated, come winter. I would be dead now, but because of you, I'm alive."

Sofia won't make eye contact with me. She's staring at the collar on my shirt. "I'm not sure you're right," she says.

"Well, I'm not sure I'm wrong, so we can disagree, or you can allow me the right to my feelings, and those feelings are that I feel very fortunate to be stuck down here with you, in one piece, with my heart still beating."

She lifts her chin and looks at me with a sense of heaviness. "Someday you might feel differently when the world unravels and reveals the truth."

I take her hands in mine, sweeping the pad of my thumb against her rigid knuckles. "That's impossible. I'm in love with you, Sofia. Nothing can change that. We are here because this is part of our life's plan, for whatever reason, for whatever lesson in life we're supposed to learn, and for whatever we will face next. And because of that, I have found something more powerful within this darkness than any of Hitler's army would want for us."

Her eyes widen, the heaviness lightens, and she looks at me as if all the previous times we told each other how we felt were just words spoken to pass the time. "What have you found?"

"The only form of love a grief-stricken person could experience while living in a nightmare." I feel ashamed for finding something wonderful in all of this, especially knowing how I've let Olivia down—as well as the pain I am surely causing her. The struggle between trying to find a glimmer of happiness and not losing sight of the grim reality is like a storm of emotions crashing into each other at every moment of the day.

Even with the dim glow from the flickering lanterns, I can see her cheeks brighten with a red tinge. "It's hard to think there was a plan for us to meet like this, in such terrible circumstances."

"The enemy can't control everything, and there are still

some things they can't take away," I tell her. "I believe our fate is part of that."

"In that case, I will never stop loving you. In fact, I will love you more every single day of whatever our forever may be."

"Forever?" I question, smiling while gazing into her beautiful, glistening eyes.

"Whatever that means—I want it with you. I want to leave Poland and go to the United States and live in a flat in the middle of New York City. I want children with you, and Shabbat dinners every Friday night, where you serenade us with the heavenly sounds of your violin. This is what I think about—it's what I want, and I yearn for it so badly. But I fear it's a wish we aren't entitled to, not when so many are grieving for love."

"Sadness for others shouldn't diminish your dreams, no matter what is happening out there." Sofia tries to smile, so I lean forward to touch the tip of my nose to hers. "You must believe what I'm saying."

"I do," she says, squeezing my hands. She peeks down at her watch like she does several times an hour. "Papa should be here shortly. He said he'd have something warm for us to eat tonight."

Friedrich has been trying his best to enhance his cooking skills, but it's been a work in progress—one he continuously apologizes for. It wouldn't matter if we were eating stale dumplings, it's food, and that's all we care about.

I think he focuses on the food so he doesn't have to wonder when someone will come knocking on his front door in search of Sofia and Lena.

Unless Sofia's watch has stopped working properly, and the mantle clock is broken, it's already well past our supper time and past the hour we normally go to sleep. From the look on Sofia's and Lena's face, it's clear they are both assuming the worst now.

"Maybe he had to work late," Lena says, peering up at the hatch for the umpteenth time.

"He hasn't worked late once since we've been down here," Sofia utters.

We know he's doing what he must to get through his work during the day, and after hours of tending to the Nazis, he still manages to wear a warm smile when he comes down here to bring us hot food, along with another load of canned goods to store, a fresh supply of water, as well as clean buckets in exchange for the soiled ones. Despite living in the house, he doesn't have it much easier up there than we do down here. If anything, he must feel like the world is weighing on his shoulders.

The minutes tick by, becoming hours, and the heaviness threatens to close our eyelids without knowing what happened to Friedrich today.

After begrudgingly digging into the supply of canned foods for supper, Sofia and I sit down against the wall, facing Lena and the ladder, keeping her company while we watch and wait for Friedrich. Lena refuses to eat.

Filled with worry for her father and mother, I'm sure Sofia has no intention of going to sleep, but her eyes are soon closed. At a closer look, I see they're clenched tightly, and tears are fighting to fall from her lashes. I know she's hurting, and the fact that I can't do anything to take the pain away reminds me of every moment I have lost with my parents.

Lena's arms are folded over her chest and her cheeks are stained red from her tears. I know she won't move from that spot, not tonight.

I adjust my back against the wall to find a more comfortable position, knowing I'm not leaving them, even for a slightly more comfortable sleeping arrangement on the quilts. I'm also pondering the thought of going upstairs to see if I can find out any information. I know Sofia would not agree and I'm aware of the danger involved, but she's in pain and I can't simply sit back and do nothing.

I question what I would see, if I were to see anything. His car would be out front if he came home. If his car is there, he may be inside, which may be a trap. If his car isn't there, he never came home, in which case, maybe there was an emergency he had to tend to at the infirmary.

"What are you thinking about?" Sofia whispers. "You've been staring at the wall in front of us for five minutes without blinking."

"I'm not thinking about anything," I lie.

"You're not going up there," she says, proving she can read my thoughts, which shouldn't come as a surprise after spending every minute with each other for the past month.

"I didn't say I was," I reply.

"I can see by the look in your eyes. You think you're staring straight ahead, but your eyes are moving just enough to tell me you're mapping something out."

I drop my gaze before looking over at Sofia. "I can't bear the thought of you being worried or upset. I want to do something to help."

"You know how dangerous that is. You can't do anything more than I can do."

I take her hand between mine and hold it against my chest. "I'm sorry."

"I know you must assume I'm thinking the worst," she says.

"Of course."

"Well, I'm not—not yet anyway. All I can think about is how I spoke to my father over the last couple of years while he was trying to play this God-awful game of keeping us alive."

"I'm sure he understands how hard this was for everyone," I tell her.

"No, I took it farther than I should have. I was sure he was becoming brainwashed until you showed me a different perspective."

"I didn't realize I was overstepping that day. I apologize."

She brushes a loose strand of hair behind her ear and shakes her head. "I needed to hear the truth, Isaac. If anything, it made me become more understanding, but there were still times we didn't agree on what was best, and it burnt our relationship at the core. The man you see when he comes down here at night is the man I knew before the war. He would go to his practice, help all the people he could help in one day and, somehow, still come home with a smile on his face just for us. He remembered everything I had going on in school. He would ask about each of my friends and their parents, remembering everyone's names and what was happening in their life. He tucked me in every night and even as I got older, he still jokingly checked under the bed for monsters before closing my bedroom door. Then the war happened, and everything felt different. Our difference in religion suddenly mattered when it never had before. Two of us couldn't live with a sense of safety, and I felt disconnected from him. It was the worst feeling, and one I couldn't move past. Now, I must sit and think about the fact that he is putting his life in jeopardy every day for us and I've just realized that I may never get the chance to tell him I understand why he did what he did, and not just say the words, but make him believe that I mean the words." Sofia places the back of her hand over her mouth and closes her eyes.

"No one knew what was happening until it happened," I say. "Even still at this moment, no one knows how much worse it can truly get and we'll still think the same way, wondering if humanity is capable of the destruction we're living through."

Her breath hitches in her throat as she looks at me, her eyes glossed over with a film of tears. "We still don't know anything, and I fear we never will until it's too late."

CHAPTER 45
FEBRUARY 1944

SOFIA

It's been an entire week since Papa has been down here with rations, clean laundry, and water. I could go on starving in filthy clothes, but we ran out of water yesterday, which means we must come up with a solution if we want to reach the end of this war. To know we can only survive for a few days without water makes the thought of Papa being okay hard to believe.

Isaac takes a seat beside me to watch the ladder sway back and forth while I nudge it with my toe. "We need to talk about this," he says.

"What's there to talk about? I was lucky, now I'm not. End of story."

"It's been days and you've hardly eaten, slept, or moved an inch from this spot. Your mother isn't doing much better, yet the two of you seem to be avoiding each other."

"It isn't avoidance, it's grief. We're sitting shiva in silence, alone, encumbering the pain from within."

"How can you grieve without knowledge of someone's passing? I haven't taken a moment to grieve either of my parents because I know that until someone tells me they have proof of their deaths, there is a chance they are still alive. The same goes for your father."

I sigh with aggravation, understanding he has been strong and brave for far longer than I have, but this is a fresh wound for me, and I'm having trouble.

"Your father had been bringing down so many extra crates of canned foods. Maybe he knew we'd be on our own for a bit and didn't want to worry you."

"We still don't know where all the extra food came from. Don't you wonder?"

"No one is able to acquire that many rations. They weren't handed to him. I can say that with surety."

When the ladder swings toward me after a final toe-nudge, I grab the bottom rung and push myself up from the ground. I hold the rope within each hand and stare up at the floorboard overhead. "I need to know where he is." I climb up two rungs, but Isaac's arm curls around my stomach and pulls me off the ladder, twisting me around and blocking me from reaching it again.

"We need water," he says. "I know this, but it's daytime, and for all you know there is someone guarding the front of your house, waiting for you to make an appearance. They won't even send you to the camp, they'll kill you right then and there."

His words paint images within my mind. Yet when someone needs something bad enough, they will do whatever is necessary —no matter the risk.

"What do you suggest?" I ask, knowing I sound bitter toward the man who has done nothing but have patience and understanding for my despondency this last week.

"Tonight, I will go up there and fetch buckets of water."

"You won't know where to find the spare buckets. I'm the one who should go."

"I'll bring the buckets from down here up to the house and refill them. It's okay, I can handle this," he says.

"Will the two of you stop arguing?" Mama hisses at us from the center of the enclosure. We both look over at her—she's never snapped at either of us while we've been down here. She points up to the ceiling. "There is someone up there," she mouths.

She quietly tiptoes toward Isaac and me, her face pale.

In the silence, I hear what Mama must have heard, but I want to pray and plead to God that it's Papa. Maybe Isaac was right, he is alive, and he's come back for us.

The thought doesn't last long as the distant sound of glass breaking travels through cracks in the foundation.

Mama clasps her hands and holds them up to her chin, still staring up at the ceiling as if it's going to break open and expose whatever it is we're listening to.

"Check the shed," a deep, authoritative male voice calls out from what sounds like within the barn walls. It's close, *too* close.

I gasp, then cover my mouth to block out any sound of air coming or going from my lungs. Sometimes I wonder if the Nazis can hear us blink. I squint my eyes close and hold my breath, feeling my heart racing through every part of me. I pray for them to leave. I pray so hard, but I've come to terms with what little my prayers seem to do.

"It's full of rats and mice," someone else says. I almost forgot they were using our shed to store some of the bodies of those who dropped dead during the day while working on our farm. It's been a few months now, but God only knows what remains were left behind.

"Did you check the loft up there?" The question comes from a different voice.

"Twice."

"Whoever tipped you off was either trying to distract you or set you off their trail."

"No, they're here—somewhere."

Whoever they are up there must be standing directly above our heads. The moment I hear footsteps, it's clear they are Nazis. There is a distinct sound that comes along with the boots they all wear. Each step sounds as if their heel has a job of destroying whatever life is beneath them.

"Well, let me know when you find them. I'll be in the car."

The smell of cigarette smoke wafts through the cracks in the floor, permeating the enclosed area. We've all moved in a little closer to one another. Isaac's arm is around me, and Mama closes her eyes and silently prays words I can imagine but cannot hear.

I close my eyes too, fearing the worst while listening to the sound of a stick thumping against the floorboards. If they hit the one that is disjointed, it will sound different. They have done this before. I'm sure they know how to seek out every potential hiding spot. They are predators hunting their prey. I imagine the top shelf of the linen closet across from my bedroom, knowing the uniform of the missing guard is folded into a sheet, hidden well. We kept it in the hope of using it to somehow save Olivia, but each plan we drew up had a greater chance of failure than success, which left us questioning if she was safer without us trying to intervene. There was, and is, no right answer—it's just too late. I want to hope whoever is up there poking around doesn't tear apart the small linen closet, but my fear is taking over the best of my bravery.

Isaac's hand clasps the back of my dress; he's holding me so tightly as if I'm a cliff he can't risk losing a grip on. I open my eyes, finding Mama's chin is trembling as if she's fighting against the emotions threatening to take her down.

I'm not sure when I took my last breath, but I've been holding the air in my lungs and I'm scared to release it. It's hard not to wonder if all of our heartbeats sound like a synchronized drum. The moment reminds me of Edgar Allan Poe's story, *The*

Tell-Tale Heart. The narrator suffers from guilt, causing a form of insanity as he convinces himself that the volume of his heart becomes louder and louder, threatening to give away his hiding place. If it's guilt that causes such an effect, why is it happening to us when we're just innocent human beings trying to survive? Papa used to tell me this story to teach me why lying can be detrimental to a person. I never wanted to lie a day in my life, thinking my mind could end up becoming my worst enemy. Yet, here I am, suffering from within.

The tapping from the stick stops, and after a long minute, heels start clacking, one after another until the sound fades into the distance.

We're all shaking from the fear riveting through our bodies. I don't know how much longer we'll need to wait before we find comfort in knowing they're gone—if they choose to leave at all.

How many more times will we have to endure this terror before one of us makes a noise? Are we just prolonging the inevitable? Are we surrounded and they're smoking us out of the hole we've been hiding in?

It seems like an hour passes before the rumbling of a car gives us a small sense of hope. Is it someone passing by, or are the Nazis giving up the search?

Without moving more than an inch, we've only been able to glance around the area in the fickle light from the lanterns.

"Your father must not be here," Mama says. "He wouldn't have let them search around the property like that."

I want to tell Mama it's obvious Papa isn't here. He would have brought us food and water if he was. It's more likely that the Nazis have been looking for us and Papa refused to turn us in. I doubt they would walk away from unanswered questions. We all knew those men would turn their backs on him the second they had a chance.

"He probably left to avoid a deep search," Isaac suggests.

"Why do they even care of our whereabouts when there are

so many others to focus on? Friedrich is still helping them, and I can't understand why that's not enough to keep them off our property." Mama's face burns with an angry red hue and she grits her teeth. "They've ruined everything and everyone. Lives are over and destroyed, and for what?" Mama takes a book she was reading and slaps it against the wall, over and over through a painful growl. I step over to her and take the book gently from her hands and hold her as tightly as I can until her breaths taper to a calm.

"I found something," Isaac whispers, bravely taking the first step away from Mama and me.

"What is it?"

He makes his way over to the small area between the storage shelves of canned food, and our makeshift washroom and toilet. He squats down, running his hand across the draped insulation Papa hung when it got colder down here a couple of months ago. Isaac pulls the heavy fabric away from the wall, exposing a small metal spout. He twists and fiddles with it for a moment, then a drop of water spills out and onto the floor.

"A pipe, which looks to be angled up to the ground's surface outside of the barn. When I turn the valve, it creates space in the pipe so precipitation runoff can drain down here." We're all a bit bewildered, wondering how Isaac thought to look beneath the insulation. "I noticed the protrusion and couldn't figure out what else it could be. Of course, your papa wouldn't have said anything. He was bringing us fresh water each night. We had no need, but he obviously thought it through while preparing this space."

It explains the nights of loud banging and the vibrations I heard. I should be ashamed for the sheer number of times I doubted him. My anger was relentless, and he continued to endure it, knowing I simply didn't understand.

Isaac tightens the valve on the spout and turns around, falling against the wall. "We're going to be okay," he says.

CHAPTER 46
JUNE 1944

OLIVIA

The week was supposed to hold good news. Rumors spread among us that the Americans had made landfall in France. They're coming to save us—or so I've been told. Of course, no one knows the truth of what is happening outside of these barbed wire gates because we're not privy to the knowledge the rest of the world receives. Therefore, any news of this sort is good enough for us. It could be an inkling of hope that the end of this horror is growing closer.

Each morning and night during roll call, I spot Ruth out of the corner of my eye, lined up in the group to the left. She has avoided me since the night I asked her to find out about Isaac. I tried to approach her a couple of times, but she left quicker than I could call out her name. I took the hint as a sign of bad news—there's nothing else to assume. She must see me for what I am—a child—one who, if I survive this, will become an orphan. It isn't her job to deliver solemn news, or perhaps she was moved to a different administration position.

I'm directly behind her this evening, in line, waiting for our nightly bread. She may not notice me since we strictly face forward as we are told to do, but I gather she knows I'm here.

"I can't bear the thought of hurting you," Ruth says, her voice carrying through a whisper I can hardly hear.

"I've already assumed the worst," I reply. "I didn't mean to make you uncomfortable."

"I'm so sorry, Olivia. I avoided you, wishing to give you more time to have hope. I'm afraid your brother's number is on the list of the perished."

I stare at the stripes of the back of Ruth's headscarf, the white polka dots sway along the black silk as I imagine a dark world, alone. I want to burst into tears and cry until the pain stops burning through me, but I can't. I must stand still and wait my turn to receive a stale piece of bread that will leave me with a scratchy throat until the morning.

I'm not sure what I'm fighting for now. I'm not sure I'm up for the fight if no one is waiting on the other side of those gates for me.

"Olivia, I can nearly hear your thoughts," Ruth whispers again. "Don't you dare give up. If you are alive at the end of this, there is a reason and purpose. You must believe that."

My eyes fill with tears and my teeth chatter. I don't want to keep going, it would be much easier to give up. "Thank you for helping me," I offer.

"Your life is not dependent upon anyone else's. You don't know what the future holds—none of us do, but I believe it holds more than what we are experiencing now. Hold on, dear. Just hold on. Please."

My shoulders collapse from the heaviness of grief, believing the words she's speaking, understanding the complexity of fighting through inhumane situations for the chance of doing something worthy of living someday. I just can't see a future, and I believe that might mean it's because this is all it will be.

CHAPTER 47
SEPTEMBER 1944

SOFIA

It's been just over nine months since Mama and I fell victim to this war, joining Isaac in hiding. It's been seven months since we've seen Papa, and my heart is still as cold as the first night he didn't come down into the bunker after dark. Mama barely talks. We had thought of at least a hundred different reasons why he didn't return, all of them avoiding a reality we can't bear to face. There aren't any sounds or hints of life within or outside of the barn. The last time we heard Nazis scouring the property was five months ago, about two months after the first time they came to search for whatever they think is still here. We're so secluded that if we didn't have a working radio, we would wonder if the world still existed.

Isaac and Mama have asked me to turn off the radio almost daily for the last few weeks—from the time the Warsaw Uprising began in August. The underground Polish resistance are fighting to liberate Warsaw. There is fighting in the streets, and it sounds like a complete massacre of both the Polish and Germans. I'm just not sure how much longer the battle will go on or if our country will come out on top. I want to have hope that the people of our country will succeed in this attack because it could give us the hope that we could be coming to the beginning of the end.

I still listen to the radio, but alone, when Isaac and Mama aren't nearby. Each night, when Mama is straightening up what never needs to be straightened, Isaac shovels waste into the one drainage hole that seeps into the ground beneath us. The smell was unbearable for a while, but we've all become somewhat numb to it—likely because we are a part of it, too. There is no additional degradation the three of us could face after all we've seen of each other down here. Privacy is something I once took for granted. I had no idea of the effect it has on a person when it's taken away. The humility and embarrassment didn't last long, but it's been difficult while undeniably falling in love with a person who shouldn't have to see me in the ways he has. How can beauty be seen through a tarnished lens?

I bring the radio over by the small spout in the wall—our saving grace. Over the last couple of weeks, we've had a lot of rain, and the runoff has been filling our metal bucket. The white noise of the stream will be enough to mask the volume of the radio. A calm, baritone male voice breaks through crackling static.

"*Breaking news: Battle ends in France—the American 7th Army forces continued their quick push up the Rhone Valley after completing their occupation of the coastal regions. This progress can offer Poland hope as American troops continue to plow their way in our directio—*"

"No, no, come back. Come back!" I slap the radio a couple of times, wishing the signal would return so I can hear more, but the silence continues.

We don't know if the Germans are causing radio wave interference or if the reception below the ground is too weak. I can only pray that tonight's update is the hope we didn't have yesterday.

I jump up from the corner and race across the bunker, past Mama, who doesn't so much as blink at my motion, and make my way over to Isaac. He has a handkerchief tied around the lower half of his face to block out the stench. "Isaac, Isaac! You're not going to believe what's happened!" I'm shouting, though trying to control my excitement, but all I've done is made him appear perplexed.

"Are you okay?" he asks, taking my arm to calm me down. "Breathe, Sofia. You're talking so fast. I can't understand—"

"I just listened to the radio for a moment. France is being liberated," I say through heavy breaths.

Isaac's eyes bulge and he places the shovel against the wooden pallet. "France is free?" he repeats in question.

"The broadcaster said this was a good sign for Poland."

"How can it not be?" he says, stifling a laugh. "My God—how did it happen?"

"What's going on?" Mama asks, seemingly snapping out of her typical daze.

"France has been freed from German occupation. Do you know what this means, Mama?" I ask, jumping up and down on my toes.

Mama seems lost, like the information is trickling in and it's taking her a minute to understand what I've said. She places her hand on her cheek and shakes her head as if the news is impossible. "France is free?"

"Yes! Yes, Mama. The American troops are pushing through. Do you think they'll free us soon, too?"

Isaac wraps his arms around me, pulling me into his chest. I close my eyes, praying harder than ever before that this might end.

"Let's pray they find the labor and death camps along their way," he says.

His words make me realize that the non-Jewish people of France were the only ones liberated. Hitler still has a hold of all Jewish lives.

I wonder if wherever Papa is, he knows what's happening, and I wonder what he might be thinking. He always had a better understanding of the news reports than me. I'd do anything to hear him say this is a turning point—maybe we are reaching the horizon of peace, but I can only imagine the words inside my head. I desperately want to believe he's still alive. Maybe he had to leave the house to keep anyone from searching the perimeter. It could have happened suddenly if they tipped him off. I know he wouldn't have risked coming down here to tell us, jeopardizing our safety, but it's been so long. It's hard to keep convincing myself of this story.

CHAPTER 48

OCTOBER 1944

OLIVIA

Some days, I feel like a rusty machine. It's as if I've programmed my body to do the same task over and over until I'm told otherwise. Other days, I feel sorry for myself, the pain creeps in like a virus and weighs every bone in my body down. I'd rather feel nothing than everything. I fixate on details, wishing I could see something different, but the scabs on my hands have become scars, my nails thin, brittle, and split, and my fingertips are raw beneath the layer of coarse skin. My bones protrude, and my wrist is smaller now than it was when I was little. It looks like it could snap if I move the wrong way. When I wipe tears from my eyes, my cheekbones ache and rub harshly against the back of my hand. Bones rubbing together—no one should know how painful it is.

"Do you hear that?" Beatriz asks.

I'm slow to look over at her, having little energy to rotate my neck, let alone my hands that must continue moving at the same pace for hours and hours on end.

After a brief moment, I comprehend what Beatriz is asking

me, so I try to listen beyond the sound of fabrics being folded, bunched, or tossed. The sound of gunshots startles me, though it shouldn't with how often we hear them. Beyond the gunshots, there is screaming and shouting—not something we often hear. The shouts are typical of the Nazis, but bellows and roars from inmates are not—we have all been subdued into silence.

Beatriz stands up from her folded knees and glances around for the guards. I didn't notice the *Wachmänner* had all left. I don't care to notice. They are gone one minute, back in another, and between blinks, I'm being dragged into a small room once again. They're everywhere, even when they're nowhere.

She makes her way over to the door and pokes her head out, then steps outside. I see women running past the barrack. I wonder how they have the strength to move so fast. Walking from here to my assigned barrack leaves me breathless.

Curious to see what's happening outside, I push myself up to my feet, using a nearby barrel for balance and shuffle over to the door. Beatriz is moving closer to the gate that leads to the gas chambers, where an endless line of unsuspecting people approach their death. Beyond her, I see objects flying in the air, gunshots are firing, people are scampering. There's a blur of chaos I can hardly make out from here.

Beatriz twists her head over her shoulder and looks at me as if she was just shot. The shock running through her eyes is alarming, yet I can't seem to muster a reaction. "The gunpowder," she whispers. Because of the commotion, I can only read her lips.

I know that a group of women have been smuggling gunpowder from the crematorium. We've even hidden some in clothing for the resistance, passing them on to others with access to a proper hiding place. I've known about the movement—the plan of resistance, but did not expect this outcome. The intention was to blow up the gas chambers, take the SS by surprise while depleting them of their biggest weapon.

From the number of gunshots firing into the air, I gather the women didn't accomplish what they intended. We knew the plan could go awry, but it sounds as if things have gone terribly wrong.

"There's a fire. I can smell it, can you?"

Anything different from the decaying odor of bodies burning is noticeable. "Yes," I whisper.

Beatriz presses up on her toes, trying to see. From the corner of my eye, I notice a group of *Wachmänner* running in this direction.

"Bea, move away, quick," I say through a heavy breath, looking back at the sight of men racing toward us. She doesn't listen, so I force myself to move faster than I think I can manage, and grab her by the back of her smock, pulling her toward the barrack we should be working in. I manage to get her inside and up against a wall as the guards run by, more concerned with whatever they are running toward than the two of us being nosey.

"The revolt didn't work," Beatriz says, her eyes glazed with tears. "Those poor women."

"We knew it was a bad idea," I remind her. "That's why we stayed away from it all."

"At least they'll die having tried to save others. We'll probably die without having even tried to save ourselves," she says, leaning all her weight against the wall.

"Don't speak like that," I reply, holding my finger up to her nose. "We promised each other we wouldn't talk that way."

Beatriz releases a sardonic laugh. "How long do you think we can survive like this? Even throughout a revolt, I doubt they were able to take down even one dirty *Wachmann* in their attempt to blow up a crematorium. We're nothing in the face of them, and we can't win. You know we're all going to pay for this now," she says, shoving her elbow into the wall.

"Let's just get back to work and keep our heads down. It's kept us alive this long," I remind her.

Beatriz falls to her knees, catching herself only by her palms against a pile of tattered clothing. "Are we even alive, Olivia? What's the difference between this and death?"

I understand her question; I stumble on the very thought every night while I try to fall asleep, hoping a dream will come to me as proof that there is life after this—that we aren't dead, and that we deserve more. Yet the dreams never come, my mind too tired to conjure them up.

CHAPTER 49
JANUARY 1945

OLIVIA

I thought today would be another typical day—the repetitive horrors revolving like a minute hand on a clock—there's never a change.

The commotion outside of the work block is unsettling after the distinct silence we've endured after the attempted revolt. Whatever is happening out there sounds different than that—the shouting is more unified and domineering. I'm not sure it's safe to stand up and look out, but I'm very curious as to what might be happening. Beatriz notices the odd change just as I do, and she peers up from the pile of clothes and stares through me while trying to piece together what she's listening to.

Without making a distinct movement, I glance around the block, finding only one *Wachmann*. Still, there is one, which means we keep working without question.

Beatriz lowers her head and continues to sort, but the lines on her forehead tell me she's worried, which causes my pulse to race a little harder. She doesn't ever seem rattled over much, so I might be underestimating the need for concern.

"*Achtung!*" A *Wachmann* appears in the open doorway of the block. "Everyone up. *Ausrichten!*"

"Why do they want us to line up here?" Beatrice mutters through a whisper.

I don't know more than any other woman here does, but I know well enough to stand and line up as they demanded.

We're all in a line, shoved into the back of one another, waiting for the next direction. My stomach tightens and my lungs feel hollow as my mind races. We're being sent to the gas chamber. That's what this is, there's no other answer.

After all this time, this is how it's going to end for us.

A hand seizes my arm, a *Wachmann* yanks me out of the line and away from the others. I want to scream and fight my way out of his hold, but I've been trained not to do so. I've also come to know that no matter what I do, it will still end the same way.

We're spinning around or maybe I'm just dizzy, but before I can find something stable to focus on, I'm thrown into the same room I've unwillingly been in day after day. Except today, the *Wachmann* is different. I remember him—he's the one who tried to take me from the one who has claimed me as his.

"Your beloved *Wachmann* is gone now," he growls. "Finally, there's nothing standing in my way."

My beloved: the one who has stolen everything I had left and stripped me of hope. What a heinous thing to say, even after all I have heard.

The small room spins around me as I come to awareness. I'm not sure when I fell or became unconscious, but my entire body aches as if I've been stabbed with a thousand knives everywhere and all at once. I try to sit up against the metal shelving behind me, but the pain is almost unbearable, and I notice a pool of blood saturating the bottom half of my smock.

He left me here to die.

For the first time in as long as I can remember, tears fill my eyes and heavy sobs buck through my chest.

I want Mama and Papa. I want Isaac.

CHAPTER 50

MAY 1, 1945

SOFIA

For almost a year, Isaac and Mama have dreaded listening to the radio, wasting the remaining batteries we have, losing the remnants of hope, gaining more fear—they felt it has been pointless to listen to the monotonous broadcasts.

I don't agree with their feelings on the matter. Personally, I need to hear every detail available through radio waves. Every word can mean something hopeful and offer a prediction to various outcomes of whatever lies ahead. I try to keep Isaac and Mama motivated with my thoughts of what I'm listening to, but deep down, I think I might only be deluding myself that there is any chance of hope left. Yet, today, something feels different.

"Just today, please. Sit with me and listen. I feel like they're about to say something important. There have been so many pauses in the broadcasts today. I feel it in my bones, Isaac. Just listen, please."

"You know I can't say no to you," he replies. "You use your big doll-like eyes as weapons on me. It isn't fair, Sofia."

"Something is happening today, I just know it," I say, ignoring his flattery.

"Okay, okay. Turn up the volume."

I twist the knob, finding static, but after just a moment, the static comes to an eruptive stop as if the radio died. We both stare at the wooden box, waiting to see what happened to the sound.

Then, our answer comes in loud and clear.

"*We have a somber and significant announcement,*" a male reporter, who sounds as if he has something lodged in his throat, warns. Stark silence follows.

CHAPTER 51

MAY 1, 1945

ISAAC

The chest-rattling sound of baritone horns and the falsetto of tubas mystify the foreshadowing of what's to come. The symphony has been playing through the speakers for over a half-hour, causing an immense amount of apprehension, making me wonder if whoever is responsible for this broadcast has intent for the way this music is making the listeners feel.

"I can't imagine why they're playing Bruckner's *Symphony No. 7* Adagio. It's like they're trying to tell us something without saying it," I mutter without losing eye contact with the radio.

"I don't understand," Sofia follows.

"Me neither," Lena says, holding her hand to her chest.

A low beat of a drum rolls through an elongated vibration, followed three more times, identically.

After months of wanting to avoid the radio, Sofia's adamance about the importance of whatever might be happening has captured my attention. I'm not sure any of us have blinked an eyelash as we've been staring at the radio, waiting for it to speak to us. My chest aches with wonder, feeling paranoid, and yet slightly hopeful because Sofia still has a look of possibility running through her beautiful eyes.

As the music fades to silence, an announcement finally begins after the torturous wait.

"The Fuhrer of the third Reich, Adolf Hitler, had fallen this afternoon while fighting at the head of his troops," the reporter says, speaking slowly as if translating words from a different language.

"Fallen?" I reply as if the man broadcasting this announcement can hear me. "They expect us to believe that?"

Hitler was not one to fight with his troops. He has always hidden behind others. I don't know who will believe any of this. Just as the thoughts ruminate, I notice the different reaction Sofia and Lena are having.

Their eyes light up like shooting stars, brightening the darkest of nights as they hug, kiss, and thank God, but none of us know what his death means—if it's even true. He had brainwashed an entire country, trained so many of them to think just the way he had. Would his army consider his death a chance for freedom, or would there be an arms race to take over, not helping those of us left as prisoners of this war?

"Isaac, didn't you hear what the broadcaster said?" Sofia asks, pulling my hands away from my hips. She's never looked so happy and I'm not sure I have the heart to tell her what thoughts are going through my mind. Maybe I'm not capable of hope anymore. I shouldn't impose that onto them.

"I'm—I'm not sure what to say or think. I think I might be in shock," I reply.

Lena places her hand on my shoulder. "This is good news, sweetheart. Very, very good news."

I want to ask her how she knows—how she can predict the future. Have I truly become this cynical?

CHAPTER 52

MAY 1945

ISAAC

Since the breaking news of Hitler's death, we've waited and listened to the radio almost every waking moment to hear what comes next. Lena and Sofia are waiting for the news they are hoping for beyond the assumptions spoken across the radio—that this state of war will all just come to an end. I want that more than anything, but I fear the thought of letting my guard down. The dread of what else could happen terrifies me, knowing we can't survive down here much longer. We need clarity before we can consider braving the outside world after how long we have remained hidden.

I've been awake for a bit and have kept the radio volume low to allow Sofia and Lena to sleep longer. Sofia's head is resting on my lap, and I've been combing my fingers through her hair for the last hour, listening to static between cut-off words.

The static grows stronger before turning silent. After several seconds of staring at the radio wondering why I can't hear a sound, a clear deep voice speaks:

"Today, on the eighth day of May in the year 1945, I am

coming to you—our nation—to announce that the unconditional surrender of the German Third Reich was signed yesterday to take effect today—officially ending the European conflict."

Uncontrollable tears fill my eyes as I grab Sofia by the shoulders and lower my head toward hers. "Sweetheart," I whisper in her ear, "wake up, wake up! It's official. The war is over."

Sofia is out of sorts as she lifts her head. "What?"

"Listen? Listen to the radio—" I turn the volume up as the announcer repeats his words again.

"Mama," Sofia cries out. "Mama!"

Lena is already awake. Her eyes are open, staring at us with tears running down her face. She sits up and wipes her jittering hands across her cheeks. "We're free?"

I feel the need to ask for validation too, but we are hiding from the Third Reich, and they have surrendered. "Yes, we're free," I answer.

Sofia pulls herself up to her knees and clamps her hands around my face, kissing me with all the strength she must have in her body. Her arms loop around my neck, squeezing the air out of my lungs. "I don't have words," she says.

"Come on, let's take that first step. There's a world out there waiting for us," I say.

"Hopefully, Olivia and Papa are part of that world," Sofia replies, holding her hand to her heart. "Please God. Please let us find them."

CHAPTER 53

MAY 1945

SOFIA

Five hundred and three days—that's how long it's been since I've seen the sun, a drop of rain falling, an innocent cloud sailing across the blue sky. With only a supply of batteries for the radio, two drum barrels of kerosene for the lanterns, and a supply of canned foods we meticulously distributed, we've collected buckets of water from precipitation runoff to keep us alive. We didn't know how long the food would last, and we were down to the last gallons of kerosene. Every day has been one with unanswered questions as we sat, confined with the worst of our imaginations.

My nightmares often included one of the three of us dying down here—it would always be someone different passing away, but in the quiet of long nighttime hours, the dreams felt so real and I would often wonder what would happen if I was here alone, the only one left. I'm not sure I could go on.

I should feel free and full of life as we make our way out of the barn. The sun blinds us all as we hold our arms up to our heads to shield some of the brightness. The farmland is brown and uncared for, but the horizon—the mountains, the beautiful clouds skating across the sea of blue sky—it's more beautiful than I remember.

The air is like ice-cold water on a hot day, filling my body with what it has desired so much. The scent of wildflowers fills the air and I want to fall to the soil and relish in all the senses I have been deprived of.

I've convinced myself Papa is hiding, even though I can't find a reason why he would be hiding in a different location than we are in. But our house awaits us and I need to see inside. We approach the back door first. My hands are shaking, just as Mama's are as we wriggle the doorknob, but it's locked.

Isaac's determination to get inside is clear, despite the back door being locked. He's stomping ahead toward the front of the house as Mama and I shuffle behind in his path. If the door isn't locked, Papa left without a choice.

As I turn the corner from the side yard to the front, I find Isaac banging on the door with his fist. "Dammit, it's locked."

My chest fills with heaviness and my heart races with optimism. Maybe I was right. He's hiding somewhere. He could still be alive.

I look over at Mama. Her hand trembles over her mouth as the sun shines down over her, accenting the white strands now woven through her coffee brown hair.

The wooden steps up to the porch feel softer than I remember, but the cedar rocking chair we've all spent many hours on still looks exactly the way it did the last time I fell into it. I kneel by the armrest and slide my hand beneath the affixed boards, finding a key we hid in case any of us ever got locked out. We never needed it. Before the war, we barely ever locked the door, and afterward, it was rare that we left the house. When we did, we had to carry more than just a key. Our papers to show origin and residency, as well as a ration card, all had to come along when we left to run an errand.

I try my best to steady my hand while unlocking the front door, but I'm scratching the metal around the keyhole.

Isaac takes the key from me and wraps his free arm around my shoulders. "It's okay," he says, unlocking the door without trouble.

He allows Mama and me to step in first. Dust covers the floor, the grandfather clock, and empty coat rack that's lying on its side across the oriental rug, which is covered with muddy footprints. All the furniture has been turned over, shoved across the room, or broken into pieces. Even with everything out of order and all our belongings scattered into disarray, the worst part I see is the dust on Papa's house slippers that he changes into from his work shoes.

I feel like a stranger inside, wishing everything felt familiar. Yet nothing does, even though the décor is demolished—I suppose that nothing will ever feel the same again. I'm not sure what we were hoping to find, but perhaps it shouldn't be shocking to discover our house the way we left it almost two years ago.

Mama walks into the kitchen, her favorite room in the house, and skims her fingertips along the counters as if she's collecting the residue of memories.

"Sofia," Isaac says, his voice soft and hoarse. He's over by the kitchen table, the placemats squarely aligned as we always left them, a vase in the center encircled by the dust of the dead forget-me-nots—the last bunch of flowers I placed there.

Isaac hands me a folded piece of paper, his hand shaking as mine was.

"What's this?" I ask.

His gaze falls away from mine as he reaches the paper out a little closer to me.

I take it, allowing the paper's crease to loosen and unfold as I lift it up.

"What is—th-a—?" Mama asks, her voice so weak she can't make enough sound to enunciate her words.

My chin quivers when I recognize Papa's handwriting. I do what I can to pull my strength together so I can read his words, sparing her the pain of having to read them, too.

"My Dearest Darlings, I pray this note finds you, which would mean you have survived, and our home is still intact. If you are reading this, you have defied many odds, and I thank God if this is the case.

"I returned from work tonight and found that someone or several people have ransacked our house. I'm not sure who was in here or what they were looking for, but along with every room, each closet and both washrooms have been torn to pieces. The Nazi's uniform is also gone, which means there is one less missing German soldier.

"There is a car parked out front, so I am writing this as quickly as I can. I'm sure they are here to collect me. I don't know what will happen, but I fear the worst.

"If I may ask one thing of you both: please don't take fault or blame for anything that has happened over the last few years. It is me who is at fault. It is me who is not Jewish, and me who tried to do what was best for our family, but me, who has failed. I would step in front of the SS for you over and over, and I tried—it's all I tried to do.

"From the time that I was a child, I wanted to care for people, save them with science, and a gentle hand, protecting people from the horrible effects of life. So, I became a doctor. Those were my only intentions until I met you, Lena, and we had you, Sofia. Then, you became my world, and I needed to be all those things to you too. I'm sorry I have let you down. Please, remember me for what I wanted, my intentions, and my love for you. Take me in your heart and keep me there always.

"I may not be sure of what's coming, but I'm certain this is not what any of us wanted.

"*My love, forget the moments of war, and remember us for the moments we could never forget.*

"*Mały myszka, I live within you and whatever you choose to do with your life, know I will be proud, and I will be by your side, watching the fruits of my labor carry on with more passion and strength than I could ever have. You are my pride, and I love you so very much. Take care, my sweetheart,*

"*Xx*"

The note falls from my grip, and I press the heels of my hands into the center of my chest. My knees weaken and threaten to give out, but Isaac wraps his arms around me. A chair from the table scrapes against the floor, and Mama collapses into the seat, her eyes wide, unfocused, but staring through the wall in front of her. Her mouth falls ajar—it's as if the shock keeps hitting her for the first time again and again. It seems Mama might have convinced herself the worst would not happen, and now she's facing a reality I wish we could both avoid.

I should be strong for her. I should hold her like Papa would, but I'm selfishly falling apart. He was her whole life—her past, present, and should have been her future. After all the suffering, there's only more to face.

CHAPTER 54
MAY 1945

ISAAC

When a reader reaches the last page of a book, the spine creaks as the back cover closes—a definitive end, and time to place the story up on a shelf for the next person. War is not like a book—there is no end. The tremors are everlasting.

It's been a couple of days to regain our bearings and scour for news and information on what's happening outside the vicinity of the farm, but it's hard to find much of what's happening locally from here. "I'm going to walk into town, toward Auschwitz, to see what information I can gather. I don't have a clue how to find lost family members. I'm hoping there's a resource somewhere that can help," I say.

"I'll go with you," Sofia says. "You shouldn't go alone. I can't imagine what's going on out there right now."

"I can't ask you to do that. Your mother needs you. You need time. This is all too much for anyone to handle."

I waited after Sofia read the letter from Friedrich, not wanting to take away from their pain, but every minute counts and I can't sit here wondering if Olivia is alive somewhere.

I don't feel right leaving Sofia behind, but I also don't want to drag her along at a time when she's being forced to accept her worst nightmare.

"Take her with you," Lena says. "There's no purpose in sitting here wondering with worry after doing so for the last eighteen months."

"Mama, I can't leave you like this. Isaac is right," Sofia says.

"Have you forgotten where half of your strength has come from?" Lena asks with tears in her eyes. "You know very well I will be fine. Plus, I have plenty to clean here, too."

Sofia bites her fingernail, making it clear she's struggling to decide what's best.

"I—" She looks between her mother and me.

"Sofia, I won't say it again. I don't want Isaac going to town alone. Two is better than one. So, please go."

Sofia drops her head and obeys Lena. Respect for our parents doesn't grow old with age, and I would obey mine if they were standing here now. I would do just about anything to see them standing here right now.

"We'll see about finding food too," I say.

Lena stands up from her chair and crosses the kitchen, reaching into a cabinet. She pulls out a can of beans, flips it over, and presses the circular bottom, showing the can has been pre-cut. A handful of coins falls into her hand, and she reaches her clenched fist out to me. "Whatever you can get, please do."

I drop the coins into my pocket and take Sofia's limp hand in mine. "We won't stay out long, I don't want you to worry," I tell Lena.

"Do what you have to do to find out about your sister. Please, don't worry about me, I beg of you."

Sofia thrusts her arms around Lena's neck and squeezes her. Their cheek-to-cheek moment sends shooting pains through my heart as I pray to feel the same if I'm fortunate enough to find Olivia.

I dip my head and pull in a deep breath before heading for the front door. When I open the door and wave Sofia out ahead of me, I realize Friedrich's car isn't here. I wonder if the SS took it, if it was stolen, or if they forced him to drive somewhere. I'm not sure we will ever find out.

Our legs struggle with each step, proving the weakness that has taken over our bodies. Though the long trek is challenging, the fresh air is a welcome change from the conditions we've been living in. Sofia is quiet, but I can almost hear her contemplating the many thoughts that must be churning through her mind.

"I shouldn't have told you not to expect the worst when you told me you were mourning your father's death," I say in a low voice. I was wrong to tell her that.

"Never say that. Your words of hope kept me alive," she says. "We have a letter, and I should be thankful for just that. Most aren't so lucky, I'm sure."

I would do anything to read a letter from Mama, Papa, or Olivia.

After a long hour of walking, we enter the village of Oświęcim. We hold each other's hands so tightly it's as if we're each other's ledge, both hanging from a cliff.

"Do you hear that?" I ask.

Sofia glances down as we continue to walk, silent as she seems to listen for the growing sound. "Are people cheering?" she asks.

"I'm not sure..."

The farther we walk, the horizon unravels the sight of people crowded in the streets. It's a sign of good, but I feel like I'm watching it all play out on a picture screen in front of me—as if it isn't real.

The closer we get, the easier it is to see that most of those who are cheering don't appear to be prisoners. Sofia and I are both trying to look in every direction at once, trying to take in our surroundings. A young boy on the side of the road is waving a newspaper around, with a dozen more folded up in his satchel. Beside him is a sign that says twenty-five grosses.

Sofia notices the boy too and reaches into my pocket for the money Lena gave us. "Information is as necessary as food," she says, sorting through the coins in her hand. She pays the boy for a newspaper and begins flipping through it while we continue to walk forward toward heavier areas of crowds. "The Soviets—the Red Army liberated Auschwitz in January," Sofia says, sounding as if she's comprehending the meaning as she speaks. "Four months ago—I didn't hear this on the radio. Why didn't we hear this?"

I stop walking, knowing there is no proper direction to head toward.

She continues to flip through the pages, and I stop myself from taking the paper, needing to know everything mentioned within those pages. "There's a rehabilitation and family connection program set up for displaced families."

"Where?" I croak out with frustration. "Where the hell will we find that?" Even after everything we've gone through, my head is reeling—I feel like I'm spinning in circles, and there isn't much preventing me from screaming for help to whoever will listen.

Sofia grabs my arm, pinching my skin. "There's a tent over there for the Red Cross. Maybe they can help."

The ground feels like it's moving against me as we walk the two long blocks, finding a line of others waiting their turn.

Sofia wraps her arm around my elbow and presses her head against my shoulder. "We're almost there."

"Where? There's no saying they'll have any helpful information." I can't help my sour attitude. I believe miracles find those with hope, and if I've lost that, I'll lose Olivia like I lost my parents.

When it's our turn to approach the woman standing at the head of our line, she clasps her fingers together and rests them over a clipboard. "How can I help you?" She speaks in English, and I search for the words to reply.

"I'm looking for my sister. She was in Auschwitz," I say, my voice stuttering.

The woman takes her pencil and flips through several pages attached to her clipboard. "What is your name?"

"Isaac Cohen, son of Ludwig and Ania Cohen, brother to Olivia Cohen from Krakow—deported to Warsaw in 1939."

She writes down the information I've given her, then reaches below the table for a binder full of papers. "Just a moment."

It takes more than a few moments before she scans through the long list of families by the name of Cohen. She reaches the end of the list and glances up at me with sorrow before looking back down again and starting afresh from the top. My heart threatens to stop beating and I feel breathless as the woman drags her perfectly shaped fingernail down the long list again, stopping just before reaching the bottom again. With a look of intrigue, she flips to another page in the binder and drags her finger down another column. "Your sister, Olivia Cohen, she is staying in a shelter in Krakow. I will write out the information for you so you can locate her."

"She's alive?" I cry out.

"Yes, sir, it says here she is alive and living at this location," the woman says, swallowing as hard as I am trying to.

She writes the location down on a small notecard and all I can do is look up to the sky and fall to my knees. Heavy sobs erupt from my throat, and I clutch my chest while rocking back and forth. "Thank you, God. Thank you," I squawk. "She's alive. Sofia, she's alive. She survived. She survived. I don't know how, but she did."

Sofia takes the card from the woman's hand and thanks her. She leans forward and takes my hands in hers. "She's waiting for you."

I push myself up to my feet and fold over Sofia, squeezing her like a flimsy blanket. The tears won't stop, and it's hard to see through the blur. I'm out of breath—numb, and yet alive, all at the same time.

CHAPTER 55
MAY 1945

ISAAC

It's very late at night by time we arrive in Krakow. We found some bread, flour, and fish to take home to Lena, had a bite to eat, and left for the train station. Lena told us not to worry about her and take our time. She said she would be busy preparing space for Olivia, and cooking with what we brought her.

I don't understand how Lena can offer to do so much for me when I've been lucky enough to receive the miracle rather than her. It's hard to comprehend what I've done to deserve it, but I'm beyond grateful for the pieces of my past that I have left, though devastated, knowing I will never see Mama and Papa again. They weren't on the list. The hope I held onto for so long —it was for nothing. I should have been honest with myself, but I don't know why God spared Olivia and me, and not them. I'm going to need to be strong for Olivia. I'm going to need to be everything she has lost, and yet I don't know how. I should assume Mama and Papa didn't make it, but I need Olivia to have a future.

"What are you thinking about?" Sofia asks, taking my hand in hers as we walk down the damp streets.

"My parents," I say. "I was foolish to think—"

"No, you weren't," she says, lifting my clenched fist to her lips. "We had no choice but to hold onto some form of hope. We would have had nothing else. We were spared of knowing the truth until we could handle it all."

"I'm not sure what I can handle, Sofia."

"My papa would have a response to your statement. When I was younger and he would tell me about new, risky medical procedures he was responsible for conducting, he told me when life feels too big to conquer, the only way through is to take one small but certain step at a time. That way, we're always moving forward, even when we don't know where we're—where—"

I twist my head to see why Sofia has stopped talking, finding her holding in a lungful of air, her face becoming red, and her brows knitting together. Her hand is burning up in mine and clammy.

"Sofia, stop—" I say, tugging at her to stop her from walking. "Are you all right?"

The movement of her head is so slight, it's not clear if she's trying to answer, but I already know she's not okay.

She sniffles and a shuttered breath catches in her throat. "He's really gone. And your parents too. How did we get here? Why? I can't understand," she questions through a raspy whimper.

I wrap my arms around her frail body, pulling her in tightly to press my lips to her head. I wish I had something more to say, but I don't. The pain is so raw, and I don't know when the gaping holes in our hearts will feel full again, if they ever will. I understand her, and she understands me. That's all we can offer each other.

"I'm sorry. I shouldn't have made this about me when you're just finding out about your parents. I'm fine."

"We're not fine, and that's okay," I tell her.

She runs her free hand beneath her eyes, drying up the tears. "Let's go find Olivia. We need some happiness."

I kiss her forehead, then her lips.

"Just hang onto me, and I'll hang onto you, okay?"

"Okay," she whispers.

The streets become darker, the farther we walk, only lit by faint streetlamps, making it hard to see which building number matches the one written on the notecard. A faded number—the one I'm looking for—comes into view and I knock on the door without a moment's hesitation.

There's a long span of silence before I hear someone rustling behind the door. An elderly woman answers, a nightcap crookedly resting on the top of her unruly white hair, and she struggles against the heavy bags beneath her aged eyes. "Can I help you?" she asks, looking between Sofia and me.

"Yes, I'm looking for Olivia Cohen, my sister. Please tell me she's here with you. Please," I beg.

The woman closes her eyes, and a small smile stretches across her lips. She presses her hands together in prayer and tilts her head toward the ceiling. "God bless you," she says, taking a step away from the center of the doorway. The inside is dark, filled with old worn furniture, lit by a few scattered candles, and smells of pipe tobacco, but it looks clean and welcoming, thankfully. "I must warn you, she arrived here in rough shape. She's been through a lot. I've done my very best to help her, but I'm not sure I've done enough. I know she will be grateful to find out you're alive. She thought you were gone."

My tongue feels swollen in my throat, wondering what any of what this woman is saying could mean. I'm terrified Olivia will be a stranger to me. I fear she may hate me for leaving her, though I never intended to. "Are you sure she'd want to see me?" I don't know why I ask because I'm certainly not leaving here without her, but I need the answer.

"I can't answer that with fairness. Olivia hasn't spoken a word since she arrived here. I was given a report on her situation through the Red Cross."

"Her situation?" I question.

"Why don't you follow me," she says.

I look over my shoulder at Sofia. She's wide-eyed—the look that tells me too many thoughts are going through her mind at once.

We follow the woman up a set of narrow stairs and in through a door leading to a another dimly lit space. It looks like a living room of sorts, one with more similar furniture to what was downstairs, but there's also a crooked oak table with one leg shorter than the other three. It's covered with books, most of which are missing half the spine's outer casing. It's a far better place than where she was—where we were.

"Wait here. Let me find her, they're all asleep."

"It's cozy here," Sofia says.

I nod, knowing anything could be described that way after the way we've been living.

The woman disappears into the blinding darkness and my heart pounds with heavy thuds, listening for the sound of another set of footsteps.

She's still as quiet on her feet as she always was. I see her before I hear her. The shadow of my sister appears in a faint light from the hallway, and she covers her mouth before squeezing her eyes shut. I try to hold myself back from running toward her, afraid of what emotional or physical state she's in. Olivia's hands drop to the sides of her pale-yellow cotton pajamas and tears fall from her eyes. "I-Isaac," she questions in hushed tones, walking toward me carefully as if I might disappear if she moves too fast. "You—you're—"

She's so much older now. She looks like Mama, just like her, and her hair has grown out, but is shortly cut to her chin. She's very thin and looks frail, and hasn't grown much taller, but there isn't a question that she is the Olivia I've always known. The sadness within her eyes is somehow encircled with a fierce inflection of strength.

I reach out for her, hoping she'll come closer. As if a rope was holding her back and was suddenly cut, she flies into my arms. I lift her up and spin her around, kissing the side of her face. "I'm here. I'm here, Lu-lu." I place her down, catching a sight of Sofia standing behind her. Sofia's hands are folded over her chest, pressing her fingernails into her skin so tightly she's going to leave bruises. "She's here. This is my sister. She's here," I tell Sofia, needing to hear myself say it out loud again.

"I thought you were dead," she cries out through hoarse words.

"No. No, I'm not. I didn't mean to leave you. I thought I could save you. I truly did, and then I couldn't. My God, I'm so sorry—I am so, so sorry."

Olivia locks her arms around my arm. "I don't care how things came to be, as long as you're alive."

"I'm alive because of Sofia, the woman beside me. She pulled me off the farm. We've been hiding in a bunker all this time."

Olivia loosens her grip around my neck and drops to her feet, taking the two small steps over to Sofia. "You kept my brother alive. I'm not sure I'll ever know how to repay you."

"Please don't think that way," replies Sofia. "Isaac has spent every day thinking of you, trying to help you out of that place."

I can't stop staring at my little sister, the woman she's become. "You're sixteen. I can't wrap my head around this. Look at you. You survived all this on your own. I can't tell you what that says about you, but, my God, you are a warrior."

Olivia's smile fades and the look behind her eyes darkens. "We all did what we had to, to survive," she says, knocking the wind right back out of me.

I take my sister back into my arms and hold her head to my

chest, hoping she doesn't see the devastation tearing through me.

EPILOGUE
MARCH 1963

SOFIA, NEW YORK

"Thank you for all your help today, Sofia. Your extra hours haven't gone unnoticed, and come later this spring, it will be our honor to have you join our staff here."

With shock running through my veins, I reach my hand out to shake Dr. Sullivan's. This was always my dream, but I couldn't fathom this day ever coming, not in a time when a woman in a doctor's coat is so rare. Papa always said if I wanted something badly enough, it would happen for me, but I didn't always believe those words to be true until now. "I'm honored for your consideration. Helping others, caring for people, and giving everyone the chance to get better—it's all I've ever wanted."

Dr. Sullivan clears his throat behind a slight smile and bounces on his toes. "You've made that quite clear through your years of hard work. I look forward to calling you Dr. Cohen soon."

My smile is stretching from ear to ear as I rush down the busy New York City streets toward our Brooklyn apartment.

We found a wonderful community, filled with others who have emigrated here over the last decade. It's a quiet spot offset from the busy streets, and the families like to congregate on the sidewalks and chit-chat on the front steps of the building. We're all like a big family here, and we each come bearing our own stories, our own scars, from our pasts before America. Though many of us choose to remain quiet about what we left behind, it's a mutual understanding.

I turn the last corner toward home and the tranquil sounds of a bow against strings swim through the air, bouncing off the other buildings. The music flows through the ground and I can feel it throughout my entire body. Listening to him play never gets old.

As always, Isaac is performing for a small audience, serenading our neighbors with his orchestral talent. I've begged him to try out for a local orchestra chamber, but he isn't interested in being conducted—he said he wants the freedom to play where and what he wants. It's something for him—and for him alone.

"Some people might enjoy a little quiet around here," I say, teasing him as I approach. "Plus, tomorrow is Shabbat, and you don't want to wear yourself out before entertaining your loving family before dinner, do you?"

"Oh, stop your kvetching," Gertrude, our eighty-year-old neighbor, says. "Listening to your Isaac is like listening to the heavens sing us a lullaby." She places her hand on her chest and swivels her head up into the air.

Isaac is grinning at the attention.

"For someone who likes to keep his talent so private, you're growing quite an audience out here," I say, leaning down to kiss my adoring husband after a long day.

"What can I say? You know I'm a blast, and the ladies love me," he coos with a cute shrug.

"Gosh, I can't imagine why." I might mind if they weren't all in their seventies and eighties, but I know he's just trying to make them all smile and laugh with his music and wit. That's what we do here—smile and laugh, all the time—whenever possible.

"The girls are finishing up their homework inside with Grammy," he says, "and dinner will be ready soon. We need to be at Olivia's showcase by seven."

Isaac stands up from the steps and bows toward the lovely ladies who are still staring at him. He extends his elbow out for me to grab and leads us up the stairs to the front door.

"Dr. Sullivan told me they will have an open position for me later in the spring," I blurt.

We stop short just inside the lobby door, and Isaac's jaw drops. He lifts me up with his one free arm and growls with excitement. "Are you kidding? Sweetheart, I'm so proud of you. I—Oh my God, we must celebrate. Your father would go crazy right now. You know that, right?" Isaac kisses me, continuing to talk against my lips. "I can't believe my wife is going to be a doctor. I'm the luckiest man in the world, and I still don't know why."

The thought of Papa makes me swallow a small lump in my throat, but what Isaac said is true, and it's all I could think about on the way home. Part of me feels like the job offer was nothing less than a miracle created by my guardian angel, who knows how much I wanted to follow in his footsteps.

Coming from a life like we did, our world here—it's perfection. It's something beyond perfection. It's hard to believe it's been nineteen years since I stared out of a window from a tall building in the middle of Warsaw. I'll never forget looking down upon fellow Jewish men and women, imprisoned by brick walls. I didn't know I was staring down at Isaac, Olivia, or their parents, nor did I understand that I was overlooking almost four hundred thousand people living on the streets or underground in the sewers, in holes in the wall, or worse.

It was then that our paths crossed, and I was none the wiser, but the pain I recall feeling in my stomach made me want to cry and plead with Papa to help those innocent people. I didn't realize I didn't have to ask because he had been quietly thinking the same.

Against all the odds, Isaac and I survived. We crossed the threshold from a nightmare to something almost unbelievable. Was it life, or are we dreaming? I still often wonder about this question when so many others didn't get a chance.

We discovered through records released after the Nuremberg trials ended in 1946 that Papa was killed on account of treason and for not surrendering information of our whereabouts. He sacrificed his life for ours. I wish I could go back in time and change so much, but life doesn't allow for those kinds of second chances, so I've done everything I can to become grateful for the one I've been given, and also to honor him in everything I do.

The more time that passed after the war ended, more information became available to us. Isaac continued to search for information regarding his parents, but it took a while to acquire documentation of what had happened to them. He learned they perished in two separate death camps, his mama in Treblinka, and his papa at Chelmno, following their days in Warsaw. I thought it would be a lot for him to handle, but instead, Isaac felt a sense of relief, knowing they hopefully didn't have to suffer as long as many did. It was the information he needed to move forward. It was time to end our story—it was the end before our beginning.

Once we start over in life, we keep moving forward. It was a pact we all made upon arriving at Ellis Island: *Never look back, only remember the good of what was left behind.*

We make the short hike up to the fourth floor and down the short hallway to our apartment.

Isaac swings open the door and places his violin in its case on the coffee table. "Hey, Ma, look what I found on the street," he jokes with Mama.

"Oy, your jokes are getting worse by the day, you know that?" she replies with a look of giddiness in her eyes. "Dinner will be ready in just a few minutes, and the girls are just about washed up, so we're all ready when Auntie Lu-lu arrives."

Mama chose the path of being the world's most wonderful mother, mother-in-law, fill-in-mother, and grandmother. I thought someday she might consider searching for a companion, especially after being alone for so long, but when I ask her if she's interested in meeting a man, she smiles and tells me she already has everything she could ask for, though I hear her talking to Papa when she thinks she's alone. It comforts me to know he's watching over her, and she feels it. What came as a surprise to me was that after all those years of parenting me, she welcomed the idea of looking after our twin girls, Layla and Lenora, while we're both at work all day. She said it would be her greatest joy to spend her days with her grand-daughters. That, and she would do anything to allow me to grow into the person I dreamed of becoming because it's all Papa wanted for me.

"Dinner smells wonderful," I tell Mama.

"It's just dumplings, something quick and easy."

"My favorite," I say, giving her a hug.

"I know," she replies, squeezing my chin between her fingers, then poking my nose.

"Mommy!" The girls run out of their bedroom, shouting for me in unison.

"How are my favorite little girls, and how was school today?" Both are dressed in their favorite black-and-white checkered dresses, their dark hair adorned with red ribbons. They like to talk at the same time, and we joke that it's because they are identical twins, but Isaac also thinks it's an inherited gene they got from me. In any case, we often can't get them to stop long enough to get a word in. Mama said I had it coming to me. I suppose I can understand.

"Someone has to take a breath," Isaac says. "The first person to be quiet for three whole seconds gets an extra scoop of whipped cream on their chocolate milk."

Both girls pretend to lock up their lips before jumping into their seats at the dinner table.

"That never works for me," I tell him.

"I didn't know you wanted whipped cream on your chocolate milk, sweetheart. You should have said something." Isaac hunches over with laughter alongside the twins falling into a fit of giggles at their dad. "I'm kidding, I'm kidding. It's because you never stop talking, either."

Mama shoves him into his chair as she walks by and mutters an insult in Polish, so the girls don't know what she's saying.

"Olivia called me on my lunch break, telling me she had the jitters about tonight," I announce while helping Mama with the drink glasses.

"I can't say I blame her, but she's ready for this," Isaac says. "The show, and the aftershow."

"She called me too," Mama adds. "She's full of nerves, the poor thing. She doesn't even know the half of it." We all chuckle, but not at Olivia's expense, only for the excitement that lies ahead.

The front door of the apartment swishes open. "The best aunt in the world has arrived," Olivia coos, kneeling for the incoming hugs from her lookalike nieces. With each hug I watch her receive, another part of me heals.

Olivia has been through more than the rest of us, and it took her years to work through the trauma she endured at Auschwitz. There was a time when no one could come near her without announcing they were close by first, and it wasn't until a couple of years ago that she was able to convince herself that all unfamiliar men are not as awful as the ones who tortured her. It wasn't something we could just tell her. Her scars run deep, but her strength is unworldly.

The thought of letting someone else take over and hold her hand through everything to come in life is hard. She's like my sister. She is my sister, but I know this is hardest for Isaac. He's been there to hold her up and to help her restore her faith in humanity as he did the same on his own—as we all did. He will laugh rather than show he's not ready to hand her over to someone, but I don't doubt that Olivia will still be here just as often as she is and always has been.

"Are you excited for your big debut?" Isaac asks his sister. "Who would have thought I'd be famous for having a famous sister?"

Olivia swats at Isaac, just like Mama does so often. "Nice try. You don't get to be famous just because you're my brother."

"I suppose, but I'm proud of you, and you can't take that away from me," Isaac says.

"Nothing sentimental tonight, you promised!" she scolds him. "I need to powder my nose. You can all start eating, I don't want to hold you up."

Everyone is quiet as Olivia makes her way to the bathroom, and we wait for the door to close.

"Is everything prepared for the end of the fashion show?" I whisper to Isaac as he serves the girls their portions from the baking dish in the middle of the table.

"She doesn't have a clue that Mason is going to pop the question tonight," Isaac says with a wry grin.

Tonight, she debuts the line of clothing she's been working on since we arrived in New York. She had no clue her designs would land her in the spotlight, but tonight's her night, deservingly so. Not only is she about to experience the true meaning of success, but also what it feels like to have a dream come true.

"I just can't wait to see the look on her face when Mason makes it the most memorable night of her life," I whisper.

He was our neighbor for a bit when we first moved into this apartment. They spotted each other in the hall as he was trying to unlock his door and she was trying to figure out why our door was locked. They've been inseparable since, and we've been eagerly waiting for him to join our family. In fact, I believe Mama took him shopping for rings a few weeks ago to ensure this would all happen according to his, or perhaps her, plan tonight.

Mama leans back in her chair to get a view of the bathroom door to make sure it's still closed. "Everything is perfectly prepared," she whispers. "Don't worry one bit."

"How many times did you talk to Mason today, Mama?"

"Yeah, Grammy," the girls echo.

"Hush, you two," Mama tells them. "At my age, a woman deserves a little fun here and there. It just so happens I have wonderful taste in jewelry, so who better to take a man shopping for our lovely Auntie Lu-lu than me?"

"Better you than me, I guess," Isaac says with a sigh. "Sofia loves the ring you chose for her too." He shoots Mama a wink, which earns him a signature eye-roll.

All I can do is smile at the man who made sure that every wish in my life has come true.

The bathroom door opens, and we all become suspiciously silent again.

"You three are up to something and I don't know if I like it," Olivia accuses us while placing her clutch down on the side table.

It's easier to simply smile at her rather than respond. Plus, she looks gorgeous in her black-and-white polka-dot tea dress with her signature contrasting accessory: a sunny-yellow ribbon tied around her waist. Her hair is short, but flipped out into a perfect wave, and the pearls Mama gave her for Hanukkah are a wonderful finishing touch to her chic look. She's certainly ready for her happily ever after. We all are.

Isaac lets out an exaggerated groan—the response Olivia so often hears from him. "Why do you always think we're talking about you? Don't you know we have other things to chat about aside from you being this big famous designer?" He jokingly rolls his eyes.

"Because I catch you talking about me at least once a day," she scoffs.

"Well, not tonight, Sis. So, you can just take a seat and eat your dinner so we're not late for your big famous debut." Not without another swat to his head does Olivia take her seat at the table in between the girls.

Our daughters both giggle at the never-ending skit and the nonsense happening between these walls. The sound of their laughter is my daily reminder of how lucky I am to call Isaac my husband—my soulmate, my very best friend, Brooklyn's most talented violinist, and one of this city's most sought-after accountants—just like his father once was. He never takes life for granted. From strolls through art museums to frequenting symphony performances, wining and dining at restaurants across the city, he lives each moment as if it's his last, all while we hold hands a little tighter each day. His hunger for life has always fueled mine and continues to do so, and he still makes my pulse race with every look into my eyes. There is life after death, happiness after misery, and the chance to create new memories that replace the old.

Our relationship rooted from something very dark and during a time that seemed like it would never end. It was hard, nearly impossible, to conjure up dreams about a future. For so long, I didn't expect to live to see the sun or sky again. Yet, here we are basking in the joy of our love that has blossomed into the most illustrious miracle—something I never could have imagined.

Just after dinner, as the girls run off to find their coats and

Mama is singing at the sink while happily soaping up dishes, I take the moment to lean in toward Isaac.

"Did you feel jittery that one starry night beneath the farmer's moon so many years ago?"

He snickers before giving me a small kiss on the nose. "Sofia, I knew we were meant to be together the day I saw you—the beautiful girl in the window—and then I was sure about it the very moment you stabbed me with a penicillin shot. You saved my life right then and there, sweetheart."

With a look of shock on my face, I can't help but laugh. "Oh gosh! I can't believe you even remember that."

"Oh, it's one of my favorite memories, I assure you," he says, sweeping his thumb across my cheek. "But, honestly, when all your dreams begin to come true, there's no way around the nerves. It's like crossing the finish line of the longest race, and even though you're there and made it, it's still hard to breathe, hard to convince yourself it's finally happened—hard to believe we were lucky enough to be there together in that place at that moment. I was more than jittery. I wanted nothing more than to start the rest of my life with you, and every second longer I had to wait felt like an eternity."

I purse my lips and place my hands on Isaac's cheeks. "Boy, oh boy, you still know how to sweep a girl right off her feet."

He curls a strand of my hair behind my ear and sighs. "Just my girl—the one who deserves the world," he says, sealing his adoring words with just one more kiss—one that makes me wonder if I am, in fact, still dreaming.

A LETTER FROM SHARI

Dear reader,

I'm thrilled you chose to read *The Doctor's Daughter*. If you enjoyed it and want to keep up to date with all my latest releases, just sign up at the following link. Your email address will never be shared and you can unsubscribe at any time.

www.bookouture.com/shari-j-ryan

The way of life and society during World War II is a topic I can't seem to learn enough about. I'm passionate about bringing these unique stories to life and keeping the history alive. My desire to focus on the Holocaust stems from my upbringing and heritage. As a descendant of two Holocaust survivors, I feel a sense of purpose when it comes to keeping the truth of their past realities alive. While the subject matter is heavy, I feel stronger at the end of each book I write.

I truly hope you enjoyed the book, and if so, I would be very appreciative if you could write a review. Since the feedback from readers helps me grow as a writer, I would love to hear what you think, and it makes such a difference helping new readers to discover one of my books for the first time.

There's no greater pleasure than hearing from my readers—you can get in touch on my Facebook page, through Twitter, Goodreads or my website.

Thank you for reading!

Xoxo

Shari

www.sharijryan.com

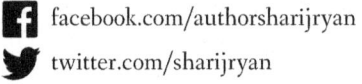 facebook.com/authorsharijryan
twitter.com/sharijryan

ACKNOWLEDGMENTS

The Doctor's Daughter was an excursion within my writing career. I pour my heart and soul into each story I write, and the characters come to life in my mind and stay with me forever.

I'd like to thank Bookouture for being an exceptional publishing house—the kindness, generosity, and compassion is something I appreciate with every exchange of communication. I'm grateful to be a part of such an amazing team. Thank you!

Christina, working with you has been like a breath of fresh air. I look forward to hearing your thoughts on every page I write and feel a great deal of inspiration from each edit and suggestion. You are incredibly gifted and talented, which has been a tremendous help to me while crafting these books. I'm so lucky to have the opportunity to work with you.

Linda, thank you for everything—for always encouraging me to grow and be true to myself. Our friendship means the world the world to me, and I don't know what I'd do without having you as a constant in my life.

Tracey, Gabby, Elaine, Heather, and Emily—thank you for sticking by my side and being my sounding board. I'm forever grateful for the time and support you offer me, but most of all, your friendship. I don't know what I'd do without you ladies!

To the wonderful bloggers and readers: Being in this community has given me a different outlook on life, and I can't think of a better industry to be a part of than this one with all of you. Thank you for your support and encouragement to continue living out my dream.

Lori, the best little sister in the universe. Thank you for always being my #1 reader and my very best friend in the whole universe. Love you!

My family—Mom, Dad, Mark, Ev, and Papa—thank you for always keeping track of my every deadline, asking me the ridiculous questions most wouldn't think to ask—like *how many words I've written today*, and telling me I can achieve anything I put my mind to—because sometimes my dreams are bigger than life. To know how greatly you love and support me gives me the constant motivation to go higher. I love you all.

Grandma—I felt like you were my biggest fan, still reading my books up until this past year. After reading, you would always look at me, nod your head with amazement and tell me I'm heading for big things in life. You would tell people your granddaughter was "famous" even though you knew it made me turn red and I would deny any part of that. Because I'm just me, doing what I love—just the way you lived your life. You might not be able to read any more of my books now, but I know you'll always be over my shoulder, giving me the strength to push forward. I love and miss you so much.

Bryce and Brayden—my wonderful boys—you have both gotten old enough to start reading my books and surprised me by reading the last. I saw a spark in your eyes after, wanting to create your own stories and write books too. All I will ever want for you is your happiness, and I hope I can inspire you the way you've inspired me. I love you so very much.

Josh, a manuscript doesn't leave my hands before I've taken a minute to appreciate the support you continuously offer me. I know I talk about fictional worlds and made-up characters, but you believe in them as much as I do, and to know you always stand behind me keeps me going every day. I won't let you forget that you motivated me to begin this journey, and I hope you know I couldn't have done any of it without you. I love you so much!

Made in the USA
Monee, IL
05 July 2022

99081084R00187